NIGHT OF THE

FÆ

Lyneal Jenkins

Edited by Amber Bungo

Contributing cover artwork by
Martine Lemmens,
H. Makridis,
And
Lyneal Jenkins.

Printed by Tyson Press

ISBN: 978-0-9926463-0-1

ASIN: B00A5S66N2

First Print Edition.

DEDICATION

For my partner Lee and all our children; Amelia, Jamie, Isaac, Gareth, Oscar, Ethan and Caitlyn.
You are all my world and I couldn't have done this without you.

Acknowledgments

Getting Night of the Fae finished was a long and demanding journey, which I couldn't have completed if it hadn't been for the support of my friends and family.

I would like to give special thanks to -

Heidi and Michael -Thank you for putting up with my rambling for hours on end, I have no idea how you both managed it.

Cheryl – Thank you for your constructive criticism and advice, I wouldn't have made it through the editing without you.

Nina – You helped me feel pride in my work, a feeling I will never forget.

Lee – Thank you for giving me the push I needed to get my work out there.

A big thank you to Tyson press for all the support and patience in getting, NIGHT OF THE FAE, printed.

Most of all, a big thank you to my three children, Jamie, Gareth and Caitlyn – I wouldn't have been able to finish this project if you hadn't allowed me the time to do so. Your on-going support is always appreciated.

I would also like to give thanks to all you readers out there. Ana's story would be nothing without your support.

ABOUT THE AUTHOR

Lyneal Jenkins was born in Shrewsbury, England in 1980. In 1996 she left home to become a Medic in the British Army. After three years she resigned the forces to start a family and begin her work with learning disabilities, which is when she was diagnosed with bipolar depression.

After a failed marriage, she moved to Spain for eighteen months with her children, taking time to reflect on where she wanted her life to go. Since returning to the UK, she began her studies towards becoming a Psychologist.

In February 2011 she sat down at the laptop with one sentence and a basic concept in mind, with no idea that she was embarking on the biggest project of her life. Night of the Fae quickly became a novel and it wasn't long before detailed notes for the remaining books in the Ana Martin series were drafted up.

To date, Lyneal is currently living with her partner in North Yorkshire along with their seven children and a crazy Springer Spaniel. Each day is a balance between normal life and writing. She couldn't be happier.

She is looking forward to writing many more books in the fantasy/sci-fi genre as this is where her passion lies.

BOOKS ALSO BY LYNEAL JENKINS

Hidden Light – Volume 2 of the Ana Martin series
Frozen Flame – Volume 3 of the Ana Martin series

NIGHT OF THE FAE is the first book in the Ana Martin series, which follows Ana as she is drawn into the secret world of the Siis, an ancient race of empathic beings torn apart by war, treachery and the consequences of past actions.

Because of the presence of the Siis, Ana soon attracts the attention of the Fae, once innocent children who are now filled with malevolent intent, and gets dragged into a war that has nothing to do with her.

Throughout her journey, she meets many new people, some of them belonging to races never encountered before. Her life becomes a tangled mess of love, friendship, loss and heartache, forcing her to find a strength and balance never needed before.

HIDDEN LIGHT, the second book in the Ana Martin series, and, FROZEN FLAME, the third book in the Ana Martin series, are now available. A synopsis for, HIDDEN LIGHT, can be found at the end of this book.

Note: the word Siis which appears throughout this book is to be pronounced as see-ass. The word Shi is to be pronounced as Shee.

NIGHT

OF THE

FÆ

VOLUME ONE OF THE
ANA MARTIN SERIES

1

I turned and sprinted towards the car. My heart beat furiously in my ears, yet the sound of his pounding steps broke through, thumping along the tarmac as he gained on me. Thick trees surrounded the car park, filled with shadows that appeared to move and flex, the darkness within a solid presence that even the moonlight shied away from. There wouldn't be any safety in them, only miles of wilderness in which he could hunt me down. My eyes focused on the dark shape of the vehicle, my only salvation, protection from the danger heading my way.

I pushed harder, speeding up my pace. He continued to close in with a bat gripped in his hands. It was as if it targeted me, following my every move, as if it were a malevolent entity with its own agenda, merely dragging the man behind it. I wasn't going to survive.

All I could think was *stupid, stupid, stupid.* I should have gone back to the car as soon as he began moving towards me. I should have headed towards the care home instead of running away. The thoughts were useless, yet they continued to gain momentum, screaming the alternatives at me as if I could somehow rectify my past.

My bag thumped into my leg, mirroring the heavy rhythm of my pace. I reached in, thanking God that I had forgotten to close the zip, and instantly felt the cool touch of metal. I pulled on the key, but it caught on the lining. My half read book and lipstick fell out, but still the key wouldn't budge. I was taking too long.

The car became more than a shadowed outline and I tugged even harder, ripping the flimsy material. The key finally came free and I pressed the button for the immobiliser. The beep pierced through the car park, the echo eerie as tight whispers, chanting, *You are all alone.*

I glanced over my shoulder, causing me to slow in my sprint. He was gaining on me. His harsh grunts and breathless mutters reached through the dim light, only overshadowed by the shambolic thud of his trainers on tarmac, uneven in their pace.

My fingers touched the handle and I pulled on the stiff door. It resisted before squealing in protest as it gave way. I was going to make it.

He reached me before the door was half way open. His feet skidded, and his body crashed into mine, propelling me forwards. The door smashed onto my hand and I screamed as the shards of broken bone ground together. The man flailed against me, his cracked nails scraping the skin off my cheek and his feet attacking my legs. He screamed, spraying spittle onto us both as the bat slipped from his fingers.

He was defenceless, scrabbling towards his weapon, cursing about how I had hurt him, how he would make me pay.

Fight! the voice in my mind screamed. I couldn't. The door had become a starving chasm, sucking the life out through my arm, laughing cruelly in a metallic groan as I fought against it. Stars exploded behind my eyes, causing my head to swim and my legs to sag as they threatened to give way. I forced life into them, demanding that they stay erect. On the ground I would be helpless. If I couldn't run, I would die.

My attacker struggled to his feet with the recovered bat in his hand. He brought it up, but the notion of running was lost, enveloped in the agony seizing my mind, becoming nothing more than a half forgotten thought, broken and disjointed as it tugged on my brain.

I needed to think beyond the swirling pit of pain that my body had become. I had to get my hand out. The door groaned once more, resisting my attempts to escape it, before screaming as the metal gave away. I fell to my knees, cradling my arm to my chest as tears rolled down my cheeks.

He hit me from behind, the wooden bat hard like concrete. I rolled across the ground and cried, the sound no more than a whimpered whisper that blended in with stillness of the night.

The man jerked as if receiving constant electrical shocks, his eyes wild as they darted around, unable to settle on one spot. He scratched at his elbow and waved the bat around, a mindless action which spoke of a junkie unable think past his next fix.

'Take my bag,' I groaned, gasping as my body threatened to shatter into a thousand pieces.

He wildly scanned the area and bent down to tug on the strap across my chest. It cut into my shoulder as he pulled it first one way, then the other, unable to release it. He dropped the strap and screeched while lifting the bat above his shoulder. I cowered into the road with my hands over my head, unable to avoid the pain heading my way.

He hit me hard. A sharp crack filled my ears and pressure rose up in my chest. Breathing suddenly hurt, each attempt resulting in blades shooting through my back and throat. I coughed weakly, choking on the blood that sprayed onto my lips.

The crazed addict lifted the bat once more.

I didn't even flinch. He had blindsided me and now I was too broken to even raise my arms in defence. The weapon made contact again and he muttered to himself, his words disjointed as if the sentence had been scattered into the wind, coming together into a random mess.

The blows turned me towards the wheels of my car. At least I didn't have to worry about changing the tyres anymore. People said that when you were going to die your life flashed before your eyes. All I could think about was the stupid tyres and how I had been worrying about paying for them. The blows continued to rain down, but the damage barely registered.

Instead, my thoughts drifted to Nora, the reason for my midnight arrival at work. I was meant to be with her right now, holding her hand and hearing her final words before leaving this world, not staring at my bald tyres. After everything I had survived in the past, dying like this seemed wrong and pointless.

A shrill scream of pain echoed out into the still night. Maybe in his crazed state the addict had hit himself with the bat. That would at least be something.

A dark smoky wave seeped over my mind, encompassing every thought, leaving nothing; no pain, no confusion, dowsing the remaining flame of hope. It was over. He had beaten me. All that remained was to die without screaming, with the dignity I had spent the last years fighting to gain. I couldn't let that go. I wouldn't be that weak again.

My eyes flickered open and I blinked several times. I almost smiled and for one crazy moment, felt a sliver of gratitude for the final blow that had rolled me onto my back. At least the stars would be the last thing I saw, perfect in their brightness against the clear midnight sky. They called to me, drawing me into their vastness where pain didn't exist.

A face came into view, blocking my vision, only an outline and the dull glint of eyes discernible in the shadows. I frowned with irritation for my spoiled view before realising that in the big scheme of things, it didn't really matter.

'It's all right,' a man told me, his voice soft and flowing like the gentle rhythm of music. 'You will be fine.'

I wanted to ask how he could possibly believe that, but liquid bubbled up in my throat, making it impossible to breathe, let alone talk.

Every inch of me screamed with pain, yet the oddest sensation overrode it, a tingling that flowed through my entire body taking away some of the agony. It cleansed me, bringing every cell in my body alive for the first time. It brought to mind the first summer sun, how I would sit out on the porch and my skin would almost sigh with relief as it drank in the strong rays after the dullness of winter. My whole body sighed with that same relief.

'Am I dying?' The blood in my lungs no longer hindered me in talking, allowing me to draw in deep, hesitant breaths.

The strange man smiled, revealing perfect teeth. 'Not today.'

'That means I have to change the tyres now,' I said, causing my saviour to chuckle.

I opened my mouth to ask him who he was, but before the words left my lips, he touched his fingers to my head.

'Sleep now,' he said.

Even though I tried to fight it, darkness claimed my thoughts and pulled me away.

'Ana, wake up,' a familiar voice called, forcing my eyes to reluctantly open. The attack came rushing back and I sat up so fast my head spun, only to see Lexi peering at me. My lungs were clear and I pressed along my body unable to feel any pain.

Was I dead?

Of course not. Lexi stood beside me, who last time I checked, was very much alive. Also, the scent of cleaning products hung in the air. As much as I loved the place I worked in, I didn't think for one minute that it would be starring in my afterlife.

'What happened?' I tried to remember the attack in detail, but a hazy film clouded my mind, making it impossible.

'You fainted in the car park,' she said with a relieved smile.

'No I didn't.' I blinked furiously, trying to clear my thoughts. 'I was attacked.' The faint taste of copper filled my mouth confirming what I knew to be true, yet when I pulled up my top, I found no evidence to support it. A deep ache permeated my muscles though, as if I had done an arduous work out the day before.

Lexi frowned at me. 'What? But the man who carried you in said he saw you pass out.'

The image of a man leaning over me flashed into my mind, the memory as fuzzy as the rest.

'Where is he?' I stood up and wobbled a bit before regaining my balance.

'He left a couple of minutes ago,' she said as I ran to the main doors.

Ignoring her call after me, I scanned the darkened green in front of the building and tried to peer over to the car park in the hope of seeing his shape. There was no sign of him, or of the man who had attacked me. But as I stood in the darkness I shivered, unable to shake the feeling that someone was watching.

'Ana?'

I jumped. I had been so focused on trying to see into the darkness I didn't notice Lexi follow me.

'Was it him that attacked you?'

I shook my head. 'My mistake.' The lie made me shift uncomfortably, but how could I explain it without looking insane? 'I must have banged my head when I fell.' I scoured the night one last time before turning with frustration, and heading back into the well-lit care home.

My bag lay on the floor by the comfortable chairs situated in the lobby, and I opened the zip, only to find that the contents were all there, even my lipstick which had definitely rolled away. I checked the lining only to find it intact. After staring at it for several seconds, I pulled the zip closed and headed to Nora's room. I had a lot to try and make sense of, but tonight my dying friend was the priority.

2

'Are you coming in?' Lexi said as I brought the car to a halt. The early hour made for an empty street, everyone having left for work. In thirty minutes the mothers would return from the school run, but for now, I managed to get a spot outside the flat.

'I wish I could,' I replied, 'but I'm already late for Uni.'

She turned in her seat and ran her hands through her long hair, untangling the red curls as she went. 'How's it going?'

'Okay, I think. Every time it starts getting on top of me I just remind myself that I don't want to be a care assistant forever.'

Lexi laughed and grabbed her overnight bag off the back seat. 'Yeah, because nurses get it so much better.'

I shrugged. 'The pay is better and I get to help people more. Anyway, it gives me something to do since I went part time.'

She laughed. 'And that's always a good thing. Did you come up with an idea for Valentine's Day?'

I groaned. 'Not yet, what do you get someone when you've only been dating a couple of weeks?'

'Richie asked me to make him a sex tape, as if I would.'

I frowned for a moment, contemplating the idea before grinning.

'Oh God,' she said quickly. 'I wasn't saying you should.'

'I do have that new editing package on the computer. And it could be fun.'

Lexi sighed. 'I've done it again, haven't I?'

'Before you say it, the idea isn't crazy. It's something I haven't done before and I'm ready for a new challenge. Uni isn't quite cutting it at the moment.' I pursed my lips and frowned. 'I will need to borrow your camera though.'

'When will I learn to keep my mouth shut?' Lexi said with a shake of her head.

I laughed loudly. 'Don't ever do that, my life would be too normal.'

'My point exactly.' She rolled her eyes and got out of the car. 'Now go to Uni and please, drive carefully.'

'I will,' I said with a grin. 'I'll pop over later for the camera.'

'Hopefully something else will grab your attention before then. If not, I'll have it ready.'

As soon as the door closed, Lexi left my mind. How could I look good for my video debut? It wouldn't do to just tape it and hand it to him. That would be amateurish. I would need to make it look professional, maybe with some background music, though none of that cheesy stuff. Then again, that could be hilarious.

Before I knew it, I reached the car park at Uni. As I took the ten minute walk to the grounds, I tried to think of how it would look. Everyone tended to find their favoured routines in bed, but for the life of me, I couldn't remember very much about what happened with him. I must get completely swept away in the moment as everything was fuzzy as if I reached through a cloud to draw on the memory. And then there was the dream I always had afterwards. Even now it tugged at my mind.

Cheryl waved and hurried over. 'Did you get your essay done?' She shifted the strap of her heavy bag and pulled her long black hair out from under it.

'I finished it last week,' I said.

She groaned. 'That's not fair. I was up till three this morning.' Her eyes were puffy and the dark smudges badly concealed. For once, I didn't think she was exaggerating.

'You should be more organised.'

'It's all right for you,' she said, 'you have your own house. I have to live with four girls who like to have parties.'

I raised my eyebrows and she grinned sheepishly.

'Okay, I have them too. That reminds me, you still haven't come to one yet.'

I laughed loudly. 'No offense, but I can't think of anything worse than a group of youngsters, drunk and drugged up to the eyeballs.'

'You're only seven years older than me and we get on fine here.'

'Of course we do. Still, I have to say no, but thanks for the offer.'

We entered the auditorium, with high ceilings and hundreds of chairs, each one raised higher than the one before so that we could all see the front. Cheryl headed for the back and I followed. My mind was off on a tangent, racing behind the scenes and I didn't want to be caught day dreaming. Before long, the lecturer, Professor Wright, a young woman wearing ripped jeans and doc martin boots, hushed us and began the lecture.

After a few minutes Cheryl nudged me with her elbow. 'Stop tapping your pen,' she said, 'it's driving me up the wall.'

I glanced at her in surprise before dropping the yellow highlighter to the desk.

'Sorry,' I whispered far too loudly. Speaking would have echoed less around the large hall. A few people turned to stare and I barely smothered a giggle. 'Sorry,' I said a tad lower this time. It was going to be one of those days in which I had no control over my actions. I already tapped my nails on the wood, creating the light sound of a drum roll.

Thankfully the time flew by, though it helped that I spent a lot of it in my own head. By the time I stepped out into the daylight, I decided that I wouldn't mention the tape to Gabriel until it was finished. He would only want to see the raw copy and that wouldn't do until all the bad bits were cut out. After all, they said the camera added ten pounds.

By the time I got to Lexi's, I was hopping with excitement and declined her offer of a drink. As soon as I saw the small case in her hands I tried to take it from her, but she kept a grip on it.

'Is there any chance I can talk you out of this?'

I laughed. 'Not today.'

'I didn't think so,' she said, still gripping the small case. 'I'm warning you, you *will* regret it in a week.'

'Who cares about in a week,' I said, tugging it from her fingers. 'It will be too late then.'

She held her hands up in surrender. 'I've done my bit.'

I gave her a quick hug, hard enough that she groaned and drove home a bit faster than I should. There was an hour before Gabriel came, which gave me enough time to set it up in the bedroom. After much silent debate and a few trials and errors, I hid it under a towel on the windowsill, making sure that the lens was free to record.

Once I finished, I entered the kitchen at the front of the house. Only weak rays of sun ever found their way through the windows, yet the pale yellow walls reflected them throughout the large kitchen creating a dazzling haze that made it homely.

I smiled, recalling how my sister and I would stand on stools at the kitchen side, helping my mother bake every Saturday morning. Even now, the memory of freshly baked cookies teased my nostrils, warming my chest with contentment.

A pan of potatoes boiled on the stove by the time Gabriel knocked on the door. I had time to take in his tall muscular frame before he slipped his arms around my waist and nuzzled my neck. My response was without restraint and it was only when my lungs cried for air that I finally released my grip.

'Are you hungry?' I panted, turning the stove down to stop the water bubbling over.

'For you I am.' He quickly turned the stove off, swept his arms under my legs and scooped me up.

'Wait,' I said as he carried me up the stairs. 'You need to give me a minute in the bedroom alone. I have a surprise.'

He nibbled on my ear. 'It sounds intriguing.'

He settled me down, though I needed to hold onto him for a moment longer as my legs quivered like jelly. I almost forgot why I wanted him to wait.

'Don't be long,' he said as I rushed into the bedroom, slamming the door behind me.

I was an idiot. Four years ago I had brought some black lingerie on a whim, only I hadn't had the chance to use it. I should have thought about it earlier. I dug around the bottom of the draw until my fingers brushed against the lacy material and I quickly pulled the tags off. It was perfect for hiding all those not so toned bits.

Once dressed, I ran my hands down my body. If only I had a mirror to check.

After pressing the record button, I lay back on the bed, trying to keep my head up so as not to form a double chin.

'You can come in now,' I called.

Upon seeing his expression my heart sped up a notch and I smiled coyly. His eyes sparkled as he took me in, with his mouth slightly agape. He took a heavy, uneven breath and slowly stepped towards me. A low rumbling started up in his throat and he ran his bottom lip through his teeth.

He pounced towards the bed, with his hands reaching out and I squealed.

'You're mine now,' he said, trapping me in his arms.

He ran his tongue up my neck causing my whole body to shiver and my insides turn to liquid. Who was I to complain?

Gabriel brushed his lips against mine before getting out of bed. 'I'll get us some bacon from the butchers.'

'Hurry back,' I said. 'I still have a couple of hours before work.'

He smiled at me, his electric blue eyes bright with warmth. 'Nothing can keep me from you for long,' he said.

I relaxed under the duvet to watch him dress. The muscles of his chest flexed with such rhythm that I wanted to demand he come back to bed at once, to forget breakfast. There would be time for that later though, so I continued to watch him with a smile playing across my lips.

As soon as I heard the thud of the door closing, I slipped out of bed, grabbed my dressing gown and went straight to the camera. It had stopped at some point during the night, though not before it recorded all I needed.

The beginning looked okay. My outfit was flattering and seductive, though I had woken naked so it must have come off at some point. Gabriel was gorgeous as always.

Ten minutes in I couldn't decide whether to blush or sigh with boredom. There were things I had never thought I could do, and some positions that I would have bet my house were impossible. But at the same time, there were also periods that we appeared to move very little, though I was embarrassingly loud. Background music was an appealing option, especially as the heavy breathing and occasional grunt made us sound like a couple of chimps.

Fifteen minutes on, my mouth dropped open. The blood rushed from my face, leaving it tingling as if I had just been slapped, and my stomach did a little flip. What I was seeing just couldn't be real. I blinked several times and touched the small screen, sure that my imagination was merely conjuring up my dream, the one I'd had every night Gabriel stayed over.

I pressed rewind and leaned in closer to watch the replay. He lay above me, Gabriel, the man who was quickly sweeping me off my feet. Then he shimmered as if a reflection passed over his skin, only it became more dazzling with each second. His body changed into a wispy brightness that trickled over my skin, only to float above the covers as it spread out over the entire bed.

My hand flew to my mouth. 'How can that be?' I whispered breathlessly. 'How the hell didn't I notice?'

I took the camera down to the lounge to hook up to the television. Surely I was seeing it wrong on the tiny screen.

I wasn't.

The big screen made it more shocking, somehow more real. So many times I had dreamt about the yellow light. Now I knew why.

After rewinding it several times, I finally managed to concentrate on what happened next.

The video showed the conclusion of our love making and Gabriel slowly retaking human form. The next thing it picked up was my dazed voice saying, 'What?' Finally I had opened my eyes long enough to see what was happening. It was about time.

The front door opened, but my eyes remained on the screen, only able to watch as he made me fall asleep with a touch of his fingers.

'Ana?' Gabriel called from the kitchen. 'I brought some mushrooms, I noticed you were out.'

My tongue glued itself to the roof of my mouth and I froze. He came through the doorway, so tall that he barely managed it without dipping his head. My paralysis finally broke. I stumbled back and grabbed the mug off the coffee table.

His eyes widened and he stepped further into the lounge. 'Why are you frightened?'

I hurdled over the back of the sofa that split the large room in two. 'Don't come any closer. I will hit you with this, don't think I won't.'

He frowned and turned to the television which still played the video on mute.

His eyes widened in surprise before he sighed loudly. 'I do wish you hadn't done that.'

'I won't just let you kill me. I *will* fight you.'

'Why in the world would I do that?'

'You're an alien.'

He took a step forward and I waved the mug at him. Would I manage to knock him out with one blow? Maybe, but he was alien. What if his head was really in his stomach, hidden under a human skin? What if he didn't have a head? He must have a head somewhere, where would his brain go?

'Do you have scales under your skin? Or two heads tucked in there?' I gagged a little. 'Oh my God, I had sex with you.' I stumbled back further. 'Is that your plan, to impregnate me? Put some sort of little bug eggs inside of me until they hatch and eat me from the inside.'

He stopped and rolled his eyes. 'You watch far too many horror movies. I am not an alien. I was born to this world.'

'Don't you try and tell me you're human. I know that's not true.'

'I'm not human either.'

My arm dropped and I nearly lost my grip on the handle of the mug. To hear it spoken so starkly suddenly made it all real.

'I knew there was something about you. Something I couldn't quite put my finger on, but this, this is insane and trust me, I know insane.'

He stepped towards me again and I threw the cup at his head. Before it reached him, it stopped mid-air and slowly lowered to the ground. I stared at it, resting upright on the beige carpet, before turning back to him.

'Oh my God! This is freakin' crazy.'

'Hear me out.'

I grabbed the cream cushions off the sofa and threw them as I backed towards the patio doors. Why didn't I have anything useful in the house? A couple of them went off course, falling to the floor well out of his reach. The others headed towards him and as with the cup, they dropped slowly to the ground by some invisible force.

He moved quickly around the sofa to stand before me and reached his fingers towards my head. I slapped them away and scrambled back over the sofa towards the kitchen

'No you don't! I saw what you did on the tape, telling me to sleep before you whispered in my ear. Is that how you made me forget for a while? Used some sort of evil mojo to make me fall unconscious so you could mess with my brain?'

He moved quickly to stand before me. I pushed hard against his chest, but he didn't shift.

'Get away!' I choked, unable to find air to breathe. I forced myself to take a deep gasped breath.

He stepped back and held his hands up in surrender. 'Please calm down.'

'Don't you tell me to be calm! I just found out my boyfriend isn't human. How can I possibly calm down?' I began pacing, so many thoughts running around my head. 'Why can't I just have a normal boyfriend? Why does something always have to be wrong with them? All I want is a normal guy, someone nice and intelligent.' I turned to him. 'Not a God damn...' I ground my teeth together, 'Urgh! I don't even know what the hell you are.'

He held up his hand and opened his mouth.

'Don't you dare speak.' I started up my pacing again. 'You aren't allowed to speak. You're not allowed to tell me anymore crap.'

'Ana,' he beseeched.

'Don't you Ana me! You need to get out now. I can't even look at you.'

His shoulders dropped and he closed his eyes. His deep sense of rejection reached to me, smothering me in a loss filled blanket. Against my better judgement, my anger began to recede. I tried to resist, but his dejected look didn't just tug on my heart strings, his feelings overpowered mine.

I stepped back. 'What are you doing? Stop stealing my anger.'

'I'm doing nothing. You are empathic.'

I stared at him incredulously. 'I know that. Do you think I'm a complete idiot? It never changes how I feel though.'

He sighed. 'I am an empathic being. It must be quite strong for you.'

'*Strong for me?* What the hell are you talking about? And how the hell do you know I'm empathic?'

I tried to cling to my anger and groaned as the tension faded with a will of its own. His feelings affected me so much more than anyone else.

'Do not end this,' he pleaded. 'I cannot live without you.'

'Live *without* me? Are you mad? We have only been together for a few weeks.'

His eyes shimmered as he looked to his feet. I took a deep breath, pressed my lips together and silently counted to ten whilst breathing heavily through my nose.

Kick him out! my mind screamed. *Report him to the authorities.*

I stared up at his eyes, his beautiful blue eyes with just a hint of lilac. They drew me in, pulling on me, begging me to fall into his arms. I stepped back.

'You need to leave,' I said. 'I need to figure this all out.' That was the understatement of the year. My hands shook as I wound them together and my heart stuttered, thrashing away as if it tried to take flight.

'Please promise me,' he said, 'phone before you make a decision, allow for me to explain.'

I wanted to say no, that he should leave and never come back. It was all too crazy for my mind to digest. Instead I nodded as if my body had a will of its own. What the hell was I doing?

He reached out to me with his fingers. I stared at them. How could I still want to touch him, feel the warmth of his skin on mine? When I didn't move, he dropped his hand down, gave one last lingering look and left. The front door closed quietly after him, leaving silence in its place.

Two days later I trudged down the stairs. A murky cloud surrounded me, affecting my every thought as if a disease had invaded my mind. *Why do you think he would want you?* my mind mocked. *You are nothing more than a waste of space, someone that people merely tolerate.*

I closed my eyes and rebelled against the familiar voice. I always fight it, thinking I can banish it for good, yet it always comes back, taunting and berating me, telling me to stay in bed and shun the world.

The voice laughed, a bitter cruel sound that tore at my confidence. *Do you really think he could love you? A sad, lonely, pathetic woman, that's what you are.* It laughed again, mocking me with its humour.

I turned the stereo on loud so as to drown out its voice. It still broke through.

How do you know you're not mad? It whispered. *This could all be an illusion.*

Its words ate away at me, throwing up questions and accusations. I watched the video again, proving that I wasn't going crazy after all. The voice continued. There was just too much for my brain to process, and each piece of information swirled around my head, leaving paranoia and confusion in its wake.

For ten days I battled the depression. On day eleven I awoke to find the sun shining. It had most likely been shining for days, but this was the first time I noticed it. The colour was back in the world and the voice once more locked in the deep prison of my mind, leaving a tonne of questions in its place.

I sat with a cup of tea on the porch, situated at the back of the house off the lounge, enjoying the sunshine after the darkness. It had been a mental darkness, but still, it felt good.

I inhaled, relishing the warm, gentle breeze that rustled the leaves and touched my hand to my face. I remembered the feel of his fingers as they caressed my skin, and how when he smiled at me, I felt like the most beautiful woman alive. God, I really missed him.

My eyes were closed when I sensed a presence moving towards me, the sound of his steps on the wooden surface barely more than a whisper. Conflicting emotions rushed through me. Could I trust him? Should I allow him into my heart?

He fell down onto his knees beside me. 'I promise I will never hurt you.'

'Oh my God,' I blurted. 'Don't tell me you can read minds too? I can't cope with that.'

His eyes widened with surprise and he burst into laughter, a gentle pleasing sound that always made me feel relaxed and buoyant. Not today.

'I can't read your thoughts.' He reached to touch my face and I leant away from him. He faltered and let his hand drop away.

I wrapped my arms around my legs. 'Why me?'

He stood up and pulled the other chair towards me, pausing to flick his dark sandy hair from his eyes.

'You intrigued me,' he said sitting down. 'Your emotions are in constant flux, more extreme than anyone I have come across before. I wanted to know more, so I followed you.'

'You followed me?' I spluttered.

He lowered his gaze and nodded.

'How long did you follow me?'

'Eight months.'

Oh my God. Was I really that self-absorbed that I hadn't noticed someone following me for that long? He sat there cautiously while the enormity of it sank in.

'I apologise,' he said. 'I have caused you more anger towards me.'

I smirked a little. Maybe he couldn't read minds after all. Then it occurred to me, 'If you were content to watch me like an experiment for eight months, why suddenly approach me?' My eyes narrowed as I glared at him. 'Did you want to examine the lab rat more closely?'

He recoiled from me, which made me want to smile once more. God what was wrong with me? The laughter bubbled up in me again as if a fizzy sweet had been set loose in my chest. He frowned and shifted uncomfortably, first back and then forwards in the chair as if unsure of what to do.

I clenched my hands and leant towards him. 'Instead of reading me, answer me.'

'Because I fell in love with you.'

My mouth dropped open. I hadn't been expecting that answer. The new information swirled around my mind. He said he loved me, but how could he feel such a way? He sat there patiently whilst everything digested. I wanted to laugh, but when my eyes met his, tears fell down my cheeks. He reached over and tucked a long strand hair behind my ear, before stroking his fingertips across my cheek. I didn't resist as he pulled me into his arms.

He kissed my damp face and told me how much I meant to him. I needed to believe him, to have faith that he wanted me as much as I did him.

He buried his fingers in my hair, pressing his lips against mine and caressed my tongue with his. My whole body swelled in response. He pulled me out of my seat and pressed his hand up against my back, forcing my body into his. The heat of his body reached through our clothes, warming my skin, pushing all lingering thoughts and doubts out. By the time he carried me through the lounge and up the stairs, I was completely his and he mine.

I lay with my head on his chest and watched the light as it trailed around his body. It looked as though the sun radiated from him, trapping dust motes in its light. His skin had no definite edge, as if the particles were not enclosed in the shell of his body, but gently spreading out, trying to escape the prison of a solid form.

I held my hand up to the light and the tiny specks rested upon my skin, making it numb and hypersensitive all at the same time. He slowly drew the light back in until he looked human once again. He watched me intently and I smiled to reassure him that everything was okay. Now I knew why he had always taken the memories away.

I pulled from his embrace and sat up, hugging the duvet to my chest. 'Please don't make me forget again.'

His chest rose as he sighed and he slid up beside me. 'That is not an option anymore, my love. You have known about me for too great a length of time now, and if I were to bury the memories, there would be too large a gap in your mind. Anyway, you have demonstrated that you are not like most people and that your mind will retrieve even the smallest of memories, even if they only come out in dreams. I doubt it would be possible to hypnotise you either as your mind doesn't take well to being tampered with.'

'Good to know I can't be made to cluck like a chicken,' I mumbled. 'Why do you glow like that?'

'My natural shape is in the form of Shi, an energy which mostly presents as light. I take human form so I can walk among you. I have also taken the form of many other species so that I can experience their lifestyle.'

'Like what?'

'Many. From a spider to a cheetah. I do enjoy being a cheetah, the speed you can reach is quite satisfying, but mostly I like to be human, the ability you have to communicate with words makes it much more interesting.'

'O-kay...' I took a moment to ponder over this. I would have to warn him not to be a spider else I will probably squash him by accident. 'So why glow again?'

'I'm not actually glowing. My molecules are reverting to their natural form.'

'Tomato, *tomato*,' I said, causing him to chuckle.

'The reason is, I find it hard to maintain this form when in your company.'

'Why is that?'

He sighed and ran his hand through his hair. 'Because of how great my love for you is. It is quite a distraction.'

Warmth spread through me causing even my toes to tingle. He loved me so much he couldn't maintain his solid form. It was one hell of a compliment. I couldn't help myself and burst into laughter.

Throughout the night we made love many times, and this time I did my best to keep my eyes open.

3

Spring had finally arrived. The daffodils peeked through the ground and the sun beat down without a single cloud to soften the heat. The tarmac shimmered, making the road appear as if it moved like the gentle waves of the sea, and the bees buzzed lazily up and down, as if the sun was a weight forcing them to the ground. The car would most likely be stifling and I dreaded the thought of touching the steering wheel, anticipating how the plastic would burn the palms of my hands.

The fridge contained nothing more than a few jars, very little for me. In the couple of weeks since Gabriel had declared his love, my head had been unable to focus on little more than him. I still had a couple of hours until I met Lexi for our weekly cup of tea, so could fit a full shopping trip in first. I composed a list of everything needed and set off into town, making sure to pack a cool box for the perishables.

The supermarket was empty, leaving me half an hour to kill before Lexi finished work. I dumped the shopping into the boot of the car and headed towards the large park filled with lots of open space and a small playground. I watched the people milling around, trying to guess who they were. A young woman jogged past, wearing tight shorts and a matching crop top, her make-up light, but expertly applied. She held an iPod in her hand and messed with the controls without pausing. Definitely an office worker on her lunch break.

An older woman walked in the distance, leading two small children towards the park. Grandma taking the kids out while their parents worked.

I'd missed lunch time, so most people were back at work leaving me with little to play with. Three distant figures gradually progressed along the path, heading in my direction. A man stood in the middle, wearing a grey suit with a mobile phone pressed to his ear. I sighed. He appeared as the usual office types that regularly strolled through the park, though he stomped instead of walked, and shouted incoherently into the phone.

The two figures around him caught my attention. They gracefully surrounded him, crouched low to the ground with their arms raised up towards his face. Their movement's fluid, like a well-rehearsed dance, they frequently leant towards him, their bodies rising as if inhaling his scent before they returned to their elegant circling.

The man appeared oblivious to their presence.

They drew closer and my back stiffened, his posture seemed all wrong. He stopped and shouted even louder into the phone. Only a scatter of his barked words reached me. He never once looked at the two figures gyrating around him.

They appeared small in stature, only a few inches taller than my eight year old niece, and wore full body leotards, similar to the dance class outfit I'd worn as a kid. I stiffened, detecting the dark purple haze coming out of their backs as if they pulled wisps of a laden thunder cloud behind them.

Without warning the female moved towards me, fast and with flair. I shrank back into the bench. Her childlike face stopped inches from mine, her breath sickly sweet upon my skin. Malice oozed from her quivering muscles and my eyes flickered around, desperately seeking a friendly face.

The angry man had passed without a glance in my direction and there was no one else in sight except for the partner of this frightening entity. He stood a few metres away, lazily taking in the surrounding area as if bored.

The power of her stare compelled me to look back into her eyes. The look of a demon full of hate and violence, set within the face of a child.

Her voice raspy and filled with venom, she spoke, 'Who are you?' My throat swelled and all moisture left my mouth, making it impossible to do anything but stare at her. 'How can you see us?'

Her teeth riveted me pausing the breath in my throat. Every single one of them were sharpened to points. They glistened with saliva which dripped off the ends. Her tongue, although human in appearance, darted out across her lips as quick as a serpent.

She inhaled deeply taking in my scent and abruptly moved back a step. 'Siis?' She dragged the word out so it sounded like 'see-ass', hissing like a snake when threatened. She turned to her companion with excitement. 'She smells as a Siis.' Her nose wrinkled as she took in another breath. 'But not quite,' she said, her face creased with confusion.

The male pranced elegantly towards me with anticipation. 'Let me see.'

My back creaked as I cringed as far back into the bench as possible. My heart raced and my head spun as I stayed motionless. Hopefully they would realise I wasn't a Siis, whatever that was.

The male gripped my face and pushed it up. He inhaled deeply, running his warm nose against my neck. 'She is human,' he disagreed.

I silently thanked God, and dared to hope that they would let me go. Surely they wouldn't harm me in such a public place. I concentrated on my breathing, forcing the air in and out of my lungs.

Their mist consisted of heavier tones than Gabriel, but contained the same tiny particles floating throughout it. Was he a Siis?

The male stepped back, the bored look returning to his face. 'We will miss the finale if we don't leave soon.'

The female didn't move.

'How do you smell of the Siis?' She drew closer again. Her clogging breath caused my stomach to roll.

'I don't know what a Siis is.'

She continued to glower at me. The silence became a physical entity, pressing, probing, demanding that I tell her everything. I wanted to tell her all I knew, if only she'd stopped looking at me in such a way. I managed to bite back the compulsion.

'Please...I just want to go home.'

The male interrupted the wordless interrogation. 'Come on, we must go.'

She gave me one last look of intense curiosity and flounced off, leaving me to breathe jaggedly as shivers racked through my body.

I eventually regained control and became aware of the scene around me. Children played and people walked their dogs in the distance, yet it was as if I viewed it from another world. The sun still beat down on me but ice threaded through my core. The hands on my watch cause me to take a second look. Only fifteen minutes had passed since I sat down. Although it had felt as if I'd been trapped under her malevolent gaze for hours, it had realistically only been a few minutes.

I pushed the feeling of quiet dread to the back of my mind and set off to meet Lexi, practicing a happy relaxed smile so as not to alarm her.

I found her in the cloakroom, retrieving her bag.

'Are you ready to go?' My voice still quivered with the remaining tension. Luckily she didn't notice.

She shifted from foot to foot and gave me a wide eyed frown, which made her nose crease up. 'I was just about to call you. Would you mind terribly if we postponed until tomorrow... that's if you're free then?'

She fiddled with the small fairy pin on her tunic. How many times had she talked of a world with fairies and unicorns? If only she knew a secret world existed, just not how she perceived it. Her face was open and her eyes innocent with no hint of guardedness, provoking the usual urge to protect her. Thank God she hadn't been at the park.

I swallowed back my sigh of relief. 'Is everything all right?'

'Yeah, it's just mum's in town for one night before heading off to Hawaii for two weeks.'

'It's all right for some. Wish I was going.'

Lexi laughed. 'You and me both. She only just got back from the Maldives and she is planning to go to New York in a couple of months. I can't keep track of her since the divorce. That's why I want to catch her while I can.'

'Tomorrow is fine,' I reassured her. 'I have stuff I could be doing anyway.'

Once back in the car, I started to shake. I rubbed my hands down my face and touched my forehead to the steering wheel.

'Are you freakin' kidding me?'

Shudders racked through my body as I remembered the touch of the male's fingers on my neck, warm and strong as if they belonged to a grown man instead of a child. Then there were the eyes of the female, which had drilled into my brain, filled with a gleaming desire to harm. The memory of them caused everything else to fade into the background as if only they existed, drawing me into the depth of their malevolence.

My breathing and mind eventually cleared. I started the car and headed towards the exit, knocking the indicator to turn left. I paused at the junction.

What had happened to my life? It was too much of a coincidence that I should meet two impossible beings in such a short space of time.

I knocked the indicator and turned right instead. I wanted my house, the safety it offered, but I needed answers first. Gabriel didn't own a mobile and it wasn't a conversation to have over his work phone.

When I arrived at the construction site, I sat gripping the steering wheel, peering through the dust filled air at the men as they built walls and joked loudly with each other over the intrusive vibration of the tools. After a few minutes, I took a deep breath to steady the left over tremors and got out.

'Hey there,' one of the men shouted, turning his drill off. 'What have we got here?'

I dipped my head and tried to continue past them.

'Hold up love,' another man said. He repositioned his hard hat and hitched his baggy jeans up, thankfully covering the top of his backside, but leaving his extensive stomach bulging over the top. 'Are you goin' to get your tits out for us?'

'I think she is,' the first man said. He took off the yellow hard hat, revealing a red rim across his forehead and slicked back his greasy hair. 'Come on now,' he said. 'What about a kiss instead?'

I gave them a scathing look and continued towards the portable cabin at the other side of the site. Animals!

I knocked twice before someone called for me to enter. After blinking several times to adjust to the shadows, I took in the stocky man before me, probably Gabriel's boss.

'You're Ana aren't you?' he said. 'Gabriel's misses?'

I shifted uncomfortably under his direct gaze. 'Yeah, would it be possible to see him?'

'Sure,' he said. 'It's comin' up to break anyways.'

I gave him my thanks as he came around the desk.

'You 'ad better stay in here,' he said. 'Can't 'av you wandering 'round the site.' He indicated to one of the chairs facing his desk. 'Park yourself there.'

Before he had a chance to leave, Gabriel entered, frowning at me with concern. They talked amongst themselves for a few seconds before his boss left us alone.

'Are you a Siis?' I blurted as soon as the door closed.

Gabriel stopped with his arms out, ready to take me in his embrace. 'Where did you hear that?'

I told him about the incident in the park and his face became still, then ashen as I explained the interest the female had in me. He stared at me intently, then scanned the cabin, pausing to scrutinise the door and windows. My heart skipped a beat in response to his reaction. I had been terrified, but I hadn't expected him to feel anywhere near the same. What were these creatures that could scare even him?

'Fae,' he replied when I asked.

'Fae?' I snorted. 'Doesn't that mean fairy?'

His face tightened and he scanned the area once more causing my muscles to tense into tight balls. 'That is the more modern translation.'

I stared at him stunned. How many times had Lexi spoken of such creatures? About the same amount of times I had laughed at her for it.

'But the stories say fairies are nice.'

'No.' He laughed humourlessly, only adding to the chill in the air. 'They are truly disturbed creatures who feed off the aggressive and hate filled emotions of others.'

The door opened and three laughing men fell in. They nodded their heads in greeting and quickly retrieved their bags off a shelf near the door. When the door slammed closed behind them, I turned back to Gabriel.

'Why did she call me a Siis? Is that what you are?'

'Yes.' The tension oozed out of him. It affected every cell in my body and I stood, looking around for something to defend myself.

'For God's sake, Gabriel, why are you so frightened?' The trembling in my voice dismayed me, as did the violent shakes that racked through my body.

He stared intently at me. 'How did you get away?'

I told him about how the male had talked about the 'grand finale'.

He sighed and his shoulders dropped down. 'You were lucky.'

'What does he mean? What is the grand finale?' My muscles began to relax as the tension drained out of them. Had the fear ever been mine, or had I merely imitated his reaction?

'The Fae are hunters, not of meat, but of the heavy energy produced by negative emotions. They have the ability to affect people's emotions as I do, but choose to use it for different purposes. If they find someone who is angry or depressed, they encourage it, pushing them to commit an act such as murder or suicide.'

The man shouting into his phone came to mind and I hugged myself. Would I see him in the paper having killed his boss, wife or maybe even his children? I leant back against the flimsy wall. What if there had been something I could have done to stop it? I clearly saw the nameless faces of his children being murdered, while the Fae stood by cruelly laughing.

Gabriel reached out his hand to touch me. 'You couldn't have done anything, even if you had known.' He spoke with tenderness, but the face of the man consumed my mind, dwelling on how the Fae had circled him. Had I witnessed them feeding?

'But why would they do that?' I choked.

'The energy they draw off it makes them strong and also... because they can.' His eyes shadowed with sorrow and I took his outstretched hand, trying to bury the face of the man. A single tear escaped, and I quickly wiped it away. Short of visiting every office within travelling distance, there wasn't anything I could do to find him.

'How did he not see them? They were moving all around him and he acted like they weren't even there.'

He sighed. 'It is one of their skills. Unless they physically touch their prey, they remain imperceptible to them. Although they can never be completely invisible as the victim will always be aware of something, a feeling as if there is someone watching them that they can't quite see. Since the beginning, they have been mistaken as demons who whisper to their victims, causing them to do harm.'

I recalled the wicked gleam in their gaze and shuddered.

'I am surprised you could see them,' he said more to himself. I wished I hadn't.

We stood in silence for a few moments before I asked, 'Why did they get excited when they thought I might be a Siis?'

'That can only be answered by explaining the origin of the Fae as they now call themselves. About four thousand years ago, one of my kind, Talamiis, formed an attachment with the children of a small settling on the outskirts of Uruk. When soldiers arrived to capture the young as slaves, he broke one of our highest laws and made them invisible to humans. As there were no young to be found, the soldiers burnt the settlement, killing several of the inhabitants as the children watched unnoticed.'

'Why didn't he just save the village too?'

'I would imagine he recognised the enormity of what he had already done, and knew the consequences he would have to face for it.'

I shuddered. The scene in my mind was vivid. Everyone running and screaming whilst their huts burnt around them. The fear they would have experienced. The children watching as their families and homes were destroyed.

'So how did they end up becoming the Fae? Did he not change them back?'

'He managed to make them visible again. However, something had gone wrong, he was unable to draw his Shi back out. Before long, the inhabitants started becoming more volatile and more often than not, it ended in violence. When this happened there would always be a child watching close by, their face a picture of wonder and glee. Talamiis realised that they had developed abilities and tried to reason with them, explaining the results of their actions. But they were children and either couldn't see the implications, or didn't care.'

'They all turned bad?'

'No. The original group separated into three factions, those who took pleasure out of causing disharmony, those who encouraged love and friendship, and the few who seemed either overwhelmed by the abilities they had, unable to control them, or unwilling to take sides, trying to continue with their life as it had been. Talamiis tried to control what was happening in the hope that the children would change their ways, but soon the settlement had become the battleground between the two main factions, the

NIGHT OF THE FAE

older dwellers their pawns. That is when he left to obtain help from the rest of us.

'The settlement was a graveyard.' His tone was low and his eyes shadowed as he recalled how it had been. 'There had been a massacre. The unchanged having killed each other in what was apparent as acts of rage. There were a few children among the bodies, but the rest had fled.'

'Did you look for them?'

His eyes darkened. 'Yes and we even found a few, but the majority had disappeared without a trace.'

'What happened to them?'

'You have to understand that there was no other option.' He looked into my eyes, trying to convey the truth of his words.

My grip on his hand tightened. 'You killed them?'

'We had to. They were no longer children but half breeds intent on destruction.'

'And what about the good ones?'

Gabriel couldn't meet my eyes, giving me the answer I really didn't want to know. I pulled my hand away.

The door opened and the man with greasy hair came in. 'Hey gorgeous.' He gave me a leery grin. My lip curled in distaste. 'Did you change your mind about that kiss?'

Gabriel turned to him with his body tense.

'I suggest you leave,' he said through gritted teeth.

The greasy man blinked several times before he finally cottoned on.

'Aw, Gabe, sorry man, I didn't realise she was your girl.' He took his hat off and scratched his hair.

'You know now,' Gabriel said.

'Sorry,' he mumbled. 'I'll get out your way.' He grabbed a small cool bag from a shelf.

'It's okay,' I said, 'I'm leaving anyway.'

I turned from Gabriel and headed out of the door. The men sat with their lunches on their laps, many of them still wearing hard hats. A few of them smiled as I passed and I struggled to return the gesture.

Half way to the car Gabriel caught up with me. He touched my arm and without thinking, I brushed him off.

'Please stop,' he said.

I didn't want too. I wanted to continue towards the car, drive home and forget this day ever happened.

His pleading eyes managed to halt me. 'Have I caused you to fear me now?'

I sighed. 'No you haven't.'

He tried to take me in his arms, but I stepped back.

'What happened to Talamiis?'

He pressed his lips together. 'He was punished for his crime.'

His tone sent a chill up my spine. I turned from him and continued to the car. 'I'll see you at home,' I shouted over my shoulder, not able to meet his eyes. At least I would have a few hours to digest the things he had done in his past and the ways of his people.

4

The wheels of the tea trolley squeaked as I pushed it into the day room of the nursing home. I grimaced, taking in the newly painted peach walls. Carl said they gave off a calm, warm feeling. They made me think of vomit.

'Morning everyone!' I called, halting the trolley in the middle of the large room. Only four of the residents had made their way out of their bedrooms so far. Three of them sat around a square table playing Rummy.

The other resident, Robert, sat in a chair by the window, a frail and extremely wrinkled man with a permanent scowl on his face. I decided to get him out of the way first and politely offered him a cup of tea.

'That's not tea,' he growled. 'I've had stronger gnats piss.' I controlled my sigh, well used to his attitude. The other residents rolled their eyes and I smothered a grin.

'I know it's terrible,' I said with a serious face. 'You should get on to management and tell them to get better tea bags in.'

'It ain't the bags, it's the staff.'

I sighed audibly. If only he would come up with something new.

'All of you are slow,' he said, 'dragging your fat arses around like slugs. None of you know how to do a hard day's work, you should be ashamed. Same as my family, no good selfish brats! They only visit so as to get their grubby hands on my money. And as for those grandkids of mine, they deserve a smack around the head.'

I shook my head. No wonder they didn't visit him anymore.

31

'So I take it you don't want one.' I held out the plastic holder, containing the disposable cup. He snatched it out of my hand as I knew he would, and turned to face out the window without a word of thanks.

Grateful to have got him out of the way, I made the three drinks the remaining residents would want.

'Thank you dear,' Hattie said as I placed her tea before her. 'You know,' she continued talking to Audrey, 'I don't know why that girl of mine bothers visiting. Every time, it's always the same. *You shouldn't be doing that mum, you know your hips will get worse if you try this.* I tell you something, I might have arthritis, but I'm only sixty five. Does she get that? No, she thinks it's time for me to die gracefully.'

'At least you have a daughter who cares,' Audrey responded with a sigh. She reached over and touched Fred's hand. 'We would have done anything for a child.'

'Ha!' Hattie snorted. 'You say that now, but I tell you something, that girl of mine has a broom shoved so far up her backside it's a surprise she can walk. I can't believe I managed to live with her for six months before coming here. I've never been so grateful as the day she showed me the leaflet, especially when I met you two. Now I actually get to have some fun.'

Fred rolled his eyes as he took the drink from me. 'Park yourself down, Ana and rest your legs for a bit. That's if you can cope with this one.'

'Now don't you start Fred Davies.'

I grinned and Hattie turned to me. 'What are you still standing there for? You heard him, sit yourself here, next to me.'

I had a quick look around. Carl didn't seem to be doing a patrol of the hallway yet, so I settled into the spare chair around the table.

'You seem to be glowing with happiness,' Audrey said.

Hattie grunted. 'That's because she's getting nookie.'

Audrey slapped at her playfully. 'Don't embarrass the girl.'

'What?' Hattie said. 'We've all been around the block.'

'Some more than others,' Fred muttered. The three of them burst into laughter and I shook my head, unable to suppress my grin.

'So how did you meet him?' Audrey asked as she put her cards down.

'Or her?' Hattie added.

Fred rolled his eyes.

'What?' she said. 'I'm up with the youth today.'

'It's a he,' I said, 'and he rescued me from an attack off damp leaves and a puddle. He even carried me all the way home because I sprained my ankle.' I smiled as I remembered that rainy night.

'Sounds like a real gentleman,' Audrey said turning to Fred. 'If only you were still that way.'

'Fifty nine years of marriage,' Fred said, 'and you're still not happy.'

Audrey reached up to caress his cheek and gave him a gentle smile. He squeezed her fingers in response, making me think of my parents.

'Hey up,' Fred said under his breath, 'warden alert.'

Carl headed towards us with his lips pressed together in annoyance. Even though short and thin, people always noticed when he entered a room, as if he sent out a silent signal announcing his arrival.

'Great, here we go.' I stood up, ready for the rant he would send my way.

'Why are you sat here?' Carl said pushing his thin framed glasses up his nose to peer at me. 'The rooms still need to be cleaned before lunch.'

'I'm just on my way,' I said.

'It's my fault,' Hattie said giving me a discreet wink. 'I was just wondering, why do we have the same dinner menu every week?'

'We've been through this before,' Carl began.

Fred silently shooed me out before Carl remembered why he came over. I gave him a quick grin before rushing off to exchange the tea trolley for the bedding one.

As I stripped the beds and washed down the tables I found myself once again thinking of Gabriel, lingering on the image of how his eyes shimmered when he gazed at me.

'You're daydreaming about him again, aren't you?' Lexi stood in the doorway, beaming at me.

I laughed. 'How can you tell?'

'Oh I don't know, maybe it's that starry eyed look you get or that stupid lopsided grin on your face.'

She ducked laughing as I threw one of the clean towels at her head.

'What about you?' I said. 'Have you got rid of that waste of space yet?'

She looked down at the floor. 'Richie isn't that bad, he just has problems.'

'Yeah, an ice cube for a personality and an addiction to drugs.'

'He's off the drugs now,' she said defensively.

'And how's it working out this time?

'He's only thrown the ashtray at me so far.'

'Well, that's okay then.'

She sighed. 'I wish you didn't hate him so much.'

'I wouldn't if he treated you with an ounce of respect.' I reached forward and pulled up her sleeve, revealing a deep purple hand print. 'And if I didn't have to see these.'

'He's getting help for it,' she said, unable to meet my eyes, 'and he was really sorry.'

'They always are, until the next time.'

'He isn't like Nathan,' she said.

'Not yet. Just give him some time.'

I spent the rest of the shift completing my chores and bantering with the residents. Finally, knock off came and after saying goodbye to everyone, I drove into town. Dinner out was just what I needed.

The traffic was light and parking easy, leaving me with time to kill before Gabriel arrived. I decided to indulge in a bit of window shopping.

A clothing shop called Mysteria had recently opened and I reluctantly considered a red, knee length dress in the window. After battling with myself for a few minutes, I reasoned that I needed a new outfit for the end of year ball for University, and entered the shop, only to turn straight back around when I saw the price. *One hundred and ninety pounds!* Who on earth would spend that much on one item?

When the time came to meet Gabriel, I made my way to the crossing closest to the restaurant. The button had already been pressed and I stood waiting for the lights to change, smiling as the cool breeze diluted the musky smell that always clung to my clothes after work. A fresh faced woman, with blonde hair scraped into a bun and thin framed glasses, joined me. She held a pram out before her, with a car seat clipped onto the top. A small boy stood at her side.

'He's gorgeous,' I told her, peering at the baby. He rubbed a tiny fist at his open mouth and blinked furiously against the sunlight.

She chuckled and bent over to adjust the baby's blanket. 'You wouldn't think that at three in the morning.'

The toddler drew my attention, his huge, deep blue eyes creased in concentration as he pursed his lips. He continually threw a tennis ball into the air and caught it against his chest, his hands too small to grasp the item on their own.

He looked up at me, causing him to miss the ball as it fell down. Neither of us moved as it hit the ground, glanced off his toes and rolled out into the road. I anticipated his actions but only managed to graze his sleeve as he ran after the escaped item.

My legs locked in place and the breath paused in my lungs as the large van bore down on him, the driver having increased his pace in the hope of getting through the amber light before it changed. The engine growled the hunger of an ancient monster approaching its prey. For a split second I didn't see the plain red van. The bonnet became a mouth, puckered with desire and the lights changed into eyes, gleaming with anticipation. The illusion went as quickly as it came, showing something even more terrifying.

I ran into the road.

At the sound of the squealing tyres, the boy looked up with wide, frightened eyes.

I managed to grab hold of his collar and without pause, yanked him backward. I thanked God before I lost my balance and stumbled forwards to take his place.

The van hit, and the ground seemed to rise up, taking me with it. My head slammed into the windscreen, shattering the glass. All the sound was sucked from the air leaving a silent vacuum, in which the sun beat down on my face, with only light wisps of clouds to block its brightness.

I hit the ground and rolled several times. My ears popped and a scream penetrated my haze, shrill and un-human in its pitch. I tried to turn away from it but couldn't move. My bones rattled as if I had been spun in a centrifuge leaving me with the notion that if I did move, I would separate and become nothing more than a heaped skeleton.

'Call an ambulance,' a man shouted. Other people also shouted, but as with the man, it sounded tinny and warbled.

Faces formed above me, blurred and distorted, making me think of the rippled glass my grandmother had had on her front door. As a child, I had always been afraid of the misshapen forms, so much so that I had hidden behind my grandmother's legs when she answered the door. Now it seemed funny, as if I was in a crazy house at a fair.

'Let me through,' Gabriel shouted. 'I'm a doctor.'

He appeared above me and I tried to talk but only managed an incoherent gargle.

His face darkened as he took in my injuries. 'Stand back,' he bellowed to the twittering observers. I tried to smile at him but the creases on his brow only deepened until his eyes became slits. I obviously hadn't managed it well.

'Why do you insist on getting into trouble?' As he spoke a tingling feeling flowed through my body as if revitalising air was being blown into my cells. A nice and somewhat familiar feeling that made me smile. My lungs cleared and I breathed in heavily, grimacing against the taste of burnt rubber that assaulted my senses.

Seconds later, my head cleared and I moved, able to feel my limbs once more. Gabriel helped me sit up and I took in the large crowd that had formed a circle around us. Most of them frowned or stared with wide eyed concern. Others looked gleeful with barely concealed smiles. Some people were such vultures.

'She's fine,' Gabriel told them all as he yanked me to my feet. The pain had gone but a deep ache made my muscles quiver and I groaned. 'Let's go,' he ordered.

The young woman stood several feet from me with the pushchair gripped in one hand while she hugged the young boy to her chest. Tears drenched her face and she shook so violently her hair vibrated in response. I gave her a small smile before Gabriel pulled on my arm.

'She should wait for the ambulance,' a woman called as Gabriel dragged me away. He ignored her and gripped my wrist harder, pulling me along so fast, I stumbled to keep up.

He didn't speak until we were away from the crowd. 'Where's the car?' he said stiltedly. I silently indicated to the end of the street and he hauled me towards it.

He remained silent as he opened the passenger door and pushed me in, before making his way around to the driver side. Once inside, he sat with his teeth clenched so hard the muscles on his face bulged. He hit the steering wheel with his fists and turned to me.

'What if I hadn't got their in time? I can't bring you back from death.'

'I'm sorry.' I leant back towards the window, watching him warily as his face convulsed. I hadn't even known he could heal me, though it probably wasn't the time to mention that.

He glowered at me and turned the key so far, the engine squealed in protest. He floored the accelerator the whole way home and only relaxed when the house came into sight. I sat quietly throughout, allowing the quiet tones of the radio, barely discernible over the sound of the rattling engine, to soothe me.

Once parked at the side of the road, he leant back in his seat and rubbed a hand across his face.

'I apologise, I didn't intend to shout.' His kind tone caused my eyes to water and I pressed my lips together in order to still my trembling chin.

'It's okay,' I said meekly as I got out of the car.

He supported my elbow as we walked the short path to the door. Once inside, I dropped into the kitchen chair, trying to still the thoughts that raced through my mind. I watched him in silence as he made us both a tea, trying to put everything that had happened into some semblance of order.

'You've done that before,' I said when he sat down opposite me, 'haven't you? After the junkie attacked me at work, ten months ago.'

His eyes widened with surprise. 'It never occurred to me that you would have remembered that. That must have been so confusing for you.'

So much for my romantic story of a rainy night, though I suppose I had to give him credit for saving my life.

'Just a little bit.' I smiled and flexed my still trembling hands. 'It caused many sleepless nights, so many in fact, I had to ban myself from thinking about it. Not an easy task I can tell you.'

Gabriel shook his head a little. 'I never heard you speak of it to anyone. If you had, I would have approached you earlier.'

I stiffened and raised my eyebrows. 'I'm going to ignore the fact that you have just confessed to listening in on my conversations.'

He grinned sheepishly.

'Instead, can you explain something to me? Lexi said the person who brought me in looked in his fifties, which you don't.'

He smiled. 'I can do more than change into another species. I can also be perceived to age or change how I look at any time.' He paused to scrutinise my face. 'Would you like to see?'

I nodded hesitantly.

His whole body shimmered as the edges of his form diffused into his yellow light. It disappeared and in his place sat someone with silver hair and deep wrinkles on the face and neck, his sparkling blue eyes being the only resemblance to the man I loved.

'Eek!' I shot up, knocking the chair down, and promptly fell back over it.

When I opened my eyes, he stood above me, my Gabriel, with his own face.

'Please forgive me,' he said, 'I didn't mean to frighten you.'

'No, it was my fault,' I tried to reassure him, though my voice shook a little. 'I'm glad you showed me, it just took me by surprise that's all.'

He helped me to my feet and picked the chair back up. We both sat back down, me trying to gain a little of my dignity back and him still frowning with worry.

'So...how does it happen? Do you just wake up one day, look in the mirror, decide you're old enough for wrinkles, and poof, you make it happen?'

'Something like that,' he replied with a small smile.

I snorted with laughter. I had heard of designer babies and now I had my own designer man. I laughed hysterically, losing all control as tears ran down my face. Pretty soon, I began to genuinely cry.

He leant towards me and snaked his arm around my shoulders, holding me tight. 'I'm sorry sweetheart,' he said as he kissed my face. 'I'm so sorry. I love you, do not cry.' I started laughing again. So much for not letting him see my worst side.

'I'm sorry, Gabriel.' I rubbed my cheeks with my sleeve. Might as well let him see all my bad habits now that he'd witnessed me losing it. Luckily, he got me a napkin to blow my nose, not a quiet task.

'It's my fault. I should not have shown you.' He tried to hold me in his arms but couldn't get a good grip with the chair in the way, so settled for kneeling on the floor. I continued to wipe the remains of the hysteria from my face.

'Please don't say that,' I said. 'I really do want to know. It's just...'

How did I explain my screwy brain to him?

'I've just been so happy and excited and have found out so many marvellous things in the last few weeks. I just hit a point that I needed to wipe the emotional slate clean and unfortunately you got to witness it.' I paused. 'On the plus side I feel a lot better now, so bring it on.'

I clapped and did a little hop in my seat. The undercurrents of energy began running around my body and I laughed in response. The sense of being in complete tune with the universe came upon me. I grabbed his arms and kissed him noisily, only to spring up giggling. A big smile crossed his face as he stood, though the furrow on his brow diminished the affect somewhat.

'What's wrong?' I tried to look concerned but didn't manage it very well. My thoughts were too scattered, erratically bouncing around like ping pong balls in a washing machine, making them impossible to catch or follow.

'I have to ask,' he said, 'how do you cope with this sudden change in mood?' He started fidgeting, like a child waiting to get the attention of their parent, shifting from one foot to another. 'Your energy is so erratic. It's as if I'm being attacked by it.'

I snorted with laughter. 'You get used to it. Can you not shield yourself from me?'

He started peeling some potatoes for dinner as we had missed our reservation at the restaurant. Maybe he wanted to put some distance between us too.

'I am able to shield myself. It's just that I have never been in such close proximity to you whilst you experience this.'

'Sorry.' I grinned. 'Can your abilities influence my emotions at all?'

He sighed. 'Emotions are tricky. Manipulating them can cause a cascade effect unbalancing your whole chemistry, though it is possible to edge your body in the direction it is already headed, or tone down the reaction to a hormone released.'

'Could you take the bipolar away for good?' I began flicking my nails together, unable to stay still.

'No, that would not be possible.'

I gave a small sigh of relief. My brain was screwy, but it was me.

On that note the conversation came to an end. We talked about work as we prepared dinner together. I thought to ask why he, an immortal being, worked in construction, and he replied that he liked to work with his hands. Throughout the evening he recounted tales of the people he had met during his life, causing me to laugh and feel in awe simultaneously.

After we made love, he held me in his arms and told me how beautiful I was. My fingers reached around to the four inch scar lining my back. I wanted to trust him, but even with a manic high upon me, I frowned with uneasiness. Experience had taught me that such words were lies. I tried to take it with good grace though and even wanted to believe.

I wanted to tell him I loved him, but did not, not on this night.

5

The steel surface of the kitchen worktops glinted as they caught invisible rays of sunlight and the fridge hummed the sound of a thousand bees, busy at work. I flicked the radio on and clapped my hands in excitement when my favourite tune blared out before making my way to the kettle, swinging my hips in time with the music.

Lexi came in and grinned. 'Thought I might risk having a drink with you,' she said. 'Carl's in a meeting.'

I grabbed her arm and spun her around. 'Dance with me.'

'Stop,' she begged. 'I'm going to be sick if you turn me anymore.'

'You're no fun,' I said, releasing her. The kettle began boiling and I threw tea bags into our cups. 'Do you want a lift home today?'

She laughed. 'Am I safe?' She reached into my cup and took the teabag out before replacing it with a decaffeinated one.

'I only drove over a roundabout once.'

'Are you forgetting all the garden fences you've hit in this mood?'

'They were rickety anyway,' I said, taking my tea off her, 'and really low to the ground. How is anyone meant to see them?' I blew the liquid and took a sip, only to grimace. Decaff just didn't taste as good.

'Yet they survived until you got near them.' She grinned. 'I will get a ride on one condition. You can't have the stereo on.'

I groaned. 'Why not?'

'Because you take your hands off the steering wheel to dance.'

'Okay, good point, no stereo. And I promise to drive slowly.' I gave her a wide eyed stare and burst into laughter. Lexi rolled her eyes and shook her head.

Carl came into the kitchen and glared at us. The meeting must have come to an early end. 'Why am I not surprised to see you two in here? The rules are quite clear, only one person at a time taking a break.'

'All the jobs are done,' I said, 'and it's too early to start lunch.'

'If you have nothing to do, the skirting boards need a wash.'

Lexi rolled her eyes from behind his back.

'Fine,' I said, 'I'll get on it now.' I grinned and he scowled.

'Make sure you get it done,' he said as he left the kitchen. I couldn't resist sticking my tongue out after him.

'Anyone would think that he owned the place,' Lexi said sitting down with her tea.

I leant back against the side with my cup in my hands. Carl wouldn't come and check for at least ten minutes.

'Do you know he gave Chloe a written warning for being late,' she continued.

'It was the sixth time in a row,' I said, 'and you have to admit, the place is a lot better since he came here.'

'Anyone would think that you like him.'

I shrugged. 'Not really, but I have to respect him as a manager.'

'Even though he doesn't have a clue how to act with the residents?'

I laughed. 'Okay, not that bit. Do you know, he came in the other day while I was washing Barbara and told me I shouldn't spend time chatting because it took too long. When I explained that it was an intimate task and that I needed to put her at ease, he just looked at me blankly.'

'My point exactly,' she said.

I shrugged. 'As long as he sticks to the books and leaves the caring to us, he doesn't really bother me.'

'Or the residents,' she said with a grin.

I laughed. 'Especially the residents.'

The rest of the shift passed in a blur of happiness. I managed to stay out of too much trouble and only broke two glasses.

When I dropped Lexi at home, she gave me a quick hug. 'Have fun feeding all those homeless people,' she said.

I stared at her in confusion for a moment before I remembered what she was talking about. 'Damn it, I'd forgotten about that.'

She laughed. 'I swear, you'd lose your head if it wasn't screwed on.'

'What would I do without you?'

She grinned. 'Walk around in a confused haze most of the time.'

I checked the time on my phone. 'I had best make a move then, I said I would help Clair get the food ready.'

She gave me a quick smile before getting out. 'Don't forget to focus on your driving,' she shouted through the closed door.

I rolled my eyes. 'Yeah, yeah.'

I took note though and forced myself to concentrate. Still, there were times I stared longingly at the stereo, wanting to fill my mind with a tune that made my body move in time.

Clair spooned some mash potato onto the plate held out before her. The man smiled in response, revealing yellow stained teeth.

'Thanks for helping out tonight,' she said to me.

I smiled at the man and forked a slice of meatloaf onto his plate. 'I just wish I could be here more often.'

'How is Uni going?

I shrugged. 'Okay. I enjoy it but wish I had more hours in the day. I feel like it's been months since I was last here.'

'It's been six weeks,' a familiar voice said. Bill stood before me, his dark hair lanky and his body odour worse than I remembered.

'Why, how are you Mr Williams? Faring well I hope.'

'All the better for seeing you again,' he said with a grin. 'Especially as you left me to the indecent intentions of Miss Gibbs here. If she had her way, we would have run off into the sunset by now.'

Clair laughed and flapped a hand at him. 'Oh you, you're such a tease.'

'Only when around beautiful women such as yourselves.'

I forked a generous helping of meatloaf onto his plate. 'Where's Dan today? I think this is the first time I've seen you without him.'

Bill frowned and fiddled with his thick, uneven beard. 'He is back at the Tannery. Things aren't right with him.'

'What do you mean?' I said. 'Is his chest okay?'

43

'Yes. He still talks about how you let him stay in your spare room while the antibiotics kicked in. That was nice of you.'

I shrugged. 'I wish I could do more to help.'

An elderly woman elbowed Bill, pushing him along a few inches. 'Come on, some of us are trying to get some tea.'

Bill gave me a wink and took his plate to the table, allowing the rest of the queue to move along. Once we finished dishing out all the food, he brought his empty plate up.

'Did you really mean it,' he said, putting the dirty dish on the side, 'when you say you want to help more?'

'Of course I did.'

'I could do with a favour,' he said, 'though it's a lot to ask.'

'Let me be the judge of that.'

'You helped Dan with all the depression stuff when he stayed with you. Do you think you could have a chat with him and do it again?'

'I didn't really do anything.'

He shrugged and helped me stack up the plates. 'He won't talk to me. I think it helped that you're a woman.'

'Is he that bad?'

He nodded as he wiped his hands down his clothes, transferring the spilt gravy into his trousers. 'He won't even eat. I'm worried about him.'

'I'll just finish up here, and then I'll come with you.'

Clair stared at me with her mouth open. 'You ain't going tonight, are you? The place is abandoned, except for all these lot.' She gestured to the remaining men and women as they finished up their dinner. 'And didn't you see the news?'

'What news?'

'About the deaths down there.'

'The deaths have all been suicides,' Bill said, with a touch of irritation. 'She won't come to any harm.'

'It's not you I'm worried about. No offense Bill, but some of the people there aren't that savoury.'

'I will ensure her safety.'

Clair shook her head and carried the trays into the small kitchen.

'Just give me five minutes,' I told Bill, collecting the rest of the trays. 'I'll finish up here and come with you.' I followed Clair into the kitchen to find her filling the sink with hot water.

44

'You're being silly,' she said as I rinsed out the trays. 'You already do too much for them. If you get found out, you won't be allowed to work here anymore.'

I stared at her pointedly. 'Who's going to tell them?'

'Look, Ana, I'll keep it to myself, but you can't feel sorry for them. Even Bill, as nice as he is, chose this way of life.'

'You don't know that.'

She shrugged and turned her back on me. 'Be it through drink, drugs or gambling, they all did something to get this way.'

'And the children?'

'They choose it.'

I pressed my lips together in irritation. 'We have both been lucky and had good families, not like some of these kids. Maybe they just need someone to be there for them for once.'

Clair sighed and shook her head. 'You aren't suited for this work, Ana. Your hearts in the right place, but you get far too emotionally involved.'

'How's that a bad thing?'

'Just be careful,' she said. 'I don't want to turn on the news one day and find you have been killed by one of them because you let them into the house.'

I groaned. 'That was a one off. He would have died if he'd stayed out in the snow. Could you really sit by and let that happen, knowing you could do something to help?'

'It's not our problem. The sooner you realise that, the better off you will be.'

We cleaned up in silence, the atmosphere tense. By the time we turned off the lights and locked up, I was glad to get out of there.

Bill stood leaning against the wall, with his thick corduroy jacket pulled up around his neck to ward off the chill in the air.

'Just give me a minute,' I said. 'I've just got to let my boyfriend know that I'm going to be late.'

I rang my house phone in the hope Gabriel had already arrived. He didn't answer so I left a message on the answering machine. He would most likely check it when I didn't come home. It would be so much easier if he would get a mobile phone.

I led Bill to my car, parked under the dusky street light. 'Excuse the mess,' I said, indicating to the empty bottles of pop on the floor. 'I'm normally very tidy, but for some reason, I always forget about the car.'

45

He rolled his eyes and laughed. 'Ana, I live in an abandoned Tannery with at least thirty other people.'

'So?' I said, blushing somewhat. 'Doesn't mean you have to put up with my mess.'

Bill shook his head and laughed again. 'You are a funny one.'

I bristled and then shrugged. It had been a bit of a silly comment considering his lifestyle.

'Can I ask you something?' I said. 'It might be a bit personal.'

'Go ahead.'

'Why do you live on the streets? I mean, you seem like an intelligent person, well-spoken and knowledgeable, so why not just get a job and a house?'

He sighed. 'It isn't as simple as that. I have no place of residence, so can't get a job. I can't get a home address without a job to pay for it. It's a vicious circle that we are all trapped in.'

'What about if you used my address?'

'Would you let me in for a shower and help me get some reasonable clothes for interviews?'

I shifted uncomfortably. 'If you want.'

He laughed. 'You really should be more careful. If people find out how generous you are, they will take advantage.'

'I wouldn't offer it to everyone,' I said stubbornly. 'I know you.'

'You don't know me, Ana. I have done some bad things in my life, hurt a lot of people.'

I gulped and gripped the steering wheel hard. 'What sort of things?' The tension tightened my voice, making it more of a squeak.

He smiled. 'Don't worry. I haven't hurt anyone in that way, well, not in this life anyway.'

I frowned, not sure what to make of that.

'I did let a lot of people down though,' he said.

'Everyone makes mistakes.'

'Yes, and they pay the price. Losing my wife and children was that price.'

'Are they dead?' I clamped my lips shut too late. Maybe I shouldn't have asked that.

He gave me a small smile. 'No, although my kids think I am.'

I wanted to ask why he didn't contact them, but figured I knew the answer to that. He wouldn't want them knowing he lived on the streets.

'I can help you,' I said instead, 'get your life together, maybe contact your children.'

'It's okay. This is my life now, has been for many years. My kids are all grown up, probably with kids of their own. I wouldn't want to burden them.'

'I'm sorry.'

'You don't have anything to be sorry for. For better or worse, I accepted it a long time ago.'

I pulled the car up near the abandoned Tannery. The dark building towered above us. Part of the roof had collapsed at some point and the rest of the brickwork appeared loose as if only the dirt held it together. I shivered and pulled my coat around me. The shadows created a sinister atmosphere, speaking of the tortured souls that called it home.

Bill thrust his hands in his pockets. 'You don't have to come in now,' he said. 'You can always come back tomorrow when the sun is out. Dan will be here, he doesn't go into town anymore.'

I swallowed. 'It's okay. I'm here now, might as well say hello.'

If only I had listened to Clair.

Light flickered through the door-less entrance, the reflection of flames only added to the bleakness. Bill led me towards the light.

Men sat huddled around an oil drum which contained a small fire, the damp wood creating more smoke than heat. The men didn't speak and only one of them glanced up as we entered. The rest continued to stare at the flames that hugged the small logs, as if it had the answer for all their woes.

A huddled figure lay in the corner, covered in threadbare blankets. They let out a dry racking cough and I took a step in that direction.

Bill gripped my forearm. 'Leave him. He isn't one you want to get involved with.'

I stepped back to Bill's side, standing so close his musky smell drifted over my skin and stung my nose. I would need a bath when I got home.

Bill led us further into the building, through small damp rooms, past many more huddled figures. Some had built some sort of protection around them, cardboard houses containing their meagre possessions which would likely be nothing more than rubbish to me.

Someone cried out. The sound cut through the air, eerie in its shrillness. I grabbed Bill and squeezed his arm through the many layers of clothing.

'I shouldn't have brought you here,' he said.

I quickly let go and straightened up. 'It's okay. I'm just freaking myself out.'

He frowned at me, then shrugged and continued forward. I kept my head down as we travelled through the rooms. Despair saturated the air, speaking of the lives ruined by bad decisions, mingling with the loss of hope. I shuddered.

'Dan's up here,' Bill said, leading me to a staircase. 'Don't walk in the middle else the step will give way.'

I followed his advice and only stood where he did, hugging the wall as we climbed. The steps creaked under us and half way up it groaned so loudly I pushed further into the dirty wall, sure that the step would collapse under me. Bill didn't stop, so after a moment to control my breathing, I hesitantly followed.

We finally reached the top and I paused to take a slow, deep breath.

'This way,' Bill said, heading into another room.

We stepped over the scattered rubble. Luckily, starlight shone through the missing roof, preventing me from twisting an ankle.

'How do you stand this?' My murmured words echoed around, returning to me as the muted whispers of haunted spirits. I shivered and clasped my bag tighter to my chest.

'It's shelter,' he said.

He halted in the next doorway so suddenly I walked into his outstretched arms.

'You need to be careful here.'

I peered into the room, taking in the missing floor. Half the wall had collapsed to the ground below, allowing the cold night air to breeze through. I raised my eyebrows in question.

'Just follow me.' He pressed his back against the wall and slowly edged around the couple of feet of crumbling floor that still remained. I stared at him without moving.

'It's safe,' he said. We definitely had different definitions of safe. He held out his hand, his fingerless gloves revealing dirty, broken nails.

'I've got it,' I said. With every step, I tested the floor, sure that it would collapse beneath me. I pressed my back so hard against the wall that crumbling bits of brick drifted down to the ground below. My coat snagged on something. My breath forced itself through my nostrils as I stood still, carefully planning how to unhook myself. After a few seconds, I back up a step to release the coat, before following Bill again. This time I made sure to avoid the protruding nail. I gave a big sigh of relief when we reached the other side.

'How far?'

What had I been thinking coming here in the middle of the night? Bill was right, I didn't know him, I didn't know any of them.

'We've done the worst bit,' Bill said. 'Not far now.'

To think, I was going to have to come back out this way. A couple of loud squeaks and a whisper of claws on brick echoed through the dusty air. Rats! My lip curled in disgust and I took a deep shuddering breath.

The faint smell of smoke disappeared and the walls closed in. The scent of damp wood filled my nostrils and I leant against the brickwork, gripping my bag to my chest, trying to banish the memories that still haunted my dreams on occasion. How naïve I'd been as a child, how easily Sonia had found it to lure me into the abandoned building on the route back from school.

Fingers touched my arm and I yelped.

'Are you all right?' Bill said.

I nodded, my throat too closed off to speak. I followed in silence, flinching with every scurry and squeak. The memory of the locked cellar stayed forefront in my mind while the imagined feel of tiny claws on my skin urged me to run from the Tannery.

A commotion started up outside, shouting and laughing, the voices coarse and raspy. The hairs on the back of my neck rose and my heart missed a beat. Something tugged on my mind, a memory that sent a shiver down my spine. I moved to the hole in the wall, once a window maybe. No frame remained, only broken brickwork with the occasional hint of an edge. Taking care not to fall out, I looked down.

Small shadows ran through the weeds and rubble. They laughed, a cold, cruel sound that froze the blood in my veins. The clouds shifted and moonlight shone down, revealing the shadows below. The black mist from their backs created a void behind them, one that no light passed through. I scanned the area, unable to breathe. About twenty figures headed to the entrance, twenty small vicious creatures. A familiar voice called out to the others, urging them on. It was the female from the park. Oh my God, it was the Fae.

6

'Oh God,' I whimpered, stumbling back from the hole. I bumped into Bill and let out a high pitched yelp. 'We need to leave,' I told him in a tight, frantic voice. 'Right now.'

He took my shoulders and moved me out of the way so as to peer down. 'You see them?'

I nodded and tugged on his arm. 'Come on,' I urged.

He resisted. 'Nobody ever sees them,' he said with wonder. 'Only ever me.'

'Bill, come on, we need to go.'

He shrugged. 'They always come here. If you ignore them, they leave you alone.'

I stared at him. 'Do you have any idea what they are?'

He pressed his lips together. 'Death, well I figure the Reapers minions at least.'

I shook my head. 'What are you on about?'

'They come sometimes, when one of us has given up. They stay while they die, I watch them.' He peered down again. 'There aren't normally this many though.'

'Don't you get it?' I said frantically, 'they kill them. They aren't nice or helpful, they are evil.'

He frowned at me. 'But they never touch a person, they only ever watch.'

I groaned through clenched teeth. 'For God's sake Bill, trust me on this one, they will kill us.'

Bill shook his head. 'I can't believe you can see them too. For so long, I thought I was going insane, but I'm not, they really are real?'

I gritted my teeth together. 'Of course they are real.' The Fae's shouts and laughter echoed through the building. They were coming. I pushed against his chest. 'We need to move, now!'

He continued to stare at me in wonder.

I quickly rummaged through my bag to get the mobile phone. Please God, let Gabriel be home. The call went to the answering machine. I called out his name, silently praying that he would answer. He didn't. I cursed, dropping the phone back into my bag. I was alone with twenty Fae heading my way. Would they ignore me like they appeared to have done Bill? Unlikely. They could somehow smell Gabriel on me, and then there was the female from the park. She had wanted to stay, find out more about me. If she saw me again... Damn, I was screwed.

I moved closer to Bill and kept my voice low. 'Is there another way to get out of here?'

He shook his head. 'Not one that is safe.'

I quickly scanned the room around me. 'What about unsafe ones?'

Bill frowned. 'They won't touch you, Ana. They never have me.'

'You're lucky.' I peered into the next room. It looked the same, broken window, filthy walls, and no stairs down. A couple of figures huddled in the corners. They looked up at me with interest at my panicked tone. 'Trust me, they won't leave me alone,' I said. 'I've come across them before.'

Bill stood, staring at me with confusion.

I grabbed his arms and shook him. 'Come on, give me a way out of here.'

He pointed back the way we had come. 'That's the only way. The fire escape broke years back.'

Damn it. I rubbed my hands over my face. If I didn't look at them, could I just walk past? Was I really willing to risk it? I looked out the large hole again. Could I maybe hang down before dropping? Maybe I would only break an ankle. Unlikely. I had more chance of breaking my neck. I pressed my palms to my head, trying to force the solution from my brain.

'Think I'll have to give Dan a miss today,' I said, turning back the way we had come. 'I suggest you get out of here too.'

What about everyone else? If I started shouting for them to get out, they would likely look at me as if I was mad. Plus, the Fae wouldn't ignore me for long if I did that.

'They won't harm us,' Bill said again.

I wanted to grab him, maybe knock some sense into his misled brain. There were just too many Fae. Even Bill appeared shocked by the amount. It was going to be a blood bath.

'I like you Bill, I don't want you to die. Come with me, humour me if you must, but leave here now.'

I headed back the way we came. Thankfully he followed. Gabriel would help the people here. Surely he knew of a way to protect everyone from the Fae. I definitely couldn't. The Fae had followed the man in the park and Gabriel's wording suggested they only ever manipulated a person's emotions. We would have time to save them. I had to believe that.

'There will be time,' I said. Who was I trying to convince?

We slowly made our way around the floorless room. The Fae's laughter became louder, more intense. The first two came into sight as we approached the stairs.

A woman sat in the corner rocking. She slapped her own face as she muttered, the pitch warbled as if she was a radio and someone was messing with the tuner. Red welts covered her arms and face, some of them speckled with blood and all fresh. The Fae hovered near, maintaining some distance yet repeating the same fluid movements I had seen before, inhaling her scent when they reached her face. She screamed, a high pitch tortured sound that pierced through the air like a knife. I jumped and grabbed onto Bill's arm.

He looked down the stairs and his eyes widened in surprise. 'There are so many. They're around everyone. They never go to everyone.'

I shushed him. The two Fae glanced at us, their eyes narrowed in interest. The nearest, a male with long blonde hair, hissed, revealing the sharpened teeth. I quickly looked down at the floor.

Please ignore me, I silently begged, watching him from the corner of my eye. He shrugged before turning his attention back to the rocking woman. The other Fae, a younger looking boy, was already leaning into her.

I tugged on Bill's arm to get his attention and pressed my fingers to my lips. He nodded and we began down the stairs, slowly and hesitantly, ensuring that we didn't make any sudden movements. We reached the bottom without incident. I pressed into the corner and gasped with horror. At least two Fae surrounded every person.

Most of them seemed unaware of what stood before them, except a young girl, maybe sixteen years old, her dirty blonde hair in a tight pony tail. She had backed into a corner and stood with her arms out, warding them off. Her wide, frightened eyes darted between the two Fae approaching her and she whimpered as they laughed.

'This one has touched us,' the small male Fae said.

His female companion laughed. 'It will make it more interesting.' She slashed at the air with her small hands, the thick nails sharpened into lethal points. The girl let out a small scream and tried to cower further into the corner causing the Fae laughed even harder.

'That's Cassy,' Bill said. 'She's new here.'

Not that new. She'd obviously been here long enough to accidently touch one of the malicious creatures, giving her the ability to see them. We had to help her.

I took a deep breath and tried to swallow back the fear that filled my throat. It remained, like an unmovable rock pinning my body in place. Cassy screamed and kicked out at the Fae. They hopped backed, laughing at her feeble attempts to protect herself.

I walked to her, keeping my head up high. The Fae moved aside and turned towards me with interest. I made sure to look through them as if they weren't there. My eyes protested, wanting to focus on the creatures before me. I resisted and moved closer to the girl so that they left my sight.

'There you are, Cassy,' I said. 'Do you know how long I've been looking for you?'

Cassy tore her eyes away from the Fae. 'Who...'

'Mum has been worried,' I said quickly, giving her an urgent look. 'She sent me to get you.'

'Ana,' Bill warned. The Fae watched me with interest. I didn't need to see them; their stare bored into the back of my head.

'I know,' I replied without taking my eyes off Cassy. I bent down and gripped her wrist. 'You're coming home right now,' I told her.

She allowed me to pull her up. 'What are they?'

'What are who?' I turned around as if scanning the building. My eyes desperately wanted to look directly at the Fae. I managed to resist the compulsion, even when they took a step towards me and inhaled deeply. 'That's just Bill.' I pointed to where he stood frowning with concern.

Cassy pulled on my grip. 'But them...' she said, pointing towards the Fae.

'Just stop it now!' I said. 'I've had enough of your stories.'

I jerked her towards me and she stumbled. When she opened her mouth to speak again, I gripped her wrist so hard, she yelled.

'We have to go now,' I said slowly through my teeth. She finally registered the urgency in my eyes and nodded. We walked past the Fae towards Bill.

'Ana,' he said. He shifted uncomfortably, taking in the amount of Fae in the large room.

'I know.' He didn't need to tell me the two Fae were following. Their malevolent interest smothered my skin like thick fog.

'She's taking our prize,' the male Fae hissed.

'No she isn't,' the female responded. As we continued to the exit, a sense of despair came over me. I stumbled under the weight of it and grabbed the wall for support. The voice in my head remained quiet, with none of the usual taunts that accompanied such a feeling. Yet my heart hurt under the pressure and my legs became heavy, threatening to give way under me. I slowed.

Move! the voice piped up. Well, that was a new one, it never normally helped. *For God's sake, you're pathetic. Move now!* I struggled forward, ignoring the tears that flooded down my cheeks and focused on the fire near the exit. I needed to keep the charade up, maybe shout at the girl for running away. I didn't even have the strength to open my mouth. It all became too hard.

'Why isn't she stopping?' the male Fae asked his partner.

The wave rushed over me again, stronger, more physical. *Why bother?* my internal demon said. *You can't do this, you're not strong enough.* So much for it helping me out, though the words somehow fuelled me, encouraging an indignant anger that gave me strength.

Over ten Fae moved around the people huddled at the fire, leaning towards them, inhaling their despair. I tried to tally up the numbers which didn't make sense. More must have come during our journey through the building.

One of the Fae looked up. Her eyes met mine and the recognition passed between us. Damn, we were screwed.

'You!' she hissed.

I grabbed Cassy's hand tighter, turned and ran towards the back of the building.

A male Fae shouted. 'But Sheah, she can't see us!'

The female from the park screamed. 'You idiot, she fooled you both.' The sound of their running footsteps followed as we bypassed the stairs. I'd seen the horror movies. There wasn't a chance in hell I was going up there.

Many of the Fae looked up as we ran into the next room, their eyes wide with interest.

'Get her!' the female Fae, Sheah, screamed from behind. Eight Fae leapt up, with their clawed hands out before them, ready to grab me. I skidded to a halt and Cassy crashed into me, propelling me forward onto my knees. My shin landed on a broken brick and I cried out. Within a second, I struggled to my feet. The Fae came towards me with no knowledge of who I was, but willing to follow Sheah's orders. I turned and ran back, dragging Cassy with me.

The Fae closed in, surrounding us. We backed up towards the stairs. There had to be another way.

Bill walked through the Fae as they moved closer, somehow managing to take no notice of them. They hissed at him but he didn't even flinch. He walked straight past me and up the stairs. Did he have something in mind?

Sheah pushed through the growing crowd. 'I hoped we would meet again.'

I followed Bill. The two Fae stood at the top, watching us with interest. They moved aside as Bill approached and peered around him so as to not lose sight of Cassy and me.

'What do we do?' Cassy said. Her voice shook and she dug her nails into my hand. I edged her up the stairs. Two Fae were better than thirty.

Where to then? my mind demanded. I ignored it. How the hell was I supposed to know?

Bill walked through the Fae and they closed the gap behind him. Had he given up on us, decided that we weren't worth the hassle? He'd been right; I didn't know him at all. He continued across the landing, taking the route we had gone before. A spark of anger exploded in my mind. The selfish git was leaving us to the Fae.

The pack of Fae approached. We backed up the stairs, closer to the two waiting Fae. How the hell did I fight them? Bill walked back out onto the landing, holding something down at his leg. The Fae didn't pay any attention to him. As soon as he reached them, he swung up a long wooden plank. They didn't see it coming. He brought it down with enough force, the smallest Fae toppled over the edge of the landing into the pack below.

All the Fae screeched as one.

Bill followed the movement of the plank through, turning on the spot. The remaining Fae didn't have time to raise his arms before Bill brought it down on his head with a nauseating crunch. The Fae dropped to the ground, unmoving, hopefully dead.

The Fae started up the stairs as one.

'Move!' Bill bellowed.

Cassy reacted first. She yanked her hand from my grip and pushed past me. I followed behind. The Fae were faster, more agile. They began gaining. Bill stood with the plank ready, resting on his shoulder with both hands gripping the base. Two steps from the top, the wood groaned and splintered, and my foot plunged through.

I held my hand out to Bill. 'Help!' My foot wouldn't pull free. The sharp splinters buried themselves into my ankle, pinning me in place.

The first Fae reached us. Sheah dug her nails into my shoulder and pulled on me. I screamed and Bill swung the plank back.

'Duck,' he shouted.

I bent down, hugging my body to the stairs and landing as he brought the plank around. It hit Sheah and she shrieked. Her nails ripped through my skin as she lost her grip and toppled down the stairs.

Bill grabbed my hand and pulled. The wood tore at my skin and stuck on my heel. Bill pulled harder and my trainer fell off. We toppled forwards to land in a heap. He rolled us over so that he lay on top of me, burying my face in his unwashed armpit before his weight lifted and I could breathe once again.

Bill didn't raise his voice in anyway, yet it carried authority like I'd never heard him use before. 'Follow Cassy now.' He held the plank ready, keeping his eye on the approaching Fae.

'Be careful,' I said.

He gave one short, sharp nod.

I caught up with Cassy in the room with the missing floor. She slowly edged her way around the small ledge.

She turned to me with wide eyes. 'Where can we go?'

I joined her on the ledge. The screams of the Fae followed us, high pitched, gleeful and filled with excitement. I hesitated.

Cassy reached the other side. 'Come on.'

'I have to help Bill. Just keep going.'

She stared at me, her eyes wide and mouth agape as she drew in deep, ragged breaths. 'Where?'

'Anywhere away from them, find a corner if you have to.' Without waiting for a reply, I started running back to the stairs. One of the missing windows had a part of its frame hanging loosely to the ground. I pulled on it, but it didn't budge.

'Come on.' I pulled on it harder. It still didn't move so I twisted it, ignoring the splinters that worked their way into my hands. It finally came free and I stumbled back.

Someone screamed, likely Bill as it sounded deeper, more human. I sprinted towards him.

The Fae crowded towards Bill as he slowly made his way back, never once taking his eyes off them. He'd dropped the plank somewhere along the way and held some sort of knife or dagger. One side curved around while serrated teeth adorned the other.

'Where did you get that?' I said.

'One of the little bastards used it on me.' He glanced down to his leg which bled profusely. 'I told you to get out of here.'

One of the Fae darted forwards and I swung the window pane around, catching it on the head. It scuttled back with a squeal.

'Don't let them touch the wood,' Bill said. 'One of them grabbed mine and the middle turned to dust in his fingers.'

'The knife?'

He shrugged. 'None of them have tried to grab it yet.'

We continued to back up through the derelict rooms. 'Something's wrong,' Bill said. 'They should be attacking us.'

'Don't complain.'

'I don't like it. They could swarm us, take us down easily. Why don't they?'

'We're at the ledge,' I told him as we entered the floorless room.

He gave a curt nod. 'Get around it, quickly.'

I began the journey. The Fae held back, many of them laughing; a hissed choking sound that sent shivers down my spine.

'Shit!' Bill said. 'They're forcing us back, cornering us.'

'Isn't there any other way out?'

He nodded. 'A dangerous one, it doesn't matter though, we won't get there.'

Cassy ran into the room with wide, frantic eyes. 'They're coming this way!' She got back onto the ledge as Fae followed her, led by Sheah. She stopped at the hole with her arms held to halt the other Fae. Her lips twisted into a cruel smile.

We were trapped with no place to go. Fae blocked us at each exit, leaving only the fifteen foot drop to below.

Cassy grabbed my arm. 'What do we do?'

What did we do? Hell if I knew.

Cassy pulled on my arm, nearly unbalancing me. 'They're everywhere. What do we do?'

I peered down. 'Sit on the ledge,' I told her. Bill stood with the knife ready. Sheah watched us with interest as Cassy did what I bid. I hunkered down next to her. Rubble scattered the floor below, but there was a clear patch, a metre of so in. Could I hold her weight as I lowered her?

The Fae buzzed with excitement. Many of them looked over to Sheah as if she had all the answers. Was she their boss? Did they have any sort of structure like that? Sheah's smiled, revealing the sharpened teeth. Her eyes shone with amusement, silently asking me what I was going to do next. I leant in close to Cassy.

'I'm going to hang you down,' I said so low I could barely hear myself. She turned her head sharply, her eyes filled with question, before glancing down at the rubble. 'I'll swing you over,' I continued quietly. 'When you get down there, run, don't hesitate, don't wait for us, just run as far from here as you can. Do you understand?'

She nodded.

'Hang yourself down, but do it quickly, before they can figure out what's happening.'

I glanced at Sheah from the corner of my eyes. She frowned and took a step towards us. At least she couldn't hear. Hopefully Cassy would get away.

You will die, the voice in my mind piped up.

'You're not helpful,' I said, drawing a sharp look from Cassy. I shook my head a little and mouthed the words *one, two....* 'Now!'

Cassy and I both fell to our stomachs. She quickly slipped her feet off the edge.

'They're coming,' Bill shouted.

Cassy hung down by her fingers. I grabbed her wrist and swung her out. She helped and kicked her feet up, pushing off from the wall. I dropped her down. She landed smack bang in the middle of the clear spot and rolled a couple of times before she came to a stop on a large brick. I held my breath, waiting for some sort of movement.

She struggled to her feet, seemingly unharmed. Thank God.

Bill yelled and slashed the knife out before him. The Fae jumped back, avoiding the wicked looking weapon. I planned to drop over the edge, use my feet as Cassy had. I didn't have time. Sheah grabbed my hair. She pulled me up with not even a hint of strain and dangled me over the edge as I scrabbled to get a grip on the broken floor. My hair ripped from its roots and I screamed as tears filled my eyes, blurring my vision.

'You want to go down?' she said with a smile. 'Let me help with that.'

She dropped me.

My fingers held onto the floor, gripping so hard the tendons screamed. She brought her heel down on them and twisted, crushing the bones. I tried to ignore the pain, keep my grip while I swung my body around. The muscles cramped and sweat poured over my eyes. I fell.

Bill grabbed my wrist, pinching the skin between his fingers and swung me out.

The Fae sprung towards him as he dropped me.

Bill turned to the Fae, with the knife held out before him. He couldn't protect both sides, leaving his back bare to Sheah. She reached towards him, with her nails at the ready, moving slowly as if she had all the time in the world, or so it seemed.

The air rushed passed me as I fell, the distance suddenly so much more than it had been. Sheah touched her hands to Bill's neck, giving me no time to shout out a warning.

I hit the ground, straight on my back. The air rushed from my lungs in one sudden gush, leaving a dull ache in its place. Bill turned too late. Sheah sunk her nails into his neck and threw him over the ledge. The Fae let out a war cry, a primal scream that pierced the air. I managed to draw in a painful breath.

Bill landed on me and the meagre air in my lungs gushed out in a grunt. He lay still, not moving at all. The Fae looked down on us laughing, all except Sheah who watched with a small smile playing across her lips.

I tried to call Bill's name but couldn't find the breath. Hands grabbed at me and I struggled against them.

'It's me,' Cassy said. She seized me under the arms and pulled. Bill shifted with us before I managed to tug my legs free. I rolled onto my knees and turned him over. His eyelashes fluttered and he groaned.

'Are you okay?' I gasped looking around.

There had once been two exits from the room, but only one of them remained. Rubble filled the other.

Bill struggled to his feet. Blood ran down his face from a deep gash on his forehead and pooled around his collar from where Sheah had embedded her nails. None of the damage seemed life threatening. He snatched the knife off the floor.

'Let's go,' he said, heading towards the exit.

We managed no more than three steps before the Fae filled the doorway. We backed up, our eyes flitting between the approaching Fae and those watching from above.

'What do we do?' Cassy said. We both looked to Bill. He pressed his lips together and scanned the room.

'Against the wall.' He pushed us back and glanced at me, unable to conceal the loss of hope that filled his eyes. I nodded and grabbed a couple of whole bricks off the floor. Cassy took one off me as we pressed our backs against the wall. The Fae smiled and moved forward, advancing slowly so as to take pleasure in our fear.

Sheah peered down. 'Don't kill the dark haired girl, I want her.'

Bill frowned. 'Why do they want you?'

I shrugged. It wasn't the time to explain my brief history with Sheah.

We were dead. We still breathed and moved, but we had nowhere to run, nowhere to hide. We had minutes at the most before they swarmed over us. Why hadn't I listened to Clair? Why hadn't I gone home? I could be in Gabriel's arms right now, talking and laughing about our day. Now I wouldn't see him again. I wouldn't feel the gentle touch of his fingers on my skin, or his breath as it flittered over my face. My heart hurt beyond any pain the fall had inflicted, a deep ache that dragged on my insides, turning them to lead.

Cassy spoke, her voice filled with confusion. 'Something's happening.' She grabbed my hand and pushed it against the wall. My eyes narrowed in confusion as the brickwork shifted beneath my touch. It vibrated as if a mild electrical current ran through it and dust drifted down.

The wall crumbled before my eyes. One second it was there, the next second a shower of thick powered brick drifted to the ground.

A figure stood on the other side and I blinked to clear the grime from my eyes.

'Gabriel?'

He gripped my arm and yanked me through the hole. 'Move! Now!'

None of us hesitated and we quickly ran out into the night. I grimaced as bits of brick dug into my shoeless foot. The Fae screamed for their escaping prey.

'The car,' I gasped as we sprinted from the building. I veered off to the right and everyone followed, including the running Fae. Could we make it? Their screams echoed out into the night, chasing us, surrounding us, taunting us. I reached for my side and cried out. My bag wasn't there.

'The keys,' I said breathlessly. 'I lost them.'

Gabriel pushed me harder. 'Just keep going.'

Cassy stumbled and fell to her knees. Without pause, Bill slipped a hand under her shoulder and heaved her up.

Gabriel grabbed my collar and threw me forwards. 'Move faster, now.'

The car came into sight and all four doors flung open on their own. I skidded to a stop, unable to comprehend what just happened. Bill and Cassy crashed into me.

'Get in,' Gabriel ordered. I dived into the front passenger seat as he took a running jump over the bonnet. Bill threw Cassy into the back and lunged in after her. We slammed the doors as the Fae reached us.

They sprang onto the car, their feet loud as they scurried over the roof, cackling with wicked joy. A male crouched on the front and hissed. Saliva sprayed onto the window and dripped off his teeth. He reached towards the glass, smiling with confidence. The engine roared into life and the tyres spun as Gabriel started the car forwards. He turned it sharply to the right and most of the Fae rolled off, unable to keep a grip. The Fae on the front sunk his fingers into the bonnet as if it was liquid rather than metal.

Gabriel sped the car down the road, taking little heed of the passing traffic. When the road cleared, he swerved the car from left to right. The Fae skidded along the bonnet, but maintained his grip as he scrambled his legs to regain his crouched position. The damn thing clung like the devil, hissing and snapping each time Gabriel managed to dislodge him. Cassy screamed as the Fae reached through the window, the glass parting around him, allowing entry to the small clawed hand.

Gabriel leant over the steering wheel and reached through the glass as the Fae had. He grabbed the creature's long, dark hair and dragged him forward. The Fae tried to turn in his grip, snapping at the hands that held him.

'Hold the steering wheel,' Gabriel shouted as he released it. I grabbed it as the car veered off to the right and tried to steady it. The Fae and Gabriel's arm blocked the window and the car swerved all over the road.

'Stop the car!' I screamed.

Gabriel ignored me and pulled the Fae towards us. He clenched the small throat in his hand, ignoring the nails that tore at his skin and twisted it sharply. A sickening snap overshadowed the roar of the engine and the wind that rushed through the damaged window. The Fae became limp and Gabriel pushed him back through the glass. He rolled off the car and under the tyres. The steering wheel slipped out of my hand as the car bumped over the body and Gabriel quickly took control. He slammed the breaks on and I shot forward into the dashboard, smacking my head so hard I groaned.

'Stay here,' Gabriel ordered as he got out of the car. I touched my head to find a lump forming. Luckily, it came away free of blood, though I was going to have one hell of a bruise.

Cassy poked her head out from under Bill's arms. 'Are we safe?'

I pressed my hand to my chest, taking deep, even breaths. 'I think so.'

She disengaged herself from Bill and peered around, checking out the darkness.

'We made it out,' she said in wonder. She started laughing, a rough sound that wavered with an edge of hysteria.

'We did,' I spluttered with my own hysteria. 'Oh my God, did you see them coming for us?' I laughed harder, gasping as I struggled to find my breath. 'And the way that one clung to the car.' It wasn't funny, but neither of us could stop the shaky laughter.

Bill frowned, not sharing in our display of relief. 'Do you want to tell me what just happened there?'

It took a few seconds to gain enough control to speak. 'I doubt I know much more than you.'

'What about that man?' he persisted. 'Who is he?'

The laughter died in my throat and I opened the door before he could force an answer from me. 'I'd better go and see what's happening.'

How could I answer his question? Gabriel would be far from happy if I filled Bill in on the truth.

Gabriel stood several feet away, his shadow taller and more dominating that I recalled. When he saw me heading towards him, he strode over and grabbed my arm too hard. 'What were you thinking coming out here at night?'

I shrank under his gaze, filled with fire that shimmered in the dark.

He shook me. 'Don't you have any concept of self-preservation?'

I pressed my lips together in a bid to keep back the tears that threatened to fall.

'How could I know that the Fae were there,' I said in a small voice. 'How were there so many of them? Were they really going to kill all those people?'

He rubbed his hand down his face and sighed. 'I do not know. It is unusual to see so many hunting together like that.'

My hand unconsciously reached for him and he opened his arms to take me in his embrace.

'If I hadn't checked your messages,' he began. 'If I hadn't come to find you...'

'But you did, and you saved us all.'

He sighed again. 'Oh yes, the others. I will need to deal with them.'

He disengaged himself from my grip and began towards the car. I grabbed onto his arm, halting him.

'Are you going to take their memories?'

He nodded.

'Why? Why not leave them. At least then they can protect themselves.'

He pulled his arm from my hold. 'They saw me using my abilities, they cannot maintain that memory.' He turned sharply from me.

'Why not?' I shouted after him. 'What does it matter if they know? Nobody will believe them.'

He whirled on me, his jaw tense and fists clenched. 'You have no understanding of our ways. You don't even understand the danger you have put yourself in by getting them involved.'

'But I didn't. They saw the Fae and helped me.'

'That may be so, however, they will need to be dealt with.'

My protests fell on deaf ears as I ran to catch up with him, hobbling as small stones dug into my foot. He cursed as he reached the car.

'They are gone,' he said through clenched teeth. Even though I believed him, I peered through the window at the empty seat. Maybe they had heard our conversation. I smiled and quickly hid it with my fingers. Hopefully they were running as far from Gabriel as possible. Hopefully Bill still had the strange knife he'd got off the Fae. I wouldn't mention that to Gabriel.

'Let's just go home,' I said getting into the passenger side. My hands still shook violently, making it a hazard for me to drive.

'I need to find them.'

'You can if you want,' I said. 'I'll just wait here.'

Gabriel grumbled something under his breath and got into the car. 'If you think I'm leaving you alone, you are sadly mistaken.'

I hid my grin behind my hands. That had been easy.

The tension finally left my shoulders as we pulled up outside the house. Gabriel ushered me in, keeping his hand on my arm as if I was going to make a break for it. Did he really think I was going to be that stupid? I thought over the things he'd already had to save me from. Okay, when I took it all into account, I could see why he was worried. It had been one hell of a busy year.

As soon as he opened the door, the smell of warm shepherd's pie filled my nostrils, making my stomach growl.

'I was cooking dinner when I checked the messages,' he said. 'Hopefully it isn't burnt.'

He gave me a disapproving look and I smiled in response.

'Dish it up,' he said. 'I have a call to make.' He stormed from the room before I could ask who.

We ate dinner in silence. So many questions bounded around my head, I didn't know where to start. It was only when we finished drying up the dishes that the tension began to recede from him and when we sat back at the table with a cup of tea, he smiled for the first time.

'So,' I said, 'that thing with the wall and car, does that mean you can change items then? Or can you only move them?'

He smiled. 'I can change nearly anything I wish.'

'Like that colander?'

I gestured to where it hung on the wall. He retrieved it from the hook and laid it on the table in between us. He held his hand out, and I became transfixed by what happened before me.

The colander shimmered and hummed, almost like it was going out of faze. It appeared to fold in on itself and within seconds a beautiful shiny swan sat in its place, small enough to fit in the palm of my hand. Gabriel watched with amusement as I gently picked it up, terrified it would crumble with my touch. I stroked along the cool metal side, able to feel the solid curves of each individual feather.

I stole a look at the man I loved and the splendour of his smile captivated me, pushing all other thoughts from my mind. I didn't deserve this wonderful creature sat before me, the man who had saved me on at least three occasions.

Tears pricked at my eyes and I turned my gaze back to the swan. In one fluid movement, he moved around the table to crouch before me and brought my chin up to look into my eyes.

'What is it?'

My chest swelled and burst. Tears flooded down my face and I sobbed in his arms.

'I love you so much.' The newly spoken words only worsened the pain, and my heart ached terribly. For better or worse, I was committed to him now.

Gabriel kissed my lips and face, trying to caress away my distress. He didn't ask about my behaviour, he probably didn't need to. He merely held me tight, kissing me and repeatedly telling me he loved me until long after the tears stemmed and calmness descended once more.

That night we didn't make love, instead enjoying the closeness of lying in each other's arms. He allowed his light to shine out, bathing my skin, and through this I felt the depth of his feelings for me. It was not the time for words, just a quiet acknowledgement that something fundamental had changed. His pulse quickened until it matched mine, our hearts beating as one, the echo vibrating between us. We were two, but also one, forever to be connected in a way that could never be broken.

7

I sat on the sofa with Uni books surrounding me. We had been instructed to read through several chapters before the next lecture. If only they were interesting. Maybe they would have been, but my thoughts kept drifting to the news I had watched in the morning.

The police were cleaning up the Tannery, moving on all the homeless people that called it home, ready to demolish the derelict building. Was that because of Gabriel? Had he called someone to sort the problem out? The news left me with mixed feelings. On one hand, the people there would probably be a lot safer, on the other, they wouldn't have a home now.

After a time of chewing on the end of my pen, I sighed. It wasn't as if I could do anything about it so I forced my mind back on track and focused on my work. I even managed to become absorbed in it.

The phone starting ringing and I considered ignoring it. With a sigh of mild regret, I reached across to the cordless handset and answered. Might as well, the shrill tone had already disrupted my flow.

A chirpy voice greeted me. 'Hel-lo, it's me.'

I smiled, glad to hear my sister's happy, yet strained voice. She didn't wait for my response.

'Are you free for a brew? I'm going to kill the little sods.' She raised her voice to be heard over the beeps and tunes from the numerous toys, only marginally quieter than the raised voices of the children. No wonder her patience had come to an end.

'Come on round,' I said, straining to be heard.

A high pitched scream echoed down the phone line and I pulled the handset from my ear. Ava was obviously struggling with her autism today. We all prayed that the older she got, the more she would be able to cope with the differences that often left her unable to communicate properly. But it had been eight years now and there was very little improvement.

'Chance to back out is now.'

'I'll pop the kettle on,' I said.

After saying goodbye, I pulled out the box of toys I kept under the stairs for such occasions and flicked on the cartoon channel. Figuring she would be in need of a boost, I started preparing a coffee.

The door flew open and in fell three kids making the noise of ten. Neave, with her bobbed brown hair and big hazel eyes reached me first and jumped up into my arms, with a force that nearly knocked me off balance.

'You're getting too big,' I told her as she kissed me.

'I'm still little,' she said, 'I'm not seven till next year.'

'Good job, else I wouldn't be able to pick you up.' I gestured to the coffee and Beth gratefully retrieved it before sinking into the closest chair, leaving the kids to bombard me.

'I'm big,' Gracey said, grabbing onto my leg. 'I'm seven too.' She brushed her dark curls from her face, revealing pale blue eyes the size of large coins.

'No you're not,' Neave told her, 'you're only three.'

'No I'm not!' Gracey pushed her sister. 'Mummy, tell her.'

'You're a big three,' I told her. 'Now, leave mummy alone, she's having a coffee.'

I touched Ava's blond hair, pulled tight into a ponytail as it was the only way she would have it. She shifted under my contact and focused her eyes on the corner of the room. I removed my hand and winked when she glanced at me.

When they had all managed to say their piece, I peeled Neave off me and ushered them into the lounge with a biscuit. As soon as they spotted the box of toys I was forgotten. It was a relief to have all my limbs back.

Closing the kitchen door to dampen down the noise level, I joined my younger sister at the table, and studied the dark smudges under her eyes. Her golden blond hair hung limply to her shoulders, though her eyes still twinkled, revealing her infectious personality. It was what captured everyone's attention, though she needed to divert most men from her breasts first.

I opened the biscuit tin. 'Bad day?'

Beth helped herself to a couple of custard creams. 'Ryan's spent the night being sick, Gracey was up at the crack of dawn and I couldn't face the housework.'

'Just think,' I said, 'you have fifteen more years until the kids leave home.'

'Yeah, and then I'll still have Ryan. He's as much of a pain as they are. I swear, he hasn't changed since I met him.'

I laughed. 'Well, that's what happens when you marry your childhood sweetheart.'

She grumbled under her breath. 'I am beginning to think that everyone was right. We were too young.'

'You don't fool me.' I leaned forward to peer at her. 'I still catch your eyes lock across a crowded room, and you laugh all the time. That's got to mean something.'

'Not laughing today. He's got a twenty four hour bug, though you would believe he was dying if you listened to his complaints.'

'That's men for you.' I laughed, while wondering if Gabriel would ever suffer from a case of man flu. Could he even get sick?

'So how is Gabriel?' she said. 'I can see you have fallen in love with him, have you told him yet?'

Nobody knew me like she did and we had no secrets from each other. The heat rose in my face and I quickly looked down to hide it. If only I could tell her the truth about Gabriel.

'I have.' An uncontrollable smile spread across my face. 'Last night actually.' I didn't tell her about the crying fit that accompanied it, she knew me well.

Beth clasped her hands together, and her eyes filled with tears. She quickly came around the table to give me a hug.

'What's that for?'

She pulled away and dabbed her eyes with the palm of her hand. 'I'm sorry. It's just, I never thought that I would see this day. After what happened, I never thought that you...' She hugged me again. 'I'm just so happy for you.'

After several seconds of being trapped in her arms, I prised her off. Thankfully, she returned to her seat but continued to stare at me with brimming eyes. I shifted uncomfortably before getting up to put the kettle on. I needed the distraction.

'Well, I figure I can't live in fear forever.'

'Does that mean you have told Gabriel about Nathan?'

I gritted my teeth together. 'It's in the past.'

She gave me a smile, intended to be loving and supportive, but came off as patronising.

We spent the next few hours talking about many things including men, the kids and anything trivial that came to mind. When it came time for her to leave, I was surprised that hours instead of minutes had passed. It helped that the kids had been little angels.

As we were getting their coats on we made plans for the girls to spend a night at mine. Neave hopped up and down on the spot, already talking about what sweets she would get. Beth sighed and muttered about how they would all be suffering from a sugar crash.

We hugged at the door and I waved goodbye as they drove off, before returning to the kitchen to wash up the few items left over from lunch. The house felt empty now they had left and my thoughts soon drifted to Gabriel.

That night I couldn't help notice the change between us. He had become my centre of gravity, and I his. When he moved, I unconsciously followed as if he was a magnet drawing me to him. We hardly spoke. Communication was achieved through contact, such as a brush of the hand or touch of the face.

It was as if a low current continually passed between us, leaving me barely able to register my surroundings. We were there, but not, drifting in a sea of fuzziness whilst feeling complete clarity in regards to each other. By the end of the night, his face was filled with as much confusion as mine.

'What..?' My voice broke as if I hadn't spoken a word for days. 'I don't understand.'

'Neither do I,' he whispered, the unsteadiness in his voice as pronounced as mine. 'It shouldn't happen like this.'

'How should it happen?' I needed to understand this phenomenon. It felt as if my free will had been taken from me, but I had not been informed and was too bewildered to truly realise it yet. A bell rang dimly in the back of my mind, telling me to be afraid and resist, but the impulse to embrace the feeling overpowered it, swallowing all doubts before they gained strength.

He went to speak and hesitated, chewing on his lip in a way that made him look like a boy. 'I think it will be easier to show you.' He gestured to the coffee table and two spheres the size of golf balls formed out of the pine wood. The act was silent and the table appeared unharmed, though I was willing to bet it was marginally lighter now.

'Imagine these spheres are each a member of my race. Throughout our existence we are free to move wherever we choose.' As he spoke the balls started rolling around the table in random directions. 'If we meet and a connection is made, call it love, we then become one.' The balls rolled towards each other and when touched, merged together to form one larger ball. 'This is a permanent connection that can only be broken by death.

'When as a whole, we cannot be separated from each other as the pain would be too great for each of us to bear. If death occurs for one of us we are ripped apart.' The ball split jaggedly through the middle and the two half's fell apart. One half dissolved into the table, leaving no sign it had ever been there. 'It feels akin to the pain of having your chest hollowed out slowly, without the release of death.' The remaining half lay broken and alone, looking so pitiful that my chest restricted and eyes pricked. 'This pain lasts for many decades before it starts to ease. Many take their own life to escape it.'

His face became drawn and pale, his eyes tight and distant. The grief radiated from him in a dense cloud that enveloped me, smothering me under its weight. I could barely breathe from the severity of it. I reached out my hand to touch him, but instead let it fall back to my lap.

'I'm sorry,'

Gabriel turned to me, the horror of losing the person he loved, and the anguish suffered because of it etched nakedly upon his face. I brushed his cheek with my finger tips and doubled over as his pain rippled through me, a twisting agony so strong, I thought I might just die. My chest restricted, making it impossible to draw breath and my soul dragged as if being ripped from my body. I shuddered. How could he endure such a pain?

I heard a low whimpering and it took a moment to realise that it came from me.

He swiftly lifted me onto his lap and embraced me, while wiping away tears I didn't know I shed.

'Don't worry my love. It won't be like that for us. I am sure of it.'

He couldn't know that the tears were not for me, but for him and others of his kind. For the anguish and pain he had suffered, the life he deserved lost, and for the nameless woman who was effectively his one true soul mate, taken away forever. I was grieving for the unjustness of life.

After a while, redness crept into my face. I had wanted to comfort him and ended up being comforted. I shifted in order to place my hand on his cheek and looked into his eyes. His face was pinched with worry for me, the signs of his suffering no longer apparent.

'I should never have scared you like that,' he said gruffly. 'Please do not worry, you are human, it will be different.'

For someone who could read emotions he sure got a lot wrong.

'It isn't that. I won't worry about what I can't change and I am in too deep to walk away now.'

'I don't understand.' He held my face in his hands, his fingers feather light. 'I have never heard you cry like that, or felt you hurt with such intensity, even when you have been at your lowest.'

I placed one hand on his heart and the other on mine. 'I felt your pain. It was so awful and sad, I couldn't bare it.'

It dawned on him what I meant and he crushed me to him, groaning loudly as he did so.

'This is wrong,' he said into my hair. 'So, so, wrong.' I tried to turn to see his face but he had me pinned to him, leaving barely enough room to breathe, causing my heart to race with panic.

'Please forgive me,' I said. 'I'm so sorry.'

He growled under his breath and tensed further, squashing me in his grip. A white hot poker seared across my brain, betraying his anger. Locked in his arms, I fought to get away. My heart thundered, threatening to explode out my chest. He released me immediately and I flew to the kitchen doorway, turning to face him in a protective stance.

I groaned upon seeing his face drawn in horror. He hadn't acted in any way that should have scared me, but his anger had been too intense and my instincts too ingrained. I wanted to put my arms around him and comfort him, to tell him it wasn't him, it was me, but my mouth remained locked closed, my lips pressed together so hard, my jaw hurt.

How dare Nathan change me into such a pathetic person! How dare he leave me as such a frightened rabbit!

Gabriel dropped his head as a single tear escaped to travel down his cheek. 'Please do not hate me. It was never my intention to scare you. I swear I would never hurt you, if you wish, I will leave right now.'

And they say females are dramatic.

I rushed over to him, all panic and anger gone. 'I don't hate you and I know you wouldn't hurt me.' I lifted his face so that he could see I spoke the truth. The emotion reading stuff just confused things.

'You cannot lie to me, I felt your fear, and saw how it caused you to react.' He choked a little as if the words stuck in his throat. 'I also felt your hate for me.'

I stiffened and quickly forced myself to relax. God knows how my frustration would complicate things.

I pondered for a moment on how to proceed. 'I felt your anger and I admit I acted badly. Please try to understand that I've learnt to fear it and my body kind of took over.' I smiled to try and make light of it. The pressure smothered me, urging me to run away from it all. I needed to see his smile, to know all was well again.

He didn't oblige.

'If that is true, why do you hate me so?'

'I don't hate you,' I said a little too sharply. 'I hate that I can still act so pathetically. I hate that the evening started so fantastically, with me feeling loved up to hell, and ended up falling apart, and I hate all this emotion reading crap, it screws everything up.' My voice increased in volume, and to make matters worse as I blinked, tears fell from my eyes. 'And I hate that my eyes won't stop leaking.'

I stomped off into the dark kitchen and slammed door behind me only to groan. The light switch was on the lounge side of the doorway. I left it off.

Time lost all meaning as I sat in the dark kitchen, trying to figure out how to make things right again. After a while extreme weariness seeped through me, coupled with a twinge of stupidity.

I sat with my arms on the table and my face pressed into them, drowsily trying to convince myself to swallow my pride and go back. I couldn't spend all night sitting in the kitchen. At the very least I would get a crick in the neck. A hand touched my shoulder and I jumped up, yelping loudly.

'It's only me. I should have spoken first.'

I reached for him in the dark and moved towards his chest. 'Please just hold me.' The needy tone made me hesitate, but only for a second. I'd gone beyond caring.

He pulled me into his arms. 'Do you forgive me?'

I snuggled closer. 'No more asking for forgiveness or apologising, there's no need. Now I just want you to hold me and tell me it's all going to be all right, even if it's not, tell me anyway.'

He chuckled. 'It will be. I promise you.'

I heard something in his voice, a set tone speaking of hidden meaning, but tiredness dragged at me, pulling me under a thick blanket of dark fuzziness.

'I'll figure it out tomorrow,' I mumbled to myself.

Disaster had been averted and I should go to bed, but I didn't have the energy to move. It had been one hell of a taxing day and night.

There was a sensation of falling, followed by a rocking motion. Some distant part of my brain had time to acknowledge that he carried me up the stairs before I fell into a deep sleep.

I awoke later that night, sat upright in bed, screaming Gabriel's name. He pulled me back down under the covers and held me in his arms as I cried. None of the dream remained, only the deep sense of loss that lingered after.

Even though the morning sun shone through the windows, shadows lurked in the corners of the room, drawing my focus away from the light. I dragged myself out of bed, groaning with how hard it was to move. Making a cup of tea was too much of a chore and the thought of eating made my stomach roll. Gabriel tried to coax some life into me, making small jokes that made no sense. I reduced physical contact with him in the hope he wouldn't be dragged into my misery. The intensity of his feelings had completely thrown me off balance and even though I used every trick in the book to alleviate the depressive bout, it barely made a difference.

Sometimes I would catch him out of the corner of my eye, holding his hand out to me and giving it a little flick. Each time, numbness spread through my mind. It didn't really make me feel any better, but I suppose it stopped me feeling worse.

My nieces came to spend the night as planned, and I managed to smile, though it was strained. Gabriel helped make their stay fun which was a Godsend as even though I participated with what happened, I spent the time distracted by my own thoughts. I acknowledged them when they talked to me, and I did my best to answer in all the right places. I even managed to laugh at times, though it sounded alien even to me. Thankfully, they didn't seem to realise anything was wrong.

We played board games with them before bed and Gabriel's laughter joined with theirs. I sat on the floor with them, but it sounded distorted and hollow, as if it had travelled down a long tunnel before reaching me. At one point whilst Gabriel laughed, I touched his arm in the hope of feeling his pleasure. Mostly I just got a sense of his concern for me, which didn't help.

The whole week was spent treading water, fighting against the impulse to give in and wallow in self-pity. Gabriel stayed every night holding me in his arms, though I couldn't focus on a single word he said to me.

Eventually I started to take an interest in what was happening around me. Colours became brighter and I could actually understand what people were saying. It had been eight days when we finally made love again and it left me feeling human once more. It felt good to be back.

Over the next couple of days I caught up on coursework, this particular essay being about personality types. I had taken the personality test a few weeks ago and scored as neurotic, no shock there, and figured it wouldn't do any harm to complete it again, this time only to discover that they now classed me as stable.

Smirking with amusement, I decided that was enough work for the day and had just finished packing my books away when Gabriel let himself in.

He held me tightly as we kissed, though remained tense in my arms. I pulled away, frowning and he shifted nervously. I stiffened in response, trying to block the sense of worry that came from him. Was it him that was worried or me? He always felt more intense when I touched him and half the time I never knew who was feeling what. I constantly had to decide how I felt before we touched. I didn't get overpowered by the sensations every time. It depended on how strong his emotions were in comparison to mine.

I bit my lip. 'What?'

'I wasn't going to bring this up until after dinner.' He pulled me to him. 'I have to go away for a while.' He gripped me tighter as I tensed further. 'Don't worry it won't be for long.'

I relaxed a little. 'Why do you have to go?'

'I have to find out what's happening between us.' He held my chin, aligning my face so as to look into my eyes. 'I am concerned about it.'

My chest restricted. 'Why?'

He dipped his head to brush my lips with his. 'I may be causing you harm and that would be unacceptable.'

77

My heart sank. 'Don't be daft, I'm hardy.' I laughed shakily and pulled away.

'I have to know. I have never heard of anyone falling in love with a human, the attraction to our own is normally too great for someone such as yourself to hold our attention, for even a brief period. I cannot believe that it hasn't occurred before and I need to know the outcome.'

'What would you do if you found out that it didn't end well?'

'I would have to leave.'

I froze solid, my blood like ice as it pulsed through my veins, sure that I would never be able to move again.

'You wouldn't?' As the words rushed out, my body unlocked and I sagged against the oak sideboard that had been passed down through my mother's family. Didn't he realise it was too late for that? We were already one. I may not be from his race, but even when he wasn't around, I could feel him as if he was stood next to me. If I closed my eyes and reached out my hand, I almost expected to find him there, smiling his beautiful smile.

'You would move on and forget me.'

His voice echoed around my head and I laughed bitterly. How could I ever move on when his presence would forever haunt me?

I took a moment to regain my posture before I moved towards him, lifted his hand and placed it over my heart. I had never done anything like this before. Would it work? I had to try.

I recalled every feeling I had ever had for him. The wonder of truly seeing him for the first time when we made love, the feeling of my heart truly coming alive when I realised I loved him, the fear of him walking out of my life like claws ripping at my chest, and the sense of loss I felt when he left a room, mingled with the notion that he was still there. There was also the lightness when he laughed, the feeling of being safe when he held me and so much more, though these were minor in comparison. I concentrated hard, pushing all of this into him, willing him to see and to understand. If he left, I would be that half sphere, lying broken and alone without the ability to heal myself.

He wrenched me into his embrace, breaking my concentration as he crushed his lips to mine.

I pulled away, gasping for air. 'Do you see?'

'I do,' he groaned.

He held me in silence. I could almost hear his brain ticking over. Too afraid to ask what he was thinking, I settled closer into his arms.

'You know I love you with everything I am?'

I nodded.

'I would only ever leave you if it would save you.'

I frowned and opened my mouth to speak. I had no idea what to say but wasn't above begging. He pressed my lips closed with his fingers.

'I must still go and find out what the others know, maybe it can be reversed.'

'What if I don't want it reversed?'

'Ana, you need to understand, your mind isn't designed to cope with emotions at such a level of intensity that you have been experiencing. Look at what happened the other week. You could barely drag yourself out of bed.'

Great, he had to go and remind me about that, as if I didn't feel humiliated enough.

'It's not like I haven't have to deal with strong emotions before.'

Gabriel raised his eyebrows in question.

'Look, I know it's nowhere near the same, what I'm saying is, I adapted to the bipolar and I can adapt to this. The other night kind of took me by surprise, that's all.'

I grinned to show I was up for the challenge and he smiled at my confidence.

'What about the other issue?' he said.

'What other issue?'

He nodded towards my arm. 'See for yourself.'

Looking at my arm I couldn't see anything. I began to think that he was winding me up, then I realised that there was something different, I just couldn't put my finger on what. He stood back allowing me the space and time to figure it out. I glanced over at his face, back to my arm and then it hit me.

'Oh my God, I'm glowing.' My mouth dropped open in surprise. There was a very subtle sheen to the skin that I would probably never have noticed without it being pointed out, but now that it had been, it was impossible to miss. I grinned. 'Am I changing into the same as you?'

'No,' he replied. 'That would be impossible.'

Redness crept onto my face. Of course not, how stupid of me to think that.

I dipped my head down. 'Then what?'

Gabriel took my hand and led me into the lounge to the sofa. 'As you know everything in life contains energy which can be transferred or shared by touch or close proximity. It can even occur over long distances if the bond is strong enough or the person doing it is well practiced.'

'Like when an old house has a good or bad feeling?'

'Yes.' He smiled. 'Then the energy has been transferred into the walls, trapping any emotions with it until such time that they are either diluted out with new energy or cleansed away. With people there is a constant energy exchange occurring.'

'Is that why I am glowing?' I wondered out loud.

'That's the problem.' He sighed heavily. 'I am an energy life form. It shouldn't be possible to share or transfer any of myself into you. I am not energy as you know it, I am composed of Shi. That is why I need to get advice.'

'Will I get any brighter?'

'I have no idea, the fact that it's happened at all astounds me.' He frowned deeply. 'I am extremely concerned, Ana, for all I know this could kill you.'

My heart missed a beat. I hadn't considered that prospect. I had gone from the possibility of living forever, to now possibly being dead.

'So no changing into a cat then?' I jutted my chin out and tried to pout. Achieving my objective, the atmosphere lightened and he laughed.

'Not any time soon.'

With disaster averted the rest of the evening became a lot lighter. Neither of us talked about the impending trip, or the implications that could arise from it.

We were in the process of rinsing out our cups before bed, when I thought of something that had bugged me on and off. 'Why does your race hide from us? Is it because you are afraid we will destroy you?'

His laugh was deep and extremely pleasurable. 'I doubt very much that your race could harm us.'

'How is that? We have some pretty awful weapons out there.'

He plucked one of my sharper knives from the rack and handed it to me. 'Try and injure me with it,' he said with a smile.

I dropped the knife onto the side with a clatter. 'No,' I said sharply. 'I'm not doing that.'

He sighed and picked the knife back up. I cried out as he thrust it into his hand.

'Do you see?'

I stared wide eyed, to where the knife penetrated his palm. He removed the blade leaving no sign that it had ever been embedded in him.

'We can move around any of your weapons,' he said with a smile. He sliced the blade across his skin and although it definitely made contact, there was no evidence to prove it.

'Okay, that's enough, you made your point. You can't be harmed in anyway.'

'I never said that.' He smiled darkly. 'Just not your weapons.'

'What then?'

'It is of no concern.'

'So why stay hidden?'

'For a long time we were peaceful,' he sighed. 'Our main focus was the evolution of our race and we had no need to interact with the lower species.'

I stiffened and then relaxed. He couldn't possibly feel that way when with me.

'And now?'

'And now things are different.'

I sighed. Maybe he would tell me more as time passed and he trusted me completely.

'What are you feeling?' he asked.

My mouth dropped open. 'I thought you could read me?'

'You are difficult to work out at times,' he said with a chuckle. 'A lot of what I get is murky. I do get a sense of your emotions when they are at a peak, but normally I believe your bipolar moods interfere with it, making it hard to read you and impossible to trust what I can.'

I grinned at him. Finally there was a positive side effect for the hell I sometimes suffered.

'I'm feeling like I want to go to bed,' I said, feeling so happy that I thought I might burst. I really did love him so very much.

9

'I will return as soon as possible,' Gabriel said as he fiercely hugged me. 'Try not to get into any trouble or hurt yourself while I'm away.'

I scowled and kissed him full on the mouth. 'How about I promise to try?' His frown caused me to laugh. 'Okay, okay, I promise.'

He lifted me up so that my feet hung several inches above the ground, and kissed me with such passion, all breath left me and my head started reeling. He lowered me down and held me steady for a few moments to ensure that I wouldn't fall over, causing myself an injury before he even left the house.

'Damn it, you're too good at that.' My vision gradually swam back into focus and I stared into his eyes, trying to conjure up a reason for him to stay. 'Where will you go?' I pulled him tighter into my arms.

'There is an old acquaintance I must find. She may be able to help.'

A spark exploded inside my brain. A female? What if he couldn't help but compare me to her?

'Is she the same as you?' I didn't stand a chance of measuring up to her if she was.

'Don't be so insecure,' he chastised.

I stiffened. He didn't seem to grasp how it was for me just being human, and knowing that I could never offer him what this woman could. I wiggled from his embrace and marched to the table to clear the remains of breakfast away.

'What happens if you get there and your attention isn't diverted by me anymore?'

He clenched his hands. 'You're being ridiculous.'

I threw the dishes into the sink and whirled on him.

'I'm being ridiculous am I?' I could already picture them together, experiencing a love connection that made what we had look like a single solitary spark dwarfed by a neighbouring forest fire, while I was left alone with my own misery and pain, never knowing for sure what had happened. 'You probably wouldn't even care what happened to me.' Tears pricked my eyes and I quickly blinked them away.

His lips pressed together so tightly that his mouth became a sharp line. 'Has it occurred to you that the reason I haven't heard of anyone having a relationship with a human, is because nobody with an ounce of sanity would put up with this.'

We stared across the room at each other, the implications of what I had done dawning on me. I wanted to reach for him and apologise.

He grabbed his bag and threw it over his shoulder. 'I'll take my leave now.'

He stamped out of the house leaving me to sink to the floor, knowing that I had ruined the only good relationship I'd ever had.

Ten minutes later, I pulled myself up and dried away the tears. My legs wobbled with weakness and I sat at the table with my face buried in my hands. Why was I so messed up? Could I not just be content with what I had?

No wonder he had walked out, I would have done the same when faced with such anger. I hadn't meant to, I just couldn't help but be aware of how much I didn't deserve him, he was so beautiful in every way and I was...well I was just me.

I recalled the anger on his face and my heart ached painfully. Why couldn't I suppress my paranoia as I always had in the past, ready to take out and examine at a later date?

Using the end of my sleeve, I dried away my tears and sat back in the seat, taking deep, slow breaths. Although he was gone, I could still feel him around me and I closed my eyes in order to relax with his presence.

'I'm sorry,' I said to the empty room.

I fantasised that he walked through the door to hold me within his arms, laughing about my stupid insecurities and paranoia, and telling me it was going to be all okay. I indulged in the illusion until I felt strong enough to face the day.

I had no choice but to survive if he didn't return. I blanched at the thought, considering the fact that I might always have to live with this pain, but I knew I would survive if only because I despised the weak person I had become.

I decided a shower was in order to wash away the remains of my feebleness, and after scrubbing away the evidence of my tears, I stepped out as a new, stronger, if not slightly tormented woman, ready to start the day.

The feeling came as I was drying my hair and I ran down the stairs, leaving the towel trailing behind. My heart sluggish with emotion, I paused at the bottom, unable to deny the evidence of the burden he also carried.

He walked towards me and took my hands into his. 'I apologise.'

My heart leapt with joy.

'I forget how hard this all must be for you.'

I withdrew my hand to cautiously touch his face, determined to keep from becoming emotional. 'You did nothing wrong, I behaved badly.'

He opened his mouth to interrupt and I placed my finger over his lips.

'Please let me finish. Irrelevant to how hard it has been, or how unusual the circumstances, it doesn't excuse how I acted. Although you have no reason to believe me, I swear that things will be different from now on. I will be that person you fell in love with again.'

He drew me into his arms and kissed my brow. 'I do not want you to change yourself. I love you so much more now than I did when we first met, do not ever forget that.' He sighed heavily, and pulled me closer into his chest. 'I am fearful about what could happen to you. I am not used to feeling this defenceless.'

'I'm sorry.'

'It's not your fault, I'm not even sure it is mine anymore.' He stroked my still damp hair, sending quivers down my spine. 'I am beginning to think that any choice I had to end this disappeared the moment we met.'

'Are you still going away for a while?' I gathered my strength, preparing for the answer.

'No.' My body relaxed upon hearing his unexpected response. 'I left a message that I was looking for her. She will be able to find me when she receives it.'

'How do you know she will come?'

A severe gleam came into his eyes. 'She owes me.'

As we huddled on the sofa, we talked about our relationship and where it was going. We discussed taking the next step and living together, which caused me to wonder about his mental state. Was he mad? After everything I had put him through lately I had to settle on yes.

I worried that moving in together while in the process of sorting my head out would only lead to seeing a lot more crazy Ana, and I'd already seen enough of her to last me a lifetime. But he claimed that my madness was worth it and I eventually agreed.

All too soon it came time for me to leave for work. Standing on tiptoes to kiss him goodbye, I had to marvel that this stunning, kind, really tolerant man was mine. How did I ever get so lucky to have him fall in love with me? I had to wonder if he realised what he was getting himself into and figured he probably had a fair idea by now.

I rushed out the door knowing I was going to be a little late, with the promise that dinner would be waiting on my arrival home.

People filled the day room, many of them carrying flowers and chocolates as they greeted their loved ones. A few kids ran around, ignoring the reprimands of their parents, already bored by the subdued atmosphere that came with visiting day.

This was the time I was meant to catch up on paperwork, but it never worked that way. I managed to get half way to the exit before Marina's daughter, Denise, stopped me.

She stood too close, with her shoulders back and her face stiff. 'Can you tell me why my mother isn't going to water aerobics anymore?' She smoothed down her already straight suit jacket and stared directly into my eyes.

'She doesn't want to go. The cool water aggravates her arthritis.'

'She doesn't know what she wants. Her mind isn't all there anymore.'

I took a deep breath to calm my irritation. 'She was quite clear in what she wanted, and there is no sign of mental impairment in her.'

Denise flapped her hand in my face. 'I am beginning to think that the care she receives here is substandard.'

Marina smiled at me apologetically from behind her.

'Why don't you talk to your mother about it' I said, trying to keep the anger from my voice. 'She is quite capable of making the decision for herself.'

'What would you know?' Denise said curtly. 'You have no qualifications.'

I bit back my words about how I had more than her in this situation and smiled disarmingly.

'Maybe so, but you mother does, it being her life and all.'

Denise glared at me with her lips pressed together so hard, the flesh around them bulged making her appear like a fish. 'I expected to receive professionalism here but if you insist on being insolent, I will need to speak to your boss.'

'Feel free,' I said. 'His office is down the hall to the left.'

She continued to glare, before turning her back to me. I sighed as she stormed towards Carl's office.

Marina hobbled over. 'Sorry about her,' she said. 'She always needs to be in control.'

I sighed. 'Do you want to go back to water aerobics?'

She laughed. 'Of course not, but it doesn't matter how many times I tell her, she doesn't listen. She has too much of her father in her.'

My eyes shifted to the door. Would Carl wait until the end of the shift to call me in, or would he do it straight away. Maybe I shouldn't have been so short with her.

'Don't worry,' Marina said. 'I'll have a word with him.'

Another family member caught my attention. I gave Marina a smile before leaving her to talk to them. At least Denise wouldn't be back for another month. I should see about organising my shifts so I wasn't working then.

The conversations were all the same. 'I think she would like this,' and, 'You should do this with him.' My job would be so much easier if any of them actually listened to their parents. I tried not to get annoyed. It was their way of showing that they really did care, even if it was misguided and the bane of my weekend.

Barbara's son, Christian, smiled at me across the room. He sat with his mother as she stared out of the window, not aware that he was there. Even so, he visited every weekend.

'How has she been?' he said when I approached.

'There are good and bad days,' I said, 'but she is hanging on.'

His eyes became downcast as he looked at his mother. 'She doesn't remember me today.'

'She doesn't remember very much anymore,' I said. 'Most of the time she seems to be in her late teens.'

'Do you think she is happy?'

I gave him a gentle smile. 'Mostly, even more so when she thinks Carl is your father.'

'That's good,' he said. 'At least she doesn't get frightened anymore.'

'Alzheimer's can do that.'

'Do you think she will ever come back to me, even for a minute?'

I shrugged. 'Sometimes they do.' I didn't add that it was unlikely. Another family member stood by, trying to get my attention. I gave Christian a reassuring smile before leaving him with the promise we would catch up before he left.

Nearly four hours later it slowed enough for me to grab a quick drink and I made my way to the kitchen. Thankfully the dishwasher had finished its cycle. There was nothing worse than trying to relax for five minutes with a horrendous rattling ten inches from your ear. I took a big slurp of my coke as Lexi poked her head around the door. We hadn't had a chance to chat yet, only managing a quick hello when I arrived.

'Are you pregnant?'

The bubbles flew out of my nose and mouth simultaneously, causing me to splutter and my eyes to water. Lexi watched as I grabbed some tissue in order to clean the mess off my uniform. Not that I cared, the yellow tunic made everyone look washed out, but I supposed I had to look presentable.

'Where on earth would you get an idea like that?' I choked, still trying to get the coke that had escaped to my lungs out.

'You haven't answered the question.' She stood with her hands on her hips looking down at me.

'Of course I'm not. Why do you ask?' I glanced down at my stomach. I wasn't looking bloated, thank God.

Lexi shuffled from foot to foot for a few seconds before answering. 'Well, you're kind of glowing.' My jaw dropped. Damn, in all the drama I had forgotten about that. 'And you have that distracted look that pregnant women seem to have, like they're constantly aware of the baby inside of them.'

Luckily Carl came into the kitchen and Lexi went back to work, saving me from having to give an explanation. What on earth could I say? I'm glowing because my mythical boyfriend's energy is rubbing off on me, oh and that distracted look is because we have this crazy bond that keeps tugging at me, making me want to throw down my tunic and run home.

Somehow, I didn't think so. Maybe she would buy that I'm glowing with happiness. It wouldn't really be a lie, more of an omission of the details. I briefly questioned whether a lie so big could be kept for long, before I rushed off to serve dinner to the ten thousand, or so it seemed.

Ten o'clock came before I knew it and Lexi had forgotten all about our earlier conversation. Years of being completely honest ensured that whatever I said was believed, which caused me to feel somewhat guilty as I finished up with hand over and collected my stuff from the cloak room.

'So when do I get to meet him?' she said, putting on her coat.

A flash of protective selfishness flared up in me. I didn't want to share the time I had with him. I sighed, 'How about tomorrow for dinner?' No use acting like a spoilt two year old not willing to share my toys.

'Fab!' She beamed at me and I nearly blushed with shame. How could I begrudge her a chance to spend some time with Gabriel? What was coming over me?

We said goodbye in the car park after arranging for her to come to mine at seven with a bottle of wine. As I drove home, the pull towards Gabriel became stronger and I even sped a bit in my haste to get back sooner. As soon as I stopped outside the house, I fell out of the car, forgetting to lock it in my haste.

I ran down the path with no control while my heart pounded like the beat of a drum roll and I breathed so rapidly, my head began to swim. I was going to fly straight into the door but couldn't stop.

The door opened and Gabriel rushed the last few metres towards me, moving in a lot more dignified manner. When I finally reached him I jumped into his arms and kissed him deeply.

'Missed you,' I breathed as he carried me into the house.

'I missed you as the birds miss the sun.'

I smirked. I actually lived with someone who said corny lines like that, though they sounded less corny and more delightful from him. He brushed his fingers over my cheek and turned me to the table. All words died in my throat, leaving me too dumbfounded to speak.

White lace covered the table, topped with several candles surrounding a solitary red rose. The surface had been scattered with rose petals, the crimson stark against the contrasting white of the table cloth. The same lace also covered the chairs. The two wine glasses looked like crystal, definitely not from my collection as I tended to opt for the cheap brands.

'It's beautiful.' I glanced down at my feet and chewed on my bottom lip. How was I supposed to react in such a situation? Words of thanks seemed too trivial in response.

'There's more,' he told me excitedly.

More? How could there be more than this?

Gabriel turned off the lights. The scene became transformed by hundreds, if not thousands, of minuscule lights flickering above as stars, causing the glasses to sparkle as did ripples of a stream caught by the sunlight.

'Do you like it? I know how much you love the stars, and as it's too cold to eat outside, I thought I would bring the night in for you.'

My voice cracked as I attempted to answer. Turning to him, I tried again, 'I don't know what to say.' I paused and put my hand to his chest. 'There aren't words to describe how beautiful it is.'

'And still it pales in comparison to you.'

I was struck speechless, making it impossible to respond to the obvious lie.

He allowed me stand in his arms for a few minutes, taking in the picture around me. I could have stood all night drinking in the splendour of it all, but he interrupted my thoughts.

'Take a seat and I'll get dinner.'

I scanned the room, feeling somewhat disorientated, before sitting down.

He filled our glasses with wine and retrieved our dinner, before joining me at the table. I had to concentrate to get the food in my mouth as it was impossible to drag my eyes away from the surrounding scene.

'I've never heard you this quiet before,' he said.

'To be honest, I'm astounded.'

My gaze shifted to his face, and I became entranced by his eyes, which blazed in the candle light. 'I could stare at them forever.'

I thought to ask how it was possible he had recreated the night sky in my kitchen, but the words never left my lips. The tiny orbs of light, floating a few feet above us were so fantastic that I didn't want to know the logical answer, the mystery only added to my awe. Once again, I had to tell myself that Gabriel was actually real, and that he was mine.

10

Gabriel and I prepared dinner together as he told me about some of the antics the men got up to on the site. Some made me laugh while others caused me to raise my eyes in question.

As usual the time flew by and after what felt like minutes instead of hours there was a knock at the door, followed by a hesitant, 'Hello?' as it opened.

'Hiya Hun, come on in.' I took the bottle of wine Lexi held out and poured her a drink.

'What a journey that was,' Lexi said dropping her overnight bag in the corner. It wouldn't contain a toothbrush as she had her own upstairs, ready for the many occasions she stayed over.

'First I get on the bus and the woman in front of me didn't have the right money and she just argued with the bus driver. But when I tried to offer her the difference, she refused and started shouting about how the elderly were persecuted in this day and age and even though she was only fifty nine, she should have free transport because she had been paying taxes all her life. Finally he just let her on, most likely to have some peace, but at the next stop some drunk guy decided to sit next to me and of all the things he could do, he fell asleep on my shoulder and when I tried to push him away he just cuddled up to me, it was disgusting.'

Finally she took a deep breath. 'Anyway, hi, I'm Lexi.'

She held out her hand to Gabriel, who pressed his lips together in a bid to control his silent laughter. I grinned without restraint. How stupid it had been to keep her away. I had only been depriving myself as she was a breath of fresh air, whose presence had a knack of bringing life into my soul.

'I'm pleased to finally meet you,' he said, taking her hand in his. 'I have heard so many good things.'

The evening flowed easily. Lexi even calmed down enough to breathe between sentences, a very good sign that she liked Gabriel, unless he was messing with her emotions. I frowned a little while watching them laugh together. Would he do that to win my friend over? Surely not.

At midnight, Gabriel retired to bed to give us time alone, an act that made my heart swell. This is what a relationship should be. Lexi had never visited while I was with Nathan as he always made the stay uncomfortable, with snide remarks and derogatory humour. How nice it was to have the people I loved in one room without problems.

'Well?' I asked once we heard the muted thud of the bedroom door closing.

'He's lovely,' she said, 'but...' She frowned. 'I'm just a little concerned with how you are with each other.'

I sipped my wine and focused on the table. As far as I could recall, we hadn't done anything untoward throughout the evening.

'Don't take offense,' she continued. 'There's nothing wrong with it, it's just strange how you act.'

'What do you mean? We weren't clingy with each other were we?'

'Not at all, it's just...how can I explain this?' Her face creased up with frustration.

I sat patiently waiting for her to find the right words.

'When Richie has drugs in the house, he is always calm and even happy,' she said. 'But when he runs out, he becomes agitated and confused as if he's lost something important. You remind me of him.'

'I love him.'

'I know you do,' she sighed, 'and I can tell he feels the same about you. But be careful please, if he breaks your heart for whatever reason, I'm not sure you will recover this time.'

I diverted the conversation onto lighter things as we polished off the bottle of wine, though her words stayed forefront in my mind as I struggled against the urge to run up the stairs into Gabriel's arms.

Gabriel stayed in bed as I drove Lexi home in the morning, complaining that the hour was too early to get up, especially as we had kept him up late with our laughter. I pulled the car up next to the long line of vehicles edging the path and sat with the engine running. There was no point looking for a parking space as it would be a miracle to find one on a Sunday.

Lexi grabbed her bag off the back seat. 'Are you coming in for a drink?'

I smiled at her apologetically.

'Of course you aren't,' she sighed. She opened the door and turned to me. 'Just do me a favour, Ana, be careful that you remember to have a life away from him, and let's not leave it so long next time.'

God, was I really that bad?

'Lexi,' I said as she got out of the car. 'They say the hot weather is going to last all week. Do you fancy coming for a barbeque in a couple of days?' She gave me such a genuine happy smile that her face lit up, and I had a flash of guilt for my recent actions, or rather, lack of them.

'Am already looking forward to it.'

I watched as she made her way to the flat door. How could I maintain some sort of balance when every cell in my body cried out to be alone with Gabriel? Lexi had been right the night before. I was an addict, and Gabriel was my drug of choice.

Once I arrived back, I found him in the lounge with two cups of tea.

'I believe I have come up with a solution,' he said.

'What solution?'

'Regarding the hue to your skin. It will involve some concentration on your part, however, I believe it can be controlled.'

I groaned and joined him on the sofa. 'Can't you just draw it out of me?' It came to mind that if he could do this I might well lose the ability to sense him, a feeling I had learnt to love and would yearn for a little if it was gone.

He sighed with some regret. 'Unfortunately I cannot. I am unable to influence particles of a similar genetic makeup. Could you imagine if a child from our kind was able to manipulate the shape of its mother or teacher? It would cause chaos.'

I stifled a giggle at the image of turning the teacher into a rabbit. What would it be like if we had a child together?

Somehow, he picked up on my stray thought and took my hand in his. 'You know I can never give you a child. I'm sorry, but it would not be possible.'

I had guessed as much, but even though I had never thought of having children before, his words caused a feeling of disappointment and regret. The feeling settled heavily in the pit of my stomach.

'Why on earth would I want my own children? I get the best of both worlds with my nieces, all the fun bits, without any of the hassle being a parent entails.'

I smiled in the hope of convincing him that I spoke the truth, but he frowned in response. It wasn't like talking about it could change anything, so before he could pursue the conversation, I brought him back on track.

'But this light has come from you. Shouldn't you be able to draw it back into yourself?'

'Even though it originally came from me, the particles have evolved, making it impossible.'

'How is that possible?'

'It's not.' His features darkened, indicating that he was starting to brood again.

I stretched along the sofa to kiss him, but my knee slipped off the edge and I promptly fell onto the floor. There was a moment of silence, in which I contemplated what an idiot I was, before Gabriel roared with laughter. Shamefaced, I returned to the sofa.

Still chortling, he leant over to give me the kiss I had been aiming for. 'I don't think I have ever met anyone who makes me laugh so much by simply being themself.'

'Glad I can be of amusement,' I muttered. 'Now, back to the point of how do I control this glowing?'

'You already use a similar technique to shield yourself from people's emotions. It merely involves a bit more concentration.' He laughed as I raised my eyebrows. 'Stop worrying, it's easy.'

'Easy for you.'

Ignoring me, he continued. 'Sit yourself comfortably as if you are going to meditate.' Once I was ready, he resumed. 'Relax until you can feel the energy flowing around your body.'

I had done this many times during meditation in the past. Previously I'd felt a tingling sensation. This time it felt as if electricity vibrated throughout every atom in my body, giving the illusion that I could be shaken apart at any moment. The hairs on my arms stood on end and the tint of my skin became a shade brighter.

'This time, instead of imagining a shield around you, pull the Shi into your solar plexus and hold it there.'

I raised my eyebrows in question. Although I dabbled in meditation, that was just gobbledygook to me.

He touched his hand to my stomach below my diaphragm. 'Here.'

I closed my eyes to concentrate and listened to the soft flow of his speech as he murmured words of encouragement. As I drew the Shi into me, my stomach rolled as if I had been riding on a rollercoaster and I heaved.

'It will pass,' he reassured me.

After a few moments it did and I cautiously opened my eyes. I held my hand up so as to view it better. The slight tinge that had been present for days had gone.

'See, I knew you could do it.'

'I can feel it sitting heavy on my stomach, is that normal?' I shifted on the sofa, careful about setting the nausea off again.

'For me, my whole body feels like it is compacted together. As for you...nothing about this situation is normal, but if I had to guess, I would say you will probably be fine.'

I decided to put my control to the test, and shifted closer to Gabriel. He perceived my intentions and bent forwards, kissing me with such force my head started spinning. With my heart racing like I'd just ran ten miles, I checked out my skin only to frown. The affect hadn't been permanent.

Gabriel kissed my forehead. 'You will get better as you practice. Anyway, I hope you wouldn't kiss anyone else in such a manner, causing such a break in concentration.'

I laughed at such a ludicrous idea and nuzzled into his embrace. Maybe he was right and it wouldn't be so hard after all, anyway it was only a slight glow. What real harm could come from it?

11

Lexi and I relaxed on the porch, enjoying the sun and the scent of the newly planted flowers that lined the edges of the garden. The fire smoked nicely and the steaks sizzled loudly, filling the garden with the mouth-watering aroma of cooking beef.

I was in the process of turning the steaks over when a weird sensation came over me as if something tickled the corner of my mind. The sky seemed to darken as if a cloud had passed over the sun. My stomach curled and my pulse began to race. Even though there was no sign of a breeze or chill to the air, goosebumps spread across my skin, and a shiver travelled through my entire body.

Seconds later I noticed a shadow by the gate. Lexi's voice faded into the background becoming nothing more than a distant drone. My throat closed up and my stomach dropped to my feet.

It was them. The Fae.

How the hell had they found me?

They moved towards us with the same flowing walk they had used before. Their features were still that of a child, and their eyes shadowed with the same desire for harm, but I didn't recognise the two approaching males. I caught a shadow through the gate as if there were more, but if there were, they didn't come into the garden.

The fork slipped from my fingers and loud spitting filled the air as the steak fell through the rack and hit the flames. I couldn't move. The underlying tone of malice and evil crept across the garden like a thick fog filled with an infectious disease that couldn't be avoided.

My legs locked tight and my lungs stopped working. The Fae glided up the two steps onto the porch and started circling Lexi while she continued to speak, completely unaware that they were there. A strangled keening found me. It was only when I took a deep, shuddering breath that I realised the sound was coming from me.

One of the males, his dark hair long to his shoulders, looked over at me and I found my voice.

'Lexi, come here.' My high pitch whisper frightened me nearly as much as the sight of the Fae did. I had lost all control of my body's reactions.

Lexi didn't move. She merely frowned, now aware that there was something wrong, but unable to perceive the real danger.

'Please,' I begged in a coarse whisper. I kept the tone low, not wanting to startle the Fae into a reaction.

How was I still stood motionless, when every cell in my body screamed for me to run? Would Lexi understand the danger we were in if she could see them? Their actions were not particularly frightening, though when they opened their mouths, the sharpened teeth would spark fear in anyone. It was their clear intentions that provoked the fight or flight syndrome in me, the knowledge that they would not only partake in evil deeds, but would get extreme pleasure from it.

How could we get away? And if by some miracle we managed to, where could we hide from the malevolent creatures?

'Please,' I said, not sure if I directed it at Lexi or the Fae.

Lexi spoke as she walked towards me, but her words escaped me. I focused on the two males who followed her with interest.

When she reached me, I gripped her hand. 'When I say go, run.'

She stiffened, finally able to sense the depth of my fear, and warily scanned the garden, unable to see the threat just three feet in front of her. I edged towards the patio doors as the gate was blocked by their approach, dragging Lexi beside me.

When we were but a few feet away from it, the panic finally bubbled over.

'Run!' I screamed, crashing through the door, only distantly aware that Lexi smacked into the frame as I yanked her through it.

I dragged her through the lounge. Had I left the keys for the car on the kitchen side? Why didn't I ask more questions when

Gabriel had spoken of the Fae? Could we make it to the car before they caught us? Hopefully, but they moved so fast. Damn, we needed a miracle to get out of this.

All thoughts stopped short when we reached the kitchen. Sheah stood silently in the front doorway, a smile of wicked amusement on her face which only enhanced the maliciousness in her eyes.

I came to an abrupt standstill, unable to breathe. Lexi crashed into me, propelling us into the kitchen side, forcing the trapped air from my lungs in one uncontrolled exhale.

Looking at the angelic appearance of the Fae, I couldn't delude myself. Begging wouldn't work, though it would possibly increase her pleasure. I shuddered, remembering how easily she had hung me over the ledge in the Tannery. She was small and slight, but if I fought against her, I would lose. I felt as a child again, only this time I had found out that the boogieman under the bed was very real, and my parents weren't around to save me.

We were going to die. The Fae weren't here to talk about the Shi within me. Gabriel's words about how they used the negative thoughts within someone filtered through my mind. With the bipolar I was a lavish buffet to them. The dark thoughts I fought to keep buried were fuel they would use against me. Would I be the one in the morning paper having killed Lexi?

Sheah grinned. She didn't just want to kill me. I had managed to avoid her twice now, and for that, she would inflict terrible pain. I scanned the room looking for an exit or a weapon or anything that would help, unwilling and unable to just wait for the nightmare to run its course.

I could scream, but the nearest neighbour lived about fifty metres away, too far to be heard properly. The chance of a passer-by was minimal, and the energy required would be best saved for if an opportunity presented itself. Anyway, I couldn't drag someone else into this. I couldn't have someone else's death on my hands.

The two males blocked the way back, the shorter haired blonde one leaning against the door frame as if this was a usual days activity for him.

Lexi tugged on my hand. 'What the hell, Ana? Let me go, you're hurting me.'

My hand cramped. I couldn't release my grip. I briefly looked into her eyes, trying to convey my sorrow for bringing this upon her.

The realisation that I had doomed my best friend allowed me to finally break my paralytic grip and I pulled her to my side, while keeping my eyes firmly fixed on Sheah.

My voice cracked as I spoke. 'I'm so sorry, Lexi.'

If I had been on my own I may have tried drastic measures such as hurling myself through the window, but with Lexi unable to see them, I wouldn't be able to get her to commit to such actions. The weight of my responsibility turned my legs to concrete and welded my feet to the floor.

My spritely friend opened her mouth to speak, but the long haired male gripped her hair and wrenched her backwards. She fell to the floor with a look of first pain, confusion and then panic as the Fae suddenly became visible to her.

She let out a piecing scream.

Anger flooded through me, fuelled by the fear. 'Let her go!'

I leapt forward to pull her free. I would fight the Fae, even if it killed me.

The short haired Fae in the doorway moved quickly, gripping me from behind. Before I could get a firm grasp on Lexi's leg, he pulled me back as I yelled and kicked. He was so much stronger than his small frame portrayed. I didn't have a chance.

'Let her go!' I shouted again, this time to Sheah as she seemed to be in charge. She just smiled whimsically, as if she held some secret that she wasn't willing to share.

Unable to move, the strength brought on by my anger drained from me. If only Gabriel hadn't gone to work on his day off. Now I would never see him again. Would he ever know what had happened to me? Or would he have to suffer the death of another that he loved, this time without knowing why? I conjured up his face in my mind in the hope it would give me the strength to endure whatever Sheah had in store for me.

'It's me you want, please let her go,' I begged, raising my voice over Lexi's wilting cries.

Sheah nodded her head in the direction of the male holding my friend. Lexi's crying abruptly stopped, though she still went through the motions. Her mouth was open wide as if she was screaming, but there was only the sound of her laboured breath being forced through her nostrils, and a look of wide eyed terror as she scratched at her neck. The long haired Fae hauled her onto her feet and threw her into the wall, pinning her by her throat as she struggled against him.

I lunged towards them and the Fae holding me sprang onto my back. He wrapped his arm around my neck, squeezing until my vision swam and my legs went from under me. I collapsed sideways onto my stomach and he released the pressure a fraction, allowing me to breathe. With a knee on my back, he gripped my hair, turning my head so that I didn't miss what was being done.

The tears flooding my face, I could only watch as Lexi silently struggled against her attacker. The Fae sank his fingers into her stomach as if her clothes and flesh were nothing more than soft butter. He moved his hand around as if rummaging through a draw filled with junk, looking for that lost and badly needed item. The blood flowed freely from her, the amount so great, it soaked her clothes in seconds before splashing onto the tiled floor.

Her body abruptly relaxed, hanging limply against the wall as her eyes glazed over. Her chest still rose and fell, but it was as if her mind had left to escape the trauma of what was happening to her.

Sheah snorted with disgust. 'Feeble human minds,' she said as her companion withdrew his hand from Lexi's stomach. At the sound of her grating voice, my captor pulled me to my feet. 'She won't be much use to me now.'

She held a dark metal sphere in one hand and an inscribed knife in the other. No, not a knife, both sides looked wickedly sharp, like a dagger.

'But at least we have quiet,' she added.

She beckoned for me to be brought towards her.

'What do you want, Fae?' Seeing the pain and then deadness in Lexi's eyes had ripped something inside my mind and my heart. Sheah couldn't cause me anymore pain than she already had.

She laughed as a snarling dog, preparing to attack and swung herself up onto the kitchen side. 'Not you.' She sat with the sphere in her lap and spun the tip of the blade on top of it. 'I just want one little thing from you and then....well, I have no need for you, so you can both go.'

'What?' I said flatly, able to detect the lie behind her words.

'Ohh, I'd like to know...' She watched the dagger spin before turning to meet my eyes with a smile. 'Where is the Siis?'

My heart dropped to my stomach and I stared at her. Of course this was about Gabriel. How could I have I missed it?

'I told you before, I don't know what you mean.'

'Oh I think you do.' She gracefully slid off the side and moved quickly to stand inches from me. 'I want the Siis who saved you.'

I gulped. 'I don't know who he is. He left as soon as we got away from you.'

She laughed. 'I know you're lying. Not only do you carry their life light inside of you.' She touched the tip of the dagger to my stomach. 'You also knew to call me Fae, and only a Siis would know to call me that.'

The strength left my body. I couldn't watch my friend die and I couldn't tell them about the man who was not only my love, but my destiny.

She watched me closely for a few moments before turning to the male holding Lexi. 'Continue.'

'No.' I hung my head. 'I will tell you. Just don't hurt her again...please.'

If it had been me they were torturing I would have gladly suffered it to keep Gabriel safe, but not Lexi. It wasn't my choice to make when she would suffer the penalty. Sheah smiled in satisfaction and held up her hand to halt her companion.

The door crashed to the floor. Gabriel burst into the kitchen, wind and the petals from the blossom tree following in his wake.

Lexi slid across the floor towards him, propelled by an invisible force. The Fae kept his grip on her throat and snarled as his legs flailed behind him. Sheah moved fast. She spun me around in front of her and moved the dagger up, pressing the flat edge across the side of my neck, in line with my jaw.

Lexi's catatonic body stopped at Gabriel's feet in a crumpled heap. He swung down and circled the childlike neck of the Fae in his hand. Yanking him with such force the Fae lost his grip, he heaved him up and dangled him out beside him. His face was full of icy rage, his eyes glinting like the steel of a blade.

'Let her go Fae.' The words spat from him like fire. Two more Fae appeared in the doorway to the lounge, crouched down with daggers held out before them.

The hanging Fae's eyes bulged and fear radiated from the other male beside me, but Sheah remained relaxed as if she had expected nothing less to happen.

'I don't think so Siis,' she said. 'There is something I want from you first and I think you will not fight us, considering what I hold for ransom.'

Gabriel stared intently at the dagger and although a slight tingle fluttered over my skin where the blade touched, nothing happened.

Sheah laughed harshly, making my skin crawl. 'It doesn't look like you're that powerful, Siis,' she sneered with contempt, taunting him.

Gabriel's lips pulled up over his teeth and his eyes narrowed even further, becoming nothing more than slits. 'What do you want?'

'Your life force of course. Your Shi will be most appreciated in creating more Fae.' She said it with an edge of disapproval as if she thought he would be most unkind to refuse.

My body turned to lead. Her words brought to mind my nieces whom I loved more than life itself. The image of the Fae creeping into their room in the deep darkness of night played out so sharply, I could almost believe I was there. The sound of the girls whimpered cries as they were taken, so real, I convinced myself that it wouldn't be some unknown child the Fae would take. They would purposely set out to track down the ones I loved as it would add to their fun.

Gabriel's eyes dropped with distress. He had no idea what to do.

Bile filled my throat. How many children would his Shi convert? Their change to malicious beings was unacceptable. The pain it would cause the remaining families could not be allowed.

Even if Gabriel somehow survived the procedure, they still wouldn't let us go. The only power they had over him was what they could do to me. Without that, he and Lexi would most likely survive. If I was lucky we would all walk away, but that was unlikely.

I shook my head, conveying that he was to do nothing. A trickle of blood travelled down my neck. The movement had caused a small cut. What did it matter? I'd most likely be dead soon anyway.

Looking deep into his eyes, I drew on my love for him and pushed it in his direction. Hopefully it would work without the luxury of touch and he'd receive my message of goodbye. I purposely glanced towards Lexi and back again to show that he was to take care of her. Mouthing the words, 'I love you,' I closed my eyes and tensed, ready to throw myself back. At the same time Gabriel roared, 'No!' and I sensed him start to move forwards. Sheah tightened her grip and turned the sharp edge of the blade into my skin.

The room suddenly filled with the sound of a silvery voice. 'Well if I'd known it was a party, I would have gotten all dressed up.'

12

Everything stopped. I remained tense, ready to push back, the edge of the dagger pressed into my neck. Gabriel halted mid-charge towards me with a look of rage and tight despair etched into his face, his body shimmering with anguish. The Fae in his hold stopped writhing and hung motionless, momentarily forgetting his desperate attempt to be free. Even the two Fae gripping me froze at the sound of the newcomer.

We all turned to stare.

Forgetting my plan to either escape or die, I stood transfixed by the angel who must surely have come directly from heaven, taking in her hair that shone like stands of gold in the light. Even in jeans and a tight fitted jumper, she could quite easily have gone to a ball and nobody would have raised an eyebrow, only able to stare with wonder at the splendour before them. She radiated beauty and happiness.

She laughed the sound of a hundred tiny bells chiming and clapped her hands as if at a child's birthday party.

'I'm sorry, am I interrupting?' She didn't look sorry. She grinned as if enjoying herself immensely. 'I can leave if it's a bad time.' She stepped back with an elegance far exceeding that of the Fae.

I wanted to touch her, confirm that the image before me was real. If I dared to hope that we were saved, would she poof out of existence? Was she merely a figment of my imagination? I reached my mind out to get a sense of her. She felt no fear, only confident amusement, and intense disgust. I sagged with relief and the blade dug further into my neck, forcing me to stand erect.

The newcomer captivated me, drawing me in so much that my fear became barely a shadow in the background. My eyes found Gabriel as a slight smile danced across my lips. His eyes were narrow and his lip curled stealing some of the light feeling. He stared at the woman as if she was a hindrance rather than our salvation.

My captors remained watchful as if waiting for the situation to develop so that they could act as needed. It seemed I was the only one mesmerised by her presence. The light shimmering around her looked the same as Gabriel's but so much brighter. She sparkled.

Sheah spoke, her voice tight with wariness. 'Who are you?'

'I am Eris,' the newcomer said, her eyes wide as if surprised they hadn't recognised her. 'But you may know me as Risa.'

Upon hearing her name, the Fae in Gabriel's grip scrabbled in the air and tried to swing behind him. Sheah pulled the dagger closer to my neck, causing the blood to flow freely down my front and shoulder. The third Fae scrambled back against the wall and the two who had recently joined us made a hasty retreat, though a strangled squealing came from their direction.

If Sheah placed any more pressure on the dagger, I would be dead. Gabriel glanced at me and his face somehow tightened further as he came to the same conclusion.

'Risa!'

'Okay, Okay.' She sighed and rolled her eyes. 'It seems that you are upsetting my friend here,' she said to Sheah. 'Do you think you could let go of that woman?' She sighed again, almost regretfully, like she wanted the scene to play out, that it would amuse her.

Sheah edged back, pulling me with her. 'This is no concern of yours.'

Eris shook her head and smiled. 'How can you be so wrong? If you truly knew who I am, you would know that you have only two choices here.'

The dagger vibrated next to my skin and the pressure released. Sheah's grip loosened in surprise as the weapon appeared in Eris' hand. Without hesitation, I pushed back and rammed her into the kitchen side, knocking all the breath from me. I staggered towards Gabriel, slipping on the blood spilt, before landing in a heap between him and Lexi.

I checked Lexi's breathing. It was scarily shallow. Gabriel grabbed my hand and pulled me up. He ground my fingers together in his tight grip and stood stiffly, his eyes darting between Eris and the Fae.

Eris laughed. 'She's a feisty one, Gabriel. I can see why you like her.'

Sheah sprung into a crouched position, with her hands curled out before her.

'Now can someone please explain what this is all about?' Eris said.

The male Fae both looked towards Sheah, who continued to glare at the beautiful newcomer, her eyes filled with vengeful hate.

Eris sighed. 'I can see I need to be persuasive.'

Eris didn't move but Sheah dropped to the ground with a high pitched scream. Gabriel continued to watch stonily, his eyes occasionally moving from Eris to the Fae.

The male Fae frantically looked around before darting towards the lounge. He managed a few steps before collapsing to the floor to join his companion in writhing agony.

Eris watched them both with a satisfied smile, before shaking herself. The screaming stopped and the Fae became motionless, though still whimpered quietly.

'Now, shall we try again?'

Sheah rose up, dragged by an invisible force. She sagged with her toes barely touching the ground.

'Why are you here?' Eris said with hope in her voice as if she wanted the Fae to disobey her again.

Sheah answered in a whisper, though still managed to maintain an air of defiance in her tone. 'To take the Siis' Shi in order to create more of our own.'

'And how would you be able to do that?'

The Fae stared at Eris, her eyes bright with hatred. Eris' grin broadened. Was Sheah really going to defy her? I had to give her credit for guts. Sheah nodded to the sphere resting on the side, obviously deciding her fate was worth more than the secrets of her trade. Eris nonchalantly picked it up and began rolling it around in her hand.

'And how does this work?'

107

Sheah glared at her before sighing with resignation. 'We use it in conjunction with the dagger—'

'This dagger?' Eris said, holding it up before her.

Sheah nodded. 'The point of the dagger is pushed into the grove in the sphere. When the Siis holds the handle, his Shi is drained into it. We use that to give children the gift of long life.'

'How ingenious!' Eris said with genuine awe. A loud crack echoed out through the kitchen and the male collapsed to the floor with his head turned at an impossible angle.

Sheah backed towards the lounge. 'Why did you do that? You said we had a choice. I told you what you wanted.'

'But you do,' Eris said. 'If you would rather a slow, painful death, I'm more than happy to oblige.'

The coldness in Eris filled me with quiet dread as I collapsed against Gabriel. Her pleasure was unnatural, leading me to wonder, was she our saviour or our damnation? The question followed me into oblivion.

Gabriel's voice broke through the haze. Hands circled my neck, the pressure light yet restricting. My eyes widened as my throat swelled and I scurried away from the touch.

'It's me. Please hold still while I heal you.'

I focused on his face, tired and engraved with worry as he smiled down at me.

'What happened?' I croaked. My neck stung sharply, mixed in with a dull throb as if my heart had travelled up. I blinked several times, trying to banish the wooziness that made it difficult to think.

'You fainted from blood loss and hit your head.'

The memories came flooding back and I quickly sat up. 'Where...?' My head spun making it impossible to finish the question.

'Risa is dealing with them.'

'You mean Eris?' I mumbled incoherently whilst swaying.

He pushed me back down. 'Only she would name herself that.'

I pressed my hands to my temples. 'Oww.' God, my skull felt like it was going to fall apart.

'Don't sit up until I have fully mended you.'

The pain in my neck receded as the tissue knitted together. 'Lexi?'

His eyes shadowed and he looked down at his hands. 'I am really sorry.'

A coil of ice made its way through my stomach. 'What do you mean you're sorry?'

'It's too late,' he replied quietly. 'She's dead.'

I rolled over, ignoring the pain in my head as it intensified. 'No!' Lexi lay on her side with her long hair plastered to her face. I shook her. 'No! You can heal her. You have to heal her.' Her skin looked ashen, but it was loss of blood, not death, it wasn't allowed to be death. I checked for any signs of breathing. 'You have to heal her now. She can't die. She can't. Heal her now.'

He put his arms around me from behind. 'I am so sorry, Ana.'

I pushed him off. 'No! You can't let this happen.'

I turned her onto her back and opened her airway. How many times had we practised this with each other, gone through all the motions during our training days at work? It was never meant to happen for real, not to each other. I started CPR. Her small chest moved too easily under my hands.

'Come on, Lexi.' Tears poured down my face and I quickly blinked them away. She would be fine, of course she would, it was Lexi. 'Damn it! Come on, it's time to wake up now.'

I forced breath into her still lungs and counted each compression out loud. Gabriel tried to draw me away and I pushed his hands off. He didn't get it. Lexi wouldn't die, she couldn't, she was just scaring me, testing me to see if I would give up.

'Stop!' Gabriel said after a time. He forced me to his chest as I fought against him.

'Get off!' Why did he want me to stop? Didn't he want her to live? He finally released me.

The minutes ticked by and my shoulders ached as I continued with the compressions. I didn't stop, I couldn't. Gabriel pulled on me again and forced me into his arms. I scratched his skin and writhed in his grip, but he only held me tighter, murmuring words of comfort.

The strength drained from me in one foul swoop and I hung lifelessly in his arms.

A sob erupted in my chest. It tore through my body, trying to rip me apart. The air stuck in my lungs and I choked. Gabriel smacked me across the back to start me breathing once more, allowing the sobbing to resume its course. At some point he healed my head wound, helping my mind to clear. The pain became even sharper and the tears fell more freely.

After several minutes it stopped as quickly as it started, leaving me hollow as if I wasn't really alive. I sat with my legs out before me and detachedly took in the carnage around me. Puddles and streaks covered the cream tiles, some of them drying to a rusted brown. Smears coated the wall, the last remains of Lexi's life. We had been sat so happy only an hour before and now she was gone. Oh my God, she was really gone.

Eris returned through the front door, smiling with triumph. 'That was fun!' She grinned wildly and delicately lifted herself onto the side. 'I found four more *just waiting* for me outside. From the scent, that was all of them.'

Gabriel glared at her as she selected an apple from the fruit bowl. The skin peeled away as she examined it.

She put a section of apple into her mouth. 'What's next?'

'We have to move her,' Gabriel said through gritted teeth.

It took a moment for his words to penetrate my haze. 'What do you mean move her?'

'We can't leave her here,' he said. 'There is no way to explain what happened.'

Eris slid off the side. 'I'll do it,' she exclaimed with enthusiasm.

I dragged Lexi onto my lap. 'No! You can't take her.' She didn't love Lexi like I did. She didn't care for her. To her, Lexi was a body that needed to be moved, not the kind, wonderful woman who was my best friend.

'We have to,' Gabriel said.

'What about the injuries?' I protested hysterically. 'People know she is here. When the police see the injuries they will come to investigate anyway.'

'Eris can change them.' Gabriel tried to disengage me from Lexi. 'Make it appear as an accident.'

His words made sense but I couldn't release my friend. Gabriel reached his fingers towards my head.

I forcefully slapped them away. 'Don't you dare,' I seethed. 'You can't just deal with me by sending me to sleep.'

He sighed and let his hand drop. 'I know this is hard, however, we need to do this.'

I glared at him for several seconds, willing him to suffer. 'I know that! Just give me some time.'

He backed away as I sat, stroking Lexi's hair away from her eyes.

'I'm so, so sorry,' I told her as fresh tears rolled down my cheeks. 'I never meant for this to happen.'

It was some time before I kissed her head and released my hold on her.

'Do it,' I told them flatly, stepping back.

Eris glanced towards Gabriel, who nodded in response. She scooped Lexi into her arms as if she weighed nothing more than a baby, her eyes still wide with excitement, though thankfully no longer smiling. I couldn't tear my eyes away from Lexi's red hair, which hung down in a mattered clump, and her limp arm that swung as it pointed towards the floor.

'I'll be back,' Eris said before gliding out of the room.

Gabriel reached out to cup my face.

'Don't you touch me. After all this, don't you dare.'

He closed his eyes against my accusing stare and I turned away.

I didn't cry as I washed the signs of destruction from the room. Instead I thought of the times I had shared with Lexi over the years. How when my parents had died, she'd taken time off work to sit with me. How she'd always known the right thing to say to draw me out of my misery or self-pity. I remembered how excited she had been when she had got the job in the care home, how she had tinkled with laughter, saying, *You have no hope of getting rid of me now.* She had been my rock. How was I supposed to survive without her? How could I live with the knowledge that I'd caused another death?

When I finished mopping the floor, I glanced towards Gabriel. He sat at the table watching me with a pained expression. How dare he look so sad and hurt. Without a word, I headed upstairs for a shower.

I stood motionless as the hot water beat at my skin, unable to drag my eyes away from the blood as it spun around the plug hole before finding its way down. I stood so long that the water began to run cool. It was only then that I found the will power to wash and get out.

Once dressed, I paused to draw on my energy reserves. The night was far from over. There was still the strange woman to deal with, and many questions that needed answers.

Eris and Gabriel sat at the table in silence, with steaming mugs grasped in their hands. They both watched me, Eris with interest and Gabriel frowning with concern, while I made a coffee to try and combat the exhaustion. Even though all my injuries had been healed, I ached painfully, so I swallowed a couple of paracetamol followed by some B12 vitamins I found in the back of the cupboard. To my astonishment my stomach rumbled. How could I feel hunger after what had happened? I prepared a plate of sandwiches before joining them. Right or wrong, I hadn't eaten since lunch.

We all sat in silence while I nibbled at the food. After a few mouthfuls, I pushed it away. It lay heavy on my stomach.

I studied the unlikely woman. Was she a friend or foe? I was only alive due to her interference, which caused me to feel grateful, yet at the same time, left a bitter taste in my mouth. The question was, did I really want her in the house? The pleasure she had received from what had happened was disturbing in the least.

'Thank you,' I told her, trying to infuse gratitude into my tone.

She shrugged and flapped her hand towards me as if to show that it was nothing on her part. I turned to Gabriel, expecting him to echo my words of appreciation. His eyes were hard and his expression firm. The animosity flooded from him as he stared at her. They must have one hell of a history.

It was irrelevant for the moment, so I turned to Eris. 'Who are you?'

She tutted dramatically. 'Did you not tell her about me, Gabriel?' She feigned being hurt. 'At least tell me you mentioned I was coming?'

'She is the one I sent for.'

I recalled the conversation. If I had known how beautiful she was then, my outburst may well have been worse, if that was at all possible. I no longer cared, though it helped that Gabriel looked at her with distain.

'Ana. I suppose you could call Ris...Eris my sister in law.' He placed his arm protectively around my shoulder.

112

I couldn't help but stare. I had already guessed he'd been married, but how he could feel such animosity for a family member?

'Pleased to meet you,' I said, holding out my hand. I had been brought up to mind my manners, whatever the situation.

Eris grinned as she took my hand. 'She really is quite funny.'

I frowned at her, unable to understand what I had done. Maybe his kind didn't shake hands.

'You can see the problem.' Gabriel indicated to me with a tilt of his head. 'I called you because I want to know what harm it could cause her, and if anything can be done.'

'Well you really have been bad, Gabriel,' she chastised him playfully. 'I would never have thought you would have it in you to change someone as you have this poor girl.'

My eyes narrowed with her amusement.

'It was an accident, Eris.' Gabriel's tone was warning. 'You know very well I wouldn't deliberately do something like this.'

She laughed. 'Well a girl can live in hope, can't she?'

He leant across the table towards her, with his fists clenched and his lip turned up. 'Well?'

She relaxed back in the chair. 'Well what?'

Gabriel remained rigid, though shocks stabbed at the air as if his rage was made up of bolts of lightning that he hurled her way.

I pulled on his arm 'Please don't. There has already been too much violence.'

'You are a priestess,' he snarled through gritted teeth. Tremors rippled through his body, so violent, my teeth vibrated with the contact. 'You have studied the ancient texts and I need you to tell me what is happening.'

'Fine,' she pouted, maybe able to see the danger she was creating for herself. 'But to be honest, Gabriel, all I know is that as with the Fae, it is irreversible.'

My throat closed up with panic. 'Will I become like them?'

Eris smiled at me as if I was an infant. 'Have you not told her anything?'

'She knows how they were created.'

'Good, that's a start then,' she said. 'You can't become Fae, that's unless Gabriel was being extremely reckless.' She smiled at him and winked. Maybe she couldn't help herself. 'When

Talamiis converted the children into the Fae, he did it by forcing his own genetic makeup into theirs, which in turn changed their DNA. That is not the case with you. Do you understand?'

I did, though still couldn't grasp the implications. Gabriel obviously felt the same. 'Will it harm her?'

'Unlikely but there is no known record of this ever happening before.'

'How did it happen?' he asked, echoing my exact thoughts.

'I'm not sure anyone can answer that. Theoretically it isn't possible.'

We fell into an awkward silence and I looked around the now clean kitchen, trying to banish the images that threatened to overwhelm me. My eyes returned to the table and I studied the sphere and dagger that lay in the middle, the cause of all the destruction that had occurred. I reached over and picked the dagger up.

It was a dull, dark grey metal, though polished, catching the light in a similar way that my leather sofa did when freshly cleaned. It was straight and extremely slim, maybe only a couple of millimetres thick. Including the handle, it was shorter than my forearm, but heavy as if it was a fully sized sword instead of a small blade. Both sides were inscribed with symbols that I had never seen before, rectangular in their design.

I held the blade out to Gabriel. 'What does this say?'

He carefully took it from me and turned it towards the light. His lip curled as he read it. 'The rough translation is, *The passage to life of the Fae.*'

As I held out my hand to take the dagger back, Eris picked the sphere up and turned it in her delicate hands.

'You know there is only one person who could create this,' Eris said as I took hold of the hilt.

'Who?' I asked, withdrawing the blade.

Gabriel hissed sharply. A single tear of blood welled over his finger, so small compared to what I'd seen so far, but the sight of it shook me to my core. The dagger slipped from my fingers to clatter to the table.

'Oh my God,' I breathed.

'It is fine,' he quickly reassured me. 'See, it has already healed.' He wiped his hand over the injury and held his finger out to show that he spoke the truth.

'But how? You can't be injured. I saw you stab yourself before and it did nothing.' Hysteria began to creep into my voice. The last grain of sand had tipped the scale and I thought that I might well snap. 'How is it that you are bleeding?'

'Calm down.' He took both my hands in one of his, while pushing the dangerous weapon into the middle of the table.

'But how?'

Eris grinned as she picked the blade up. 'I take it she doesn't know about Daku.'

Gabriel kept his hands on mine and spoke in a way that calmed the storm within. 'Remember I said that we could not be harmed by any weapons known to man?'

I nodded.

'Daku is a metal that can only be found deep beneath the earth's surface, and it is rare enough that humans have not come across it yet. It is the only material that I cannot manipulate.'

'But I don't understand. Even if you can't manipulate the dagger, why couldn't you just move yourself around it like you did the kitchen knife?'

He sighed deeply and pressed his lips together. Eris watched us with interest.

'Because when it has contact with us,' he finally said, 'we lose all our abilities. If in human form, we are effectively human, with human strength and speed, and we can be damaged as a human can be.'

'So Daku is your kryptonite then?' They both frowned with confusion. 'Never mind,' I said. 'Can I ask you something Eris?'

'Of course,' she responded, the playfulness back in her voice.

'How is it that you could move the dagger and Gabriel couldn't?'

Gabriel stiffened and clenched his hands together.

Eris sniggered. 'She hit a sore spot there didn't she, Gabe?'

He glowered at her.

'I'm a priestess,' she said proudly.

I looked at her blankly.

'I trained for many of your lifetimes to learn the secrets of the elders and now I can manipulate pretty much anything with concentration. Gabriel here was also studying before....well before he stopped,' she added, her voice dropping in volume.

'You know why I did.'

Eris hesitantly reached her hand towards him. 'I'm sorry for what happened.'

I shifted in my seat and looked down at the table, aware I was witnessing a private exchange. She dropped her hand as if she had just become conscious of my presence.

'It's all in the past now,' she said. She beamed at me but I detected sadness in her, also betrayed by the shadow in her eyes. 'Anyway, I had best take my leave. It's been fun and extremely interesting.'

Even though her words caused a spark of anger within me, I thought to ask if she wanted to stay, after all she had saved my life. But Gabriel sat in stony silence, ensuring the words never passed my lips.

She skipped to the door. 'Oh and Gabriel.' She stopped and turned to face him. 'Be careful. You know what will happen if they find out.' With that final warning she left.

'What did she mean by that?'

He pulled me closer. 'Nothing.'

Somehow, I didn't believe him.

'Where did she put Lexi?'

'Somewhere she will be found soon. She also thought to appear as Lexi in public, so that there will be no suspicion on us.'

I should have pushed to find out how Eris had changed her, and what cause of death she had staged, but I couldn't deal with the lie right now. 'I'm going to bed,' I said instead.

Neglecting to brush my teeth, I slipped under the covers, hoping to be instantly swept away into oblivion. I was disappointed. Continual flashes played across my mind. Every time I tried to direct my thoughts, they returned to Lexi and how I had caused her death.

I heard the knocking sound before I realised that it was the echo of my teeth chattering. My whole body was frozen as if I had been out in the snow all day, leaving my hands and feet so numb I couldn't feel them. Gabriel held me tenderly within his arms, tucking the covers up around us. I didn't cry. I wanted to, if only to release the knot in my chest. But for once my tears wouldn't fall, instead choosing to stay locked inside.

13

I spent the next day in a haze. Gabriel cooked but I didn't eat. He tried to engage me in conversation but I wasn't interested. I sat on the sofa with my arms wrapped around my legs, staring off into space, not really thinking of anything, but allowing all my thoughts to flow over my mind, each one never quite catching hold. Sometimes the grief overwhelmed me. Each time, numbness spread over my mind, signifying that Gabriel was trying to dull my pain.

At ten, I turned on the night news to find the story of a hit and run several miles from my home. They didn't release the name of the victim, but I knew it was Lexi and a pressure built up in my chest until I thought I might explode. When I went to bed, I lay with Gabriel's arms around me, not able to sleep until the early hours.

I awoke after a couple of hours fitful sleep, with my lips pressed together in order to contain the scream that my nightmares caused. As if it hadn't been awful enough living through it the first time, my mind wanted to assault me with the memories once again.

Taking care not to disturb Gabriel, I slipped out of bed and made my way downstairs. I avoided looking at the photo of Lexi and I, taken on one of our rare nights out, and collected all my Uni books before settling onto the sofa.

At seven thirty someone knocked on the door. To my surprise, I found Carl stood nervously on the door step.

He withdrew a piece of cloth from his pocket and started cleaning his glasses. 'Can I come in?'

I stepped back to allow him entrance and he stopped just inside the door.

'Ana, I'm so sorry. I heard on the radio this morning that Lexi died in a hit and run accident.'

I already knew this, but the news hit me like a sledge hammer and tears sprung from my eyes as my chest heaved. It was actually real. Lexi was really dead.

'I didn't want you to hear it at work,' he continued as he fiddled with his glasses. 'I know how close you both were.'

'Thank you,' I choked. My relationship with Carl was strained at the least, and it touched me that he would come out of his way like this.

'I have covered your shifts for the week. If you need more time I can organise something.'

I took a deep uneven breath. 'I don't want time off,' I told him with more force than I intended.

He shifted uneasily as he studied me, taking in the tears that although had slowed, still silently fell. 'Okay, but I don't want you in for your late today.'

'But—'

'No buts,' he said.

My arguments would fall on deaf ears, so I nodded meekly in agreement. He was probably right.

I thought to offer him a drink, but he declined, saying he had to get to work. He gave me his condolences in such a heartfelt manner, I realised I didn't know the man who had been my boss for over a year. What I had always thought of as coldness was really only professionalism.

When he left, I took a moment to gather my strength before returning to my Uni books. Gabriel came down minutes later, having been woken by the thud of the front door closing.

'You do not need to worry about your studies right now,' he said.

'I have exams soon,' I replied without taking my eyes off my work. 'The world doesn't stop because I don't feel like participating in it.'

He wanted to say more, but thankfully kept it to himself.

Focusing on my work helped and the haze began to dissipate. I still felt somewhat disconnected from the world, but Gabriel managed to provoke a weak smile at times.

I had just put my books away for the evening when Gabriel looked up, with his head on a slight angle.

'You know how you have always wanted to meet my friends?' He had a distant look to his face that sent a cool shiver down my spine.

'Yes,' I said uncertainly.

'Now's your chance.'

He grinned and turned towards the lounge door. I waited, my apprehension growing by the second. A massive figure stepped through the doorway, so large he had to dip his head in order to fit.

They smiled at each other and Gabriel crossed the room towards the tall man. They held out their hands as if they were going to shake, but instead gripped the tops of each other's arms and bumped shoulders. They laughed easily and Gabriel gazed at the man as a younger brother might, with respect and admiration. A warm feeling reached across the room from Gabriel confirming his deep sense of love for the man. Unlike everyone else, nothing came from the stranger.

Gabriel slapped the man's back. 'How are you old friend?'

'Good as always,' the stranger said with a husky voice.

They released each other and Gabriel placed his hand on the man's shoulder to guide him in my direction. 'What name do you go by now?'

'Adam. What about you? Are you still using Gabe?'

Gabriel chuckled. 'You know me. Never did like change.' He laughed again and the feeling began to infect me, almost like a bubble had exploded inside my body, sending fizzy tingles throughout every cell.

The man stood four inches taller than Gabriel. I took in his short, dark hair and chiselled looks. Hardness carved his features, the complete opposite to Gabriel's softness. The white t-shirt clung to his muscles, rounded and defined, rippling with every movement. Everything about him screamed *dangerous,* and I took a step back.

'This is my oldest and dearest friend,' Gabriel said.

His chest puffed out with pride for me as he introduced us and my heart swelled in response. I had been so closed off to him for the last couple of days. I touched his hand to convey my feelings, before turning to face the person who obviously meant the world to him.

I became locked in his stare as he scrutinised me, his eyes the colour of liquid chocolate, so dark, they almost blended in with the pupil. He glared as if my presence offended him.

Unable to breathe or speak, I nodded in acknowledgement, shocked by his attitude and the fear it caused in me. Gabriel was so absorbed with his own happiness that he didn't sense my distress. He finally freed me from his gaze and I sighed with relief as he turned to Gabriel.

'So this is *what* caused the problems with the Fae?' His words dripped with distain.

'Don't be like that,' Gabriel quietly beseeched. 'It was not her fault.' He pulled me into his arms. 'Anyway, how did you find out about it?'

'Eris.'

Gabriel's eyes tightened. 'I should have known she couldn't remain silent.'

'She is concerned for you.' Adam spoke gently, but when he glanced in my direction, his lip momentarily curled with contempt. 'You have to forgive her, Gabe.'

'Sirus died trying to rescue her,' Gabriel said, his tone louder and tinged with anger. 'All because she was arrogant enough to think she could complete the mission on her own.'

'There was no way to know that Vakros was there. Eris paid greatly for her mistake and not only with Sirus' death.'

'He is dead because she believed she is better than us.'

'She was young and reckless as we all once were and Sirus knew the risks when he went in. Anyway, we both know that is not the problem.'

Gabriel clenched his fists and leant towards Adam. 'She could have prevented Deonti's death.' His pain cut into me, raw and jagged, similar to the night he had spoken of the love between his kind.

'You know what Deonti was like, Gabe. Nothing could stop her when she had her mind set on something.'

Gabriel opened his mouth to speak. Instead his eyes narrowed and he turned towards the lounge. 'You brought her here?'

I followed his gaze in time to observe Eris enter through the doorway, where she paused, her face still supporting a mischievous grin, only this time edged with apprehension.

'You are not welcome here!' Gabriel stated stiffly.

How could he be so rude? He had initially called her *and* she had helped us.

'Please, Gabriel,' she said, the smile gone from her face. 'I only want to talk.'

Gabriel tensed as if to launch himself at her.

I quickly put my hand on his chest and spoke to Eris. 'Come to the lounge with me please.' My voice cracked with tension and I threw a glance in Adam's direction. He may hate me for whatever reason, but he obviously cared for both Gabriel and Eris, and I needed him to calm Gabriel down. I walked past Eris and she followed me to the sofa.

Once we were both seated I studied the strange woman, unsure as how to proceed.

'I know what it's like to blame yourself for someone's death,' Eris said.

'Did you kill your best friend too?' I said with more bitterness than intended.

Eris sighed. 'What happened to you was a case of wrong place, wrong time. I did so much more than that. That's one of the reasons Gabriel finds it impossible to talk to me.'

'Who is Deonti?' I had a good idea but wanted it confirmed.

Grief shadowed her face. 'She is my sister.'

'I'm sorry,' I said, partly for bringing it up and partly for her grief.

'Don't be.' She gave me a small smile. 'There was a great battle within our race, about two thousand years ago. There were those that believed that we were superior because of our abilities and immortality, and that the human race was there to serve us. The rest of us didn't think like that, we liked our solitude and had no wish to dominate others. There were also those that wished to study the evolution of humans as it gave insight into our own earlier evolution.'

I stared at her with my mouth open. 'You were human?'

She laughed at my expression. 'No we weren't. However, we were solid forms once, some millions of years ago.'

I wanted to ask what they looked like and how they had evolved, but now she had started her story she wanted, maybe even needed to finish it.

'The talks about whether we should show our true selves to humans broke down. The ones who agreed with it eventually got tired of our opposition, and took matters into their own hands.'

She gazed towards the far wall, though I suspected that she was focused inwards, rather than taking in my many photos.

'Many of us had formed a settlement of sorts in order to figure out how to deal with the situation before it got out of control, bringing our families, including the children to it, in order to keep them safe. We did not expect them to attack, but word came that many of them were headed our way. We had no time to evacuate the children and some of us stayed behind to protect them, while the rest set off to fight.' She paused. 'Deonti was Gabriel's life partner and he had specified that she was to stay and protect their child.'

I nearly choked.

Her eyes widened with surprise. 'Didn't you know he had a daughter?'

I shook my head in answer, not able to speak as the new information vibrated around my brain.

'I'm sorry. I thought he would have told you by now.'

I shook my head again, still unable to speak, and gestured for her to continue.

She studied me for a moment before shrugging. 'Deonti was a great warrior and she believed that she would be better able to protect her daughter by fighting against the Others, which is what we call them. After Gabriel had left, she begged me to look after Suraya and I agreed willingly. I understood that she needed the chance to fight for her daughter's life. I was wrong. I could have stopped her, yet I didn't. Because of me, my sister was killed in battle.'

I reached forward to touch her hand. The contact brought her back to the present and she smiled.

'So now you know the person I am and why Gabriel holds such animosity towards me.'

'It wasn't your fault.'

'Yes it was,' she argued without strength. 'I will never forget my part in my sister's death, but thank you for your kind words.'

She squeezed my hand a fraction before pulling away to stand. 'I should leave. It doesn't look like he will see me today.'

'Please come back again,' I begged. I had so many more questions for her.

'I don't think time will change how he feels about me, but thank you for the invitation. You never know, I might take you up on it one day.'

'I'll talk to him,' I said. There was something about her that made me want to keep her in my life and my anger towards Gabriel only reinforced the feeling. Who was the man I had fallen in love with? Not only had he hidden a daughter from me, but he blamed Eris for something I may well have done myself.

'Good luck with that.' She laughed, all signs of her sorrow now locked away. 'By the way, Ana...you really need to get your ability under control before someone notices it.'

I looked at her dumfounded.

'You must have noticed that you can read people's emotions much more now.'

I had noticed, but had put it down to the bond between Gabriel and me. When I thought about it, I realised that I could also sense other people more than usual.

'Oh my God, is that because of the Shi in me?'

'Yes and it will probably get stronger. You need to be careful when around those of my kind as we can detect the changes in you, in response to what you're feeling.'

My throat restricted and I gulped. 'Is that dangerous?'

'It could be,' she replied grimly, 'but don't worry about it now.' She smiled easily again. 'Just learn to protect your mind and if anything else comes up, let me know.'

With those parting words she skipped out the open patio doors, leaving me to speculate what else could possibly come up.

I reluctantly returned to the kitchen to find Gabriel smiling once more. After offering them both a drink, I joined them at the table. I really wanted to shout and scream at him for keeping his daughter from me, but I had been brought up better than to air my dirty laundry in public. So keeping my mouth closed, I took Eris' advice and tried to shield my feelings from them.

Both of them laughed easily, though Adam seemed a lot more in control than Gabriel.

I shifted on my seat and looked at them suspiciously. 'What's so funny?'

'Adam here has been filling me in on what he's been up to for the last few years. It's hilarious.'

'What would that be?'

Even though Gabriel must have filled him in on the details of our relationship, Adam's eyes were still full of contempt for me. I shrank back in my seat. Why did he scare me so much?

'Say hello to the Beast of Bray Road. He's been scaring the Americans by changing into a werewolf. He even jumped onto the back of one of their trucks.' Gabriel laughed so boisterously I thought he would fall off the chair. 'I wish I had been there to see it.'

I scowled. 'That's not very nice!'

Adam's eyes narrowed further and shone with annoyance. Why the hell did I speak? Determined not to shrink under his glare, I stared back at him trying to be bold, but secretly shaking inside. Why wasn't Gabriel picking up on my distress?

'Why do you say that?' he asked me. He held me in his gaze, making it impossible to pull away.

Trying to force my breath calmly in and out, I answered. 'Just because you have powers doesn't mean you have the right to use them.'

Adam opened his mouth to respond, but Gabriel interrupted him. 'Come on, Ana.' He laughed as he pulled me closer to him. 'It's just a bit of fun.'

'I don't see how scaring people is fun.'

Adam's lips curled further. 'Do you really believe that I would spend my time scaring the locals for amusement?'

Gabriel tensed. 'Adam,' he warned.

I tried to ignore the narrow eyed scowl coming from Adam. 'What is it?' I asked.

'For some reason you claim to *love* this human,' he said to Gabriel, emphasising the word love as if he was saying something distasteful. 'Maybe you should tell her what our world is really like.'

Gabriel slammed his hands down on the table. 'No!'

'How about you tell me?' I couldn't manage the same level of distaste as Adam, but I made a good attempt.

Adam lent forward on his chair, decreasing the distance between us. His intense stare pinned me once more. I really should have kept my mouth shut.

'The reason I did it was to claim another Siis that was hiding out as a deer. The human male had collected him off the side of the road believing he was dead, when he was only injured.'

'Why would you be hunting a Siis?' I frowned at Gabriel. How could he be friends with someone who would kill his own kind?

'You do not know?' Adam said.

I shook my head to indicate that I had no idea what he was talking about. He studied me in silence.

'There is a war going on,' he said eventually. 'One that we have to protect you humans from.'

'That is enough,' Gabriel said sternly. 'It's nothing to worry about, Ana. It has no bearing on us.'

I wanted to believe him. My head already buzzed with the information about his daughter. One problem at a time was more than enough to keep me occupied.

Adam continued to watch me as if he expected me to jump up and do something wrong. The weight of his stare frayed my nerves.

'I'm going to bed,' I said stiffly, standing up. I gave Adam a curt nod and stalked out of the kitchen.

Gabriel caught up with me as I headed up the stairs. 'What's wrong?'

What could possibly be wrong? His friend looked at me as if I was nothing more than faeces, and I had just found out he had been keeping secrets from me.

'You know that talk about war was just talk,' he continued. 'There really is no need to worry about it.'

The war was the furthest thing from my mind.

I took a deep breath and turned to him, only to find him looking at me with big doleful eyes. My resolve broke and I joined him at the bottom of the stairs, allowing him to take me in his embrace.

'I'm fine,' I reassured him. 'I'm just tired and I really want to do some more Uni reading.' I smiled at him and locked my real feelings inside.

He visibly relaxed, obviously more willing to believe the lie than the truth betrayed by my emotions. 'I will be staying up with Adam if that is okay?'

'That's fine, like I said, loads of reading to get through.'

'Do you mind if he stays in the spare room?'

I stiffened and then sighed. The downside of living with someone was that you didn't get a choice in who they let into the house.

'Of course not.' I smiled, indicating badly that it would be a pleasure.

I reached up on my toes to give him a kiss good night, with the knowledge that it would probably be the early hours before he came to bed.

Half way up the stairs he stopped me. 'Ana. What happened with Eris?' He stood tense, waiting for me to answer.

'We'll talk about it tomorrow.' I continued up the stairs, not really caring what he took from my answer.

I opened my books with every intention of reading, but my thoughts kept wandering. How could he not tell me he had a daughter?

The question continued to race around my head, but after a while, my anger gradually dissipated. It wasn't as if he had a small child I would have to care for. She would be at least two thousand years old now. Hopefully we could be friends.

My mind eventually quietened and by the time Gabriel slipped in the bed beside me, I was dozing. He wrapped his arms around me and I snuggled into his embrace, no longer feeling anything except the pleasure of having him to myself.

'Has something upset you?'

'Not upset, just disappointed.'

'Why? Is it Adam?'

I bristled at the sound of his name. Forcing myself to relax as there were other things I wanted to discuss, I turned to face him. 'I know about your daughter.'

Gabriel stiffened. 'She shouldn't have told you about Suraya.'

'She thought I already knew. To be honest I would like to know why I hadn't heard of her before.' His anger towards Eris only fuelled my earlier irritation and I sat up in order to see his expression better. 'Well?' I urged.

'I apologise, it never came up.'

'How can you having a daughter not *come up*? It's the sort of thing you tell someone on the first date. We have been together for months and in all that time it never *came up.* How is that possible?'

Gabriel waited until some of the anger drained from me before answering. 'Is it a problem that I have a daughter?'

I groaned and pulled even further from him. 'It's not that you have a daughter that bothers me. It's that you never told me about her that's the problem. I thought we were closer than that. You know everything about me, even what my uniform for secondary school was like. But I don't know about the most important thing in your life.'

He gave up trying to pull me into his arms, and sat up with a sigh. 'Really?' he said calmly. 'If that is so, then how did you get the scar on your back? And why won't you let me heal it?'

I stiffened, unable to prevent the flash of memory that forced its way from the depths of my mind. Bradley Carmichael, his eyes wide with surprise as he collapsed onto the floor, blood gushing from the hole in his chest. I had only ever smiled at the man a couple of times in the street, yet he had come running when he heard my scream. Why had he done that? Why had he given his life so easily?

'Well? Gabriel prompted.

I slumped back against the head board. 'That has no bearing on what's happening now,' I said. 'You hiding a daughter from me does.'

He groaned. 'It's not like that.'

'Why don't you tell me then, what is it like?'

'You have to understand what time is like for me. Five months is so long for you, but I have lived for thousands of years.'

'So this relationship is like having a holiday fling for you?'

He rolled his eyes. 'Don't be irrational. You know how much I love you and that will never change. Even if I live for a further hundred thousand years, you will always be in my heart.'

'I know.' I sighed. 'You still should have told me about her. Do you not want us to meet?'

'Of course I do. Looking back in hindsight, I realise that I should have told you earlier. Strangely Adam and I were having a similar conversation tonight.'

'Oh, and what did *he* have to say?'

'He only asked if you knew about her.' He paused to study me. 'What is your problem with him?'

'He scares me and I know he doesn't like me.'

He looked at me in astonishment. 'Why on earth would you think that?'

'I don't know.' I looked at my hands. Away from Adam's crushing stare I began to feel a little bit foolish. 'He just seems so hard and dangerous, and you have to admit that he doesn't like me.'

'Give him a chance. He has only just met you. I am sure he will grow to love you as I do.'

I almost shivered at the thought.

'He's just so...' I paused to find the right words. 'Un-human'

Gabriel bellowed with laughter. 'I'm not human either you know.'

'Yeah, but your more human than he is. He's more...animal. You know what I mean, he's darker and harder and.....' I flapped my arms in frustration. 'I don't know. He's just scary.'

'There is good reason he is that way.' His smile faded and a shadow crossed his face. 'He has lost more than most and in the most horrible of circumstances.' He stared off, lost in thought, before smiling. 'Anyway, that is not a conversation for the night. Especially when there is a beautiful woman lay next to me whom I hope has forgiven me my actions.'

I giggled as he pulled me towards him, though suspected it was his happiness that affected me, rather than my own state of mind.

Gabriel's breathing settled into a relaxed rhythm as his eyes closed and he dropped off into a peaceful sleep. He seemed much happier having Adam around, and I silently vowed to make it as easy as possible for him, even if the man did grate on me something chronic.

Unfortunately, sleep evaded me. The doze I'd had gave me enough energy to keep going, and thoughts of Lexi were keeping my mind active. I slipped quietly out of bed so as not to disturb Gabriel, retrieved my glass from the bedside table and silently made my way downstairs. Hopefully some milk would help.

The heavy closed curtains shrouded the house in shadows, making it only just possible to detect the furniture. I left the lights off and entered the kitchen in darkness.

'Who are you?' a voice said from the shadows.

I jumped and dropped the glass. It shattered on the floor and I automatically reached down for something to use as a weapon. My fingers touched a large part of the base which had survived and I quickly scooped it up.

'Who's there?'

A shadow rose up by the table and without any control, I stumbled back.

'Adam,' he said quietly as he walked towards me.

My heart picked up its already thundering pace. A trickle of blood rolled down my hand as I gripped the broken glass tighter, but I couldn't relax my hold. My mind tried to reason that he wouldn't hurt me, if only for Gabriel's sake. My body refused to listen, arguing that he was angry enough to do it and he would have the abilities to leave no trace of what happened.

He stopped so close that his breath stirred my hair, and even in the shadows his eyes burned into me, making it impossible to turn away. Maybe his stare was one of his abilities, being able to paralyse his prey, making it impossible for them to flee from him.

'What do you want with Gabriel?'

I stood trapped by his gaze, unable to speak.

'Why you?' he said.

I forced open my grip on the glass before I caused myself more damage. The deep silence allowed me to hear the splash as my blood hit the tiles below. He reached out and easily plucked the glass from my hands before taking a step back.

'I will be watching and will work it out.'

He left silently and I slumped against the kitchen side.

Once my breathing settled, I set about bandaging up my hand. I could get Gabriel to heal it but didn't want to wake him, especially as he would be able to sense my lingering distress. If I told him what had taken place he would probably laugh at me. He wouldn't understand that it wasn't so much what Adam had said, but the intent behind it. He had made it very clear that he would be staying around.

How was I going to hide my true feelings from Gabriel? Hopefully his ability to acknowledge only what he wanted to, coupled with his failure to read me properly would be sufficient enough to conceal the depth of my fear of his friend.

I retrieved the dustpan from under the sink to clean up the broken glass. I frowned with confusion and looked around the room until I found the glass set upon the side in one piece. Adam had obviously fixed it. I grabbed a cloth to clean away the only remaining evidence of the incident, my blood.

14

Work was awful. My body dragged with exhaustion and every time I walked into a room, I kept expecting to find Lexi there. Sometimes I saw her, laughing as she pulled the covers from the bed, or biting her lip in concentration as she counted out the medication. Then she would be gone, reminding me of what had been lost.

By the end of the shift I felt weepy and drained. Thankfully Carl agreed for me to leave thirty minutes early as I wasn't needed for handover.

As I approached the cloakroom someone inside spoke my name, halting me in my tracks. My mother had always told me that you never hear anything good when you eaves drop, yet I couldn't force the door open and instead hovered outside listening through the gap.

'Well, I don't see how she gets special treatment,' Michelle sniped.

'Wasn't she close to Lexi though?' Chloe said, her young sweet voice clear in the small room.

'So,' Michelle moaned. 'It's not as if I didn't like Lexi too, but I don't get a day off for it. It's not as if her sister died or something, but Carl is treating her as if it was. It's just not fair and we should complain.'

Unable to prevent myself, I opened the door. 'You have no idea what you are talking about.'

Pauline stood in the corner, a quiet woman in her late forties, her thick curly hair greying prematurely. She averted her eyes to her hands.

I took a step towards Michelle. 'Do you think that I spent the day shopping?' My voice became loud in the small room. Chloe stepped back with her mouth hanging open. 'Or maybe I spent all day in bed with my boyfriend, laughing about how you lot had to work.' My fists clenched so hard, the nails bit into my skin.

Michelle stumbled back against the shelves containing our bags. 'I'm just saying.'

'Maybe you should stop *just* saying and start thinking,' I said. 'You're a mother for God's sake. Is this the sort of role model you want to be for your little boy?'

Her wide eyes flickered to the other women in the room, before settling once more on me.

'You can't speak to me like this,' she said in a small voice.

'Why not? You spoke to your ex-husband like crap all the time. We all heard you. You didn't even have the decency to keep it behind closed doors. And as for how you speak about the residents, you should be ashamed of yourself. They are not decrepit old fools here for your amusement. And about what I heard you say the other day, about how they should do us all a favour and kill themselves.' I flexed my fists and stepped closer, taking deep heaving breaths. 'Don't ever let me hear you say it again. Do you hear me?'

Tears tracked down her cheeks and she nodded furiously.

I stepped aside to give her access out of the cloakroom. She didn't move. Her eyes continued to flicker around the room as if she waited for someone else to take the lead.

'Go,' I told her.

She didn't need telling twice. She edged her way around me, taking care to avoid any contact, and ran from the cloak room. Chloe gave me a wide eyed, unblinking stare, before she hastily followed, leaving me alone with Pauline.

'That probably wasn't the best thing to do,' I said, collecting my bag off the shelf.

'Maybe not, but it was nice to see her taken down a peg or two.'

I threw my bag over my shoulder and pulled my coat off the hanger. 'How are you doing?'

She gave me a strained smile. 'I'm as good as ever. Why ever do you ask?'

'It's the anniversary of David's death tomorrow, isn't it?'

She looked down and chewed on her lip. 'I can't believe you remembered that with everything going on.'

I shrugged. 'So? How are you?'

'I'm doing okay. You would think after two years, it would be a bit easier.' She sighed. 'Marley is being great. It's like he knows what time of year it is. As soon as I walk in the door he's glued to me, purring away as he licks my hand. He's also taken up sleeping on my neck again.' She paused and scrutinised my face. 'How are you holding up?'

'I've had better days.'

I walked from the room, leaving her to frown worriedly after me.

Once outside, my eyes welled up. Determined to hold it together, I rushed to the car, blinking back the tears that threatened to overwhelm me. Driving soothed me a little and by the time I got home I figured I might be able to hold off the crying until I was in Gabriel's arms. At least it was Saturday and he would be home.

I let myself into the house only to find Adam stood waiting for me.

'Where's Gabriel?' I said through gritted teeth.

'He was called into work.'

My jaw clenched so hard, my teeth creaked and stomped off to the medical cabinet, situated in the kitchen due to the multitude of accidents that I incurred there.

I pulled out new bandages to change the damp, chemical smelling one that hung limply off my hand. The tape got stuck behind a box and I pulled on it. Everything in the cupboard fell down on me. I stared at the mess. It wasn't fair. Michelle shouldn't be such a cow. Chloe shouldn't follow her around like a sheep. Pauline should have a husband to go home to at the end of each shift, not only several cats to comfort her. Lexi shouldn't be dead!

'Do you want me to help you with that?'

I jumped and swung around only to smack straight into Adam's solid chest.

Refusing to look up at his eyes in case I became transfixed again, I shouted, 'Do you get off on intimidating women or something? Move the hell back.'

I lifted my arms and went to push against him with all my strength. He took a step back and I ended up pushing against thin air. I stumbled forward, only to trip over his feet and land heavily on the floor, cracking my head against the tiles.

'Damn!' Sharp, stabbing blades radiated over my head.

Adam stood over me. Did the corners of his mouth just twitch?

'Let me help you with that,' he said seriously causing me to question his amusement.

With effort, I sat up and brushed his hands away from my head. 'Get off!' I tentatively touched the base of my skull only to find it wet and groaned.

'Hold still,' he said. 'Unless you would rather go to a doctor to have it stitched.'

I glared at him. Had Gabriel told him how much I hated hospital waiting rooms? He continued to stare at me passively.

'Fine,' I grumbled.

My skin prickled as the tissue knitted together, but it felt different to when Gabriel healed me. It contained none of the fuzziness or sense of emotion that it did with him. It felt clinical as if he had filtered out everything before it got to me. Maybe he didn't have anything to send in the first place.

He finished and indicated to the ugly red gash on my hand. I nodded for him to get rid of that too. Why not, it was his fault I had cut myself anyway.

When he finished, I mumbled a thank you and stood up. I shifted uncomfortably under his stare. Being in the cloakroom with my work colleagues would be preferable to Adam's presence. Thinking of them brought thoughts of Lexi back into my mind and I pressed my lips together, trying to still my trembling chin.

'Do you want to talk about it?' he said.

'Yes,' I retorted. 'Can you please stop standing so close to me, it makes me nervous.'

His eyes widened with surprise for a second, before returning to the usual tightness that made the corners crease.

'I will try to refrain from unnerving you in future, however, I did not mean that.'

I flopped into the kitchen chair ready to tell him no, but I didn't just want to talk, I needed to.

I told him everything that had happened since first meeting the Fae. Even though he had probably heard most of it from Gabriel, he sat silently as I got everything off my chest, finishing with what had happened at work. He sat with his elbows on the table and his fingers pressed to his lips as I controlled my breathing, forcing the tears to stay locked inside. As I calmed, I realised with surprise that I felt better, not brilliant, nor anywhere near my old self, but still, better than I had.

We sat in silence for a few minutes as I ran my hand thoughtfully around the circular coffee stain on the table. I was about to excuse myself to get changed when he spoke.

'Why did you not ask Gabriel to take your memory of it?'

'Didn't he tell you? My memories refuse to stay buried.'

Adam stared at me for a few moments. 'I could try and repress them far enough that they will not come back.'

I looked at him expectantly. Every time I tried to sleep, the Fae came back to haunt me. And Lexi, her lifeless eyes filled my dreams, how I'd pushed my hands into her chest, refusing to acknowledge the stark truth before me. How nice it would be to forget everything.

I sighed regretfully. 'I can't.'

'Why not?'

'Because I need to know what threats are out there. If I don't remember the Fae, how will I know to avoid them?'

'Even if it means that you will always blame yourself for her death.'

His words stung.

'Especially because of that,' I answered stiltedly.

He leaned forward and stared at me intently. 'Why do you do it?'

I shifted on my seat and crossed my arms. I averted my eyes as I replied, 'Do what?'

'Why stay with him?' He paused as if trying to find the words. 'Now that you know of some of the dangers there are, why not leave and protect yourself from it?'

'Because I love him.'

Adam leaned back in his seat and studied me. I shifted in my chair once more. This was beginning to feel like an interrogation.

I wrung my hands together. 'May I ask something?'

He gave a slight nod of his head.

'Why do you dislike me so much?' I bit my lip and kept my eyes steady. I wasn't going to be intimidated again.

His eyes burned into mine. Okay, maybe I was a little intimidated.

'Why do you ask that?' he said.

'Because of....of...' I couldn't keep my thoughts straight when he pinned with his gaze, so closed my eyes. 'Will you stop putting your evil mojo on me, it's not nice.'

As I turned to face the end of the table, I caught his scowl out of the corner of my eye, most likely annoyed because I'd caught him out.

'Just admit you don't like me.'

'You are right. I do not.'

My head snapped up to stare at him. I had expected him to lie. 'Why?' Stupidly, I was going to cry again.

He relaxed back in his seat. 'Because you are dangerous.'

I stared at him with my jaw hung open. I went to demand he explain, but a warm feeling spread through my body. Gabriel would arrive home soon.

I stood and smoothed myself off as if I could wipe away my sadness by straightening my clothes. I threw Adam one last withering look and forced a smile onto my face.

Gabriel pulled the car up as I reached the door. Lightness flowed from him and I ran towards him, drawing off his mood to help banish the darkness within. He barely had time to close the door before I threw myself into his arms. In his embrace I could almost forget the day. His smile was like a ray of sun breaking through on a stormy afternoon. So what if he didn't always understand what went on in my head. Although he was an emotion reading entity, he was still essentially a member of the male species.

Once in the kitchen, we kissed while Adam stood watching us unemotionally. I drew away from Gabriel's embrace and smirked at Adam. If he was going to be here, he would just have to put up with what we did.

I left the men alone whilst I changed out of my work clothes. Thanks to Adam I no longer had a burning need to talk. I wasn't sure what to make of him. He obviously had a strong relationship with Gabriel and how he had listened to me ramble on showed that he had a decent side. Then again, he had openly stated that he thought I was dangerous, so maybe he'd done it to gather information.

I dropped onto the bed and groaned loudly. I was tired and my body hurt from all the tension I'd been carrying around. If only life wasn't such a chore at the moment. It didn't help that the first of my exams was in the morning and I didn't feel at all prepared. As it had been weeks since I had last seen Beth, I made a plan to visit her when I finished. I needed to spend some time back in normality where problems centred on money and kids.

Someone touched my face and I sat up so fast my head became woozy.

'I didn't mean to wake you.' Gabriel sat on the edge of the bed watching me. I had fallen asleep fully clothed on top of the covers.

'I'm glad you did,' I said stretching. 'I must have been more tired than I realised.'

'How are you?'

Maybe things didn't escape him as much as I thought.

'I'm okay, I think.'

'Do you need to talk?'

I didn't really, but I filled him in on the details about my day including what happened with Adam. His face tightened as I mentioned Adam's comment about me being dangerous.

'Why does he think that?' I said, snuggling into his arms.

'He shouldn't have said that.' His words came through gritted teeth. 'Don't believe what he says, he is just being overprotective.'

'But *why* would he think that?'

'No reason.' He kissed my brow. 'Try not to worry. I will have a word with him.'

'Don't do that.' I quickly pulled away, only able to imagine how bad it would get if Adam thought I had been telling tales on him. Gabriel sat ridged, his silence telling me that he would do it anyway. 'Please, Gabriel,' I begged. 'It's not that big a deal. I just wanted to know, that's all.' I smiled, trying to hide my anxiety from him.

He shrugged. 'Would you like something to eat?'

'Think I'll give it a miss tonight, am too tired. Will you cuddle up to me while I fall back to sleep?'

He cupped my face and smiled heart-warmingly at me, before helping me to strip out of my clothes. Once I crawled into bed, he lay on top of the covers, pulling me close to him as I drifted into sleep, feeling safe and protected with him there.

Muted voices roused me. They came from downstairs and Gabriel's voice was raised in anger. As sleep began to claim me again, Gabriel spoke my name, but before I could grab hold of what he was saying I was taken away on a sea of mist into a thankfully dreamless sleep.

15

I sat in my seat at the individual table in the middle of the hall, staring at my pen, pencil, ruler, eraser and sharpener. The sound of scuffling feet and quiet, nervous chatter filled the room as everybody waited for the papers to be handed around. The fear hung thick in the air, like moisture on a muggy day. After everything that had happened, it seemed silly to be afraid of an exam, but still, my hands shook somewhat as I manoeuvred my stationary into a neat line at the edge of the wooden desk.

Tension oozed from the other hundred plus people in the room, prickling my senses and overwhelming my mind. Eris was right. I could definitely sense emotions more now.

One of the lecturers, an elderly professor with grey speckled hair, started handing out the papers. Several muffled coughs echoed around the hall as if people were trying to clear their throats before silence was demanded of them. When the lecturer slid the paper onto my table, I forced myself to stop chewing my nail. I wasn't ready for this at all.

The time, 09:30, had been written on the white board at the front of the room, under the large round clock, followed by 12:30. Three hours seemed so long and I already regretted that second cup of coffee I had drunk.

'You may open your papers now,' the lecturer said clearly.

The rustle of paper was loud as the edges were torn. Taking a deep breath, I used my pen to open the edge of mine. There were only two sides of printed words, which made it worse as it would mean that they expected long, detailed answers. I tried to focus on the questions, but everyone's fear crushed me. I'd become a magnet, drawing it all in. It intensified my own anxiety until it was sharp enough to affect my breathing.

Protect your mind better, Eris had said. I focused on her words and took a deep breath as I imagined a bubble around me, blocking the sense of everyone else. Almost a minute later, the tension began to fade out as if it was chatter instead of emotions and I was moving out of range.

I sighed loudly as the pressure lifted, causing the lecturer to glance in my direction. I looked back at the paper and gave a twitch of a smile. I could focus once more.

The time flew by, and I finished and checked my paper with fourteen minutes to spare. Leaning back in my seat, I studied everyone around me. Some still wrote furiously, the scratch of their pen on the paper loud, desperate to write those last words before time ran out. Others sat back in their seats with a smile on their faces, echoing my own sense of relief.

Once the hand of the clock reached the designated time, the lecturer spoke. 'Pens down now everyone.'

Several people groaned as they dropped their pens and someone gave a relieved laugh. The papers were collected and we were given permission to leave. The sound of scraping chairs and chatter filled the room as people made their way to the back to collect their bags.

'How did you do?' Cheryl said, her young face flushed with excitement.

'Okay, I think. You?'

'It was awful,' she moaned. 'I'm dreading the next one.'

She walked with me to the exit of the building, chatting about which parts she found most difficult.

'Are you coming to the end of year ball?' she asked.

Damn, I'd forgotten all about that.

'I'm afraid I can't.' I shuddered, thinking of how many Fae I'd seen at the Tannery. What if they followed me to the ball? So many people would be at risk. 'But you enjoy yourself,' I said, turning towards the car park.

The car was due its yearly safety check, so I dropped it at the garage with crossed fingers that there was nothing wrong with it, and walked the short distance to Beth's.

As I listened to her talk about all the problems with the kids, everything that had happened faded into the background. We didn't talk about Lexi. She knew what had happened, but also knew that I would talk about it if I needed. It was nice to pretend for one day that everything was normal.

I had hoped that I would have the car back in time to drive home, but I should have known better, an old banger like mine had zero chance of sailing through the test. After talking to the mechanic for several minutes, I got off the phone with my bank account two hundred and sixty pounds lighter and no car for two days. I left a message on the house phone for Gabriel to pick me up. The car had already dented my savings and I didn't want to waste any more money on a taxi.

When it came time to leave, Beth hugged me fiercely at the door. 'You know where I am if you need to talk.'

How I wished I could tell her everything that had happened. Even with Gabriel there for me, loneliness left me feeling hollow and disconnected from the world.

When we arrived home, I caught Adam watching us through the open window.

I scowled. 'Is *he* staying for long?'

Gabriel's eyes narrowed with irritation. 'Is there a problem if he does?'

'No,' I mumbled. 'Just wondering.'

He gave me a long stare before getting out of the car and starting down the path. I needed to rush to catch up.

'I just wanted a bit of time on my own with you to talk.'

He stopped only a few feet from the door. 'About what?'

'Eris.' I kept my voice low in the hope that Adam wouldn't hear us.

His lips tightened. 'What about Eris?'

'I think you should try to make amends with her.'

'You have no idea what you're talking about. You don't know what happened.'

'Actually I do.' I stared at him pointedly and stretched up in the fruitless hope of reaching eye level. 'She told me about it.'

His lip curled and he turned towards the door. 'You heard her side.'

I grabbed his arm in order to pull him back, having to plant my feet so as not to be dragged along with him.

'Why don't you tell me then? She seems to think that she is to blame.'

Gabriel stiltedly told me his version. 'Now you see?' he said with a touch of smugness.

'No I don't. That is exactly what Eris told me and to be quite honest I'm disgusted with you.' He recoiled from my words, causing me to regret the harshness. 'She is your *wife's* sister. Do you think she would approve of how you are treating Eris?' He stood staring at me with a hurt expression on his face. I had hit a sore spot. 'You know I love you,' I reassured him, 'but the way you treat Eris makes me wonder how you would treat me if I ever caused you pain.'

'It's not the same and you know it.' The arrogance had been replaced with a stiff monotone.

'Maybe not, but it does make me question your character.' I challenged him with my stare. I had experienced the unjust blame Eris held for herself. Gabriel should have freed her from it.

'Ana,' he pleaded, the stiffness gone. 'I don't think I can forgive her.'

'Have you even tried?' I said. 'It happened a very long time ago and it's about time you did.'

'I don't know how.'

'How about you start with inviting her for dinner?' I was pushing him too fast, but there were enough things to worry about without their animosity.

'Why does it mean so much to you?'

'Because whether you like it or not she is your family. If something were to happen to her, you would never forgive yourself.'

Gabriel pulled me into his arms. 'I love you, you know. I will try, if only for you.'

I kissed him and said, 'Find out when she is available for dinner.' Ignoring his pained expression, I pulled away to enter the house, only to come face to face with Adam's cold stare.

'Fantastic,' I muttered. A vague memory of hearing them arguing the night before came back to me. Damn it, Gabriel must have gone against my wishes and talked to him.

I gave him a sharp nod and retrieved the sandwiches I had made earlier from the fridge. When I offered him one he just continued to stare at me frostily. It was worse than having in laws, at least they went away.

Making the excuse of Uni reading, I retired to the lounge with my food and retrieved my books with displeasure as I really did have work to do.

The time passed quickly and I jumped when Gabriel kissed me on the neck. 'I'm going up. Are you coming?'

I gazed longingly at him before sighing loudly. 'I will be soon. I just have to finish this chapter. My next exam is in a couple of days and I don't think this one will go as well.'

'You will be fine.'

He kissed me with a passion that almost made me throw the books to one side and chase him up the stairs, but I was in the zone and needed to at least finish the section I was on. I groaned as I pushed him away.

'Go before I change my mind.'

'Would that be a bad thing?' His breath intoxicated me, making it hard to remember why I said no.

'Umm...'

He laughed and kissed me once again. 'I'll be waiting.'

Once alone, I tried to focus on my reading but it was too late. My mind was already upstairs with Gabriel. Sighing, I collected my plate and took it to the kitchen.

'Why did you do it?' Adam's voice startled me and I nearly dropped the plate.

'For God's sake, why do you do that?'

'Do what?'

'Creep up on me in the dark.' I reached around to flick the light on, marched to the sink and threw the plate in.

'I did not *creep*. I have been sat here the entire time.'

My teeth ground together as I whirled on him. 'Do you always have to sit in the dark?'

He shrugged. 'I do not need the light as you do.' When I turned to leave he asked me again, 'Why did you do it?'

I groaned. 'What could I have possibly done now? If this is about what I told Gabriel, I told him not to say anything.'

'No. It is about Eris.'

There was a moment of silence, in which the conversation with Gabriel ran through my head. 'What's the problem?' I said. 'I thought you would be happy about it.'

'I am.'

'So what's the problem then?'

'I want to know *why* you did it.'

'Go to hell. You want to be suspicious of me fine, but I don't have to put up with your crap, especially as my meter has reached its limit for the week. So unless you tell me what it is you want to know, I'm not interested anymore.'

My anger escalated and my mind reached out. I wanted to know what he found so disturbing about me. My ability to read emotions had gotten stronger and I figured it couldn't do any harm to try. At the very least I could work out the level of his distrust.

Touching him felt like nothing I had experienced so far. Everyone's emotions were like waves in the sea, flowing and changing as their thoughts did and if I paid enough attention, I could sense when they changed. Adam's mind felt like having a metal door slammed in my face, cold, hard, impenetrable. Not even a wisp of feeling got through as if they were locked up tight.

'It will not work on me,' he said, making me jump.

He moved forwards and I cringed against the kitchen side as he paused only a foot away from me.

'So you *are* getting abilities then?'

Too late I remembered Eris's warning about how a Siis could tell.

'I'm sorry.'

He stared intensely at me and I averted my eyes, partly with guilt and partly to prevent being trapped by his gaze. I sensed him shift and when I finally found the courage to look up, he had gone.

'I screwed up,' I admitted to Gabriel as I cuddled up to him in bed.

'How is that possible?' He laughed as if the idea was absurd.

I hesitantly told him about what had happened. Once finished, I bit my lip, waiting for his response.

He sighed. 'That is not going to help matters.'

'What do you mean?'

'You know you asked why Adam distrusted you.'

I nodded, though he definitely felt more than distrust.

'It's because he is concerned about what you may become.'

'You mean like the Fae?'

He pursed his lips and sighed through his nose. 'You have to understand that as far as we know, there has never been another like you. The closest to what you are, would be the Fae.'

An equal measure of fear and hate coiled in my stomach at the thought of the child demons. 'But Eris said I couldn't become like them.'

'You won't.' He pulled me tighter into his arms. 'As far as I have been able to tell, absorbing my Shi has only increased your natural ability, that being your empathy. I do wish you hadn't used it on Adam though, I have been trying to keep it hidden from him.'

I stared at him with wide eyes. 'You knew what I could do?'

'Of course I did. Do you really think I would not notice you mirroring me and the occasions that you have connected to see what I'm feeling?'

I had thought I had been so clever and discreet.

'Will he tell the rest of your kind? Eris told me they wouldn't be happy.'

'Eris talks too much.'

'Well?'

'It's very unlikely. However, I'm afraid he will watch you closely to make sure that nothing else occurs.'

My gulp was loud in the quiet room.

'You worry too much,' he said. 'It will all be fine, I promise.'

If only I could believe him.

16

It was the day I had been dreading. Gabriel booked the morning off work so that he could accompany me to the church. The sun shone brightly causing the light mist of raindrops to sparkle and small rainbows to appear low in the sky. He led me up the long path lined with ancient gravestones, keeping a tight hold on my hand.

Gargoyles and high arches decorated the old stone building. I had visited Saint Mary's many times in the past. The services held no interest for me, but I always enjoyed the quiet peacefulness the empty church offered.

When we reached the heavy doors, I pulled back.

'I can't go in there,' I said. 'How can I face Margret? How can I face Lexi's dad?' The thought of coming face to face with Lexi's parents caused my heart to beat erratically and my palms to sweat. 'What if they can see my guilt?'

Gabriel sighed and numbness spread throughout me. 'It will be over soon,' he promised as he led me through the doors.

The lengthy church was barely half filled, many of the occupants fidgeting and murmuring to each other. Michelle sat near the front with Chloe and Carl. She glanced over at me and I met her stare. She quickly turned back to the front. The rest of their pew was empty. I ignored it and sat in a vacant seat near the back. I wouldn't be able to witness Margret's grief up close and Michelle's bitterness was draining, even with the distance.

The controlled numbness continued throughout the service, making it impossible to cry, even when the priest spoke kind words about Lexi. Gabriel kept a tight grip on my hand as the mahogany coffin was carried back up the aisle. I kept my head bowed as Margret past, her grief so intense that I recoiled from it.

We followed the procession to behind the church to the freshly dug grave. Gabriel tried to coax me to the front, but when I saw the deep hole it all became too much.

'I can't do this.'

I stumbled back and bumped into a weighty man, with fine hair brushed over his balding head. His beady eyes glanced up from where he cleaned his thick glasses on the bottom of his shirt.

'Watch it,' he grumbled as I pushed past him.

I ran towards the exit of the graveyard trying to banish the memory of the open pit, so deep and dark, making it all too final. Lexi had dreamed of being married with kids, and of having a long life filled with laughter. It wasn't fair that the future she had planned had been ended so abruptly and with so much pain.

Why? I silently demanded of God. *Why would you take her?* There were so many nasty people in the world, how could it be that someone so innocent, with so much love to give, could be taken so early?

Half way down the path, Gabriel grabbed my arm, pulling me to a stop.

'Get off me!' I yanked myself from his grip. The numbness spread across my thoughts once more and I pushed hard against his chest. 'Stop doing that! Stop trying to make everything better.'

He stood back and raised his arms in surrender. 'I only want to help.'

'Well you're not. I just want to grieve without you manipulating me.'

I turned from him and continued on my way at a march. He followed behind, matching my pace.

When I reached the heavy iron gates, decorated with metal leaves and topped with dark angel figureheads, I turned to him.

'Just leave me alone, Gabriel.'

His shoulders dropped down and his eyes to became shadowed and pinched, dulled by his sense of rejection.

'Look,' I said in a softer tone. 'Just go to work. I'm going to go for a walk and I'll see you at home later.'

He held his hand out to me. The compulsion to be in his arms was so great that I nearly relented.

'Go,' I told him before I gave into the unnatural desires that governed me.

He hesitated before dropping his hand down. 'Phone the site if you want me to come home,' he called as I walked away.

I didn't answer. He remained motionless as I left the church grounds and his gaze stayed heavy on me until, with relief, I turned the corner.

I wandered the streets with no specific destination in mind, ignoring the drizzle that covered my face in a light sheen. Every time I tried to remember Lexi laughing, I saw her lifeless eyes. When I remembered how her face had lit up when we had visited the city, it was ruined by the sight of her hand hanging limply in Eris' arms. Away from Gabriel's control, the pain in my chest increased, so much so, that I thought I might choke on it at times. But the tears didn't come.

After a time, the discomfort from my new shoes broke through my haze. I looked around, taking in my surroundings. I was on the road towards home. The sky had filled with thick, laden thunder clouds and the air had become muggy. It was probably time to go back to reality.

About half way home something touched me, a cloud of red hot rage that restricted my chest. I opened myself up to my new ability and followed the scent as such, to a rundown apartment just off the main road.

My hands shook as I cautiously opened the door, making it possible to hear a man shouting, the fury evident in his voice and emotions. I also sensed the presence of another person. I followed the voice up the stairs, breathing short shallow breaths in order to avoid the stench that filled the hallway. I needed to step over a puddle of urine, causing me to mutter with disgust and consider turning around.

The man resumed with his furious threats compelling me forwards, past a clear bag, the contents of which looked suspiciously like used, broken needles. I halted in front of the first door I came across.

The different hormones told me that the other person was female. I frowned. She felt strange, not like anyone I'd come across before. I hesitated outside the door, not sure how to proceed. Did I call the police? Maybe Gabriel?

The man shouted, 'I am going to kill you!' He really meant it.

Taking a deep breath to steady my nerves, I knocked on the door, with no idea of what to say.

The flat fell silent and I had to knock again before the door was thrown open with so much force, it rebounded off the wall before being stopped by the mammoth body that stood before me. He was a bull. Although not much taller than me, every part of him dominated the doorway. I couldn't drag my eyes away from the bulging muscles in his neck and arms, and the swollen purple veins that spread over his skin like the roads on a map. I gulped loudly.

'What?' he roared.

'Hi,' I said weakly, still with no idea what to say.

I peeked into the flat behind him to see a small, sparsely furnished lounge. A burnt orange sofa sat in the middle of the room, old and lumpy with stuffing poking out of one of the corners. It was situated in front of a small scuffed coffee table with magazines strewn across it. Stacked moving boxes filled one wall. Some of them with the flaps open as if they had been emptied as the items were needed.

A petite brunette stood behind the far sofa, her hair short and spikey, the ends tinted with several different colours. Three or four piercings decorated her ears and when she moved, the light caught another piercing in her nose, a delicate diamond. She beamed as if unaware of the situation around her. The angry bull turned to follow my gaze.

'Hey, Ana,' she said chirpily. 'Glad you could come.' She grinned and pranced towards me. 'Is Gabe on his way over now?'

I stared at her, wondering who the hell she was and how she knew me. The Bull's questioning glare bored into the side of my head and I quickly nodded. If only I was telling the truth.

'You had better get out of here, Ron. Gabe is a cop and he won't think twice about slinging your ass back into jail.'

The Bull, who was Ron, stood clenching his fists. The indecisiveness rolled off him in sickly waves, probably wondering if he could kill us both before Gabriel turned up.

With his teeth audibly grinding, he hissed at the petite woman, 'Mark my words bitch, I'll be back to finish this.' With that he stormed past, slamming me into the door frame.

'Come on in, Ana,' she beckoned, her eyes bright with excitement. 'Watch you don't trip over the stuff on the floor.'

She disappeared through a doorway, leaving me to stare at the clutter around me. Her stuff I could see, the floor not so much. Piles of clothes lay over the sofa and filled every corner of the room, scattered amongst the shoes and boots. Dirty dishes and cups lay in every available space, and half burnt candles stood on every surface, giving the room it's only light as the curtains were still closed.

I stood awkwardly by the still open door. A few minutes passed before she returned, carrying a tray with the makings of tea on it. After pushing the magazines onto the floor, she laid the tray down and turned to me.

'Were you born in a barn?' she said.

I looked at her dimly. There had been many occasions in my life that confused me but this was probably the most mystifying experience I had ever had.

'Close the door silly.'

I pushed the door closed. Maybe I was still in bed having some mad dream my mind had conjured up in order to cope with the craziness in my life. Then again, even in my dreams, I couldn't imagine such a mess.

'Do I know you?' I said as she pushed the unfolded clothes to the end of the sofa.

'Now you do.' She laughed excitedly as she patted the seat.

I ignored her plea to sit. 'I'm sorry, but who are you?'

She was like a whirlwind, her energy flying off in all directions like sparklers.

'I'm being rude aren't I? I'm Maria. Come, sit, we have so much to talk about. I can tell you, we will be the best of friends.'

Reserving the right to make that judgement for myself, I perched on the edge of the cushion and watched her carefully as she poured the tea.

She held up a small bowl. 'Sugar?'

Indicating no, I waited for her to finish before talking again. 'How do you know me and Gabriel?'

'Oh I don't really,' she said, settling back onto the sofa, 'but I knew you were coming.'

I shifted uncomfortably. 'How? I didn't even know I was coming this way until twenty minutes ago.'

'My spirit guide told me.'

I nearly snorted, but she looked at me so earnestly, I swallowed it back. She actually believed what she was saying.'

'O-kay. And did this spirit warn you that you were going to get killed today?'

She laughed and flicked a corner of toast off the arm of the sofa to the floor. I stared at where it landed on a strewn out jumper, back to her and down at the floor again. Really?

'Nah, she just said what you looked like and that you would come and look, here you are. Good timing too.'

She didn't seem at all concerned that she had nearly been killed or at the very least beaten to within an inch of her life.

'And what about Gabriel? He isn't here today, so how could you have known his name?'

'I was told it. Like I said, you and me are going to be great friends.'

Even though I accepted the concept of spirits, I found her words difficult to believe, leaving me to speculate whether she was even human. My mind reached out and I tried to get a sense of what she was. There were definitely no signs of her being a Siis or Fae, but a weird hum came from within her, making me feel jittery.

'What do you know?' I said.

She sighed. 'Not really anything. I was just told that you would both come into my life.' She paused to stare at me before continuing. 'She didn't think to share with me that you would be different.'

I frowned, trying to ignore the spider that looked down at me from the large dusty web in the corner of the ceiling. 'What do you mean?'

'I can read auras,' she told me chirpily.

I raised my eyebrows in question.

'You know, I can see your energy field.'

She looked at me expectantly and it hit me what she was referring to. She could see Gabriel's Shi within me. The blood drained from my face.

'Don't worry,' she said quickly. 'I won't say anything to anyone.'

I stared at her numbly. How did my life keep getting more and more complicated? Gabriel had never warned me about how to deal with someone like Maria. How could I keep a secret when the cat was already poking its head out of the bag?

'I'm not sure what you mean,' I said too late.

'I get it.' She leaned towards me and her voice became a dramatic whisper. 'It's a secret.'

I picked up my tea in the hope of having a moment to clear my mind, and took a sip before speaking. 'Can I ask, what you did to make him so angry?'

'Ron?' She laughed. 'Why, I made him think his penis was rotten and told him I gave it to him.'

The tea stuck in my throat and I snorted with surprise causing the hot liquid to spray everywhere. 'What?' I choked.

'I just put a little spell on him to make him believe it was rotten.'

'Spell?'

'Oh didn't I say? I'm a witch.'

Her chest puffed out with pride and she grinned. I was definitely dreaming. People just didn't have lives like mine.

'Unfortunately I didn't actually turn it gangrene. That would probably have been wrong.' Regret lay heavy in her voice. 'But I sure would like to be a fly on the wall when he goes to the doctor.'

Laughter burst out of me before I even had a thought to rein it in. All I could see was Ron with his trousers around his ankles, arguing with the doctor that his penis was rotten and how could he not see it. The laughter became so hysterical, tears started falling and my jaw began to ache. It was minutes before I managed enough control to speak.

'Will he always think that?'

'No it will probably wear off as soon as he believes what people are saying, but how much fun would it be if it didn't?'

I burst into another fit of giggles, in which more tears flowed from my eyes. Whoever the strange woman was, she had managed to lift my spirits higher than they had been in a long time. When I calmed enough, I took another sip of my remaining tea, most of it having spilt on to my lap during my fit.

'You look like you needed that,' she said.

'I did,' I replied, wiping my tears away. 'Why did you do it?'

'He cheated on me with the tramp downstairs.'

'Oh my God, what did you do to her?'

'Let's just say she will be sat next to him in the clinic.' A wicked gleam came into her eyes and I started laughing again. I would have to keep her away from Gabriel, but it would be worth it to be able to laugh in such a carefree manner.

The afternoon flew past with lots of giggling and some more hysterics. She told me how she came from a long line of witches dating back many hundreds of years, but unfortunately most had passed on now leaving only a few distant relatives in America that she had never met.

When I asked about the stacked boxes, she laughed, saying, 'I only just moved in three months ago.' She smiled at me in a way that a sister might, easily and without restraint, and I relaxed further in her presence.

Eventually I had to leave, and after swapping numbers she hugged me goodbye at the door. It felt natural.

The pavement was wet as it had rained heavily whilst I'd been inside, though had now died back down to a drizzle. A blue car raced down the road and through a large puddle. Dirty water splashed onto my legs but I didn't even grumble. Somehow the darkness had left me and I felt brighter than I had in over a week. During the walk home I couldn't stop smiling.

Whilst fishing for my keys, I realised that I had left my purse at Maria's. I groaned with annoyance. I'd only just replaced bank cards after leaving my bag in the tannery. I decided to dry off before going to retrieve it, and pushed open the door while trying to pull the keys out of the stiff lock.

I sensed him too late as I was pushed violently from behind. I fell into the kitchen with a yelp as the air was knocked out of me, only managing to turn once I landed heavily on my knees.

A cold dread filled me as I stared up at the massive figure in the doorway. It was The Bull; Ron. The rage rolled off him in waves of sickly darkness, and I almost gagged on the intensity of it. His eyes burned with a craziness that was worse than the Fae's and murder filled his heart.

17

'You interfering little bitch!' he snarled.

He followed me as I scurried across the floor, attempting to find my feet without losing any speed. I screamed as he grabbed my hair, pulling me up to face him.

'I'm gonna kill you!'

He circled my throat and threw me against the wall with enough force that my frame rattled. I kicked and clawed. He slammed me into the wall once more before releasing my hair to reach behind him.

He pulled a gun from his waist band.

I froze, only able to stare at the dull glint of the barrel as he swung it round, the hole of the shaft deep and dark, as if it was the entrance to hell. As he looked me over his emotions shifted and he smiled. Lust crept in, travelling over my body, making the hairs stand on end. He ran the cold barrel of the gun up my thigh, pushing the black skirt with it. His eyes sparkled with excitement.

'Maybe I'll have me some fun first!'

Panic bubbled over, breaking my paralysis. I fought with every ounce of strength I had, but my blows were ineffective against the solid slab of his body and he pushed the gun into me, tearing me from the inside. The pressure on my throat only allowed harsh grunts instead of a scream to escape, while my panic and fight only caused him to become more aroused.

The door swayed a fraction in the breeze, allowing a sliver of sunlight to enter. If I could just hurt him enough to free myself, I could run into the safety of the road. But he was stronger and merely laughed coldly at my attempts.

'Ana, you left your purse...' Maria's voice faded off as she stepped into the house.

The pressure released as he withdrew the gun and swung it in her direction. Everything was so clear. She clutched my new driving license in her hand telling me that's how she had found me. Drops of dew scattered her shoulders and hair, sparkling in the remaining sun. Her friendly smile dropped away, leaving recognition in her fear filled eyes.

'What the fuck did you do to me, Witch?' With a wave of the gun he directed her into the house. 'Get the fuck in and close the door.'

She cautiously moved further into the house and the grip on my neck increased. He didn't need to play with me anymore as the object of his wrath was within reach. Unable to scream as there wasn't any air to breathe, I bucked and clawed, trying to force myself away from the wall. His body remained unmoveable.

Suddenly, he was gone. In his place stood somebody else, somebody from years before who still haunted my dreams on occasions. Ron's murky brown eyes had been replaced by the speckled green I knew so well and when he turned towards me, I knew that I was going to die, for this was my punishment for escaping him the first time.

The image left as quickly as it had come. It wasn't Nathan. This wasn't then. But the situation was just as dire and I needed to fight.

Maria shouted and pleaded with Ron, but my brain could only focus on one thing, air. I kept thinking, *That's enough now, stop, I need to breathe,* as if my mind wouldn't accept that it was real, that the idea he would kill me was too absurd to comprehend.

The scream of my chest overrode the agony in my neck and the blood rushed to my head, pounding in my ears, drowning out all other sounds. My head swelled with heat and pressure, and I distantly wondered how nice it would be to place my face against the cool wall.

My vision closed in, the edges of the picture first becoming red with flashes of light, before changing into a grey then black nothingness. I could see down a dark tunnel with such clarity that I observed the build-up of wax within his ear and each individual poker scar across his cheek. How had Maria ever come to be with him?

Fight! my mind screamed. *Don't just give in.* I tried to lift my arm, but it hung dead and without feeling, a leaden weight that pulled me down. When had I stopped moving?

The tunnel became smaller and the pain became more distant. Maria continued to shout, though it sounded as if water filled my ears and her words escaped me, only audible as a muffled echo. I wanted to tell her it was okay. I didn't hurt anymore. Even the voice in my head was losing the battle and had faded into the background. It was all right, there was no pain or worry. I was drifting off into a peaceful sleep.

Irritation flooded through me as something disturbed my peace. Then agony racked forcefully through my body, bringing every cell alive with pain. My lungs instinctively drew in short ragged breaths and claws raked through my throat and chest. Even my teeth ached. My body sung with relief as life was sucked back into it.

Someone else started shouting, their words drowned out by the rushing blood within my ears. My mind began to clear and the will to survive became stronger. Suppressing the panic, I controlled my breathing, forcing each breath slowly in and out, past the pain of the claws shredding my throat, each one leaving red hot tears in its wake.

'Ana? Ana? Can you hear me?' As the words broke through so did everything else and I cringed away from the loudness of it all. A terrible scream vibrated through my body, setting my teeth on edge, drowning out my own harsh breaths.

'Wha....' As I tried to speak the claws became hundreds of blades slicing me from the inside, preventing the croaked words from being completed. Thankfully the screaming stopped. I slumped with relief and tried to turn my head towards the person shouting at me, but it wouldn't comply, as if the muscles no longer worked.

Everything was a blur. It took seconds of blinking away the tears formed from the pressure of his grip, before my vision began to clear. Somehow I knelt on the floor in the middle of the kitchen with my hands in front supporting me.

When I forced myself to sit, I saw it was Maria who shouted at me. I tried to put my hand to her lips to quieten her, but only managed to wave it uselessly in her direction, the action jarring every bone in my body.

'It's over now, Ana. Adam has him.' Thankfully her voice was quieter, though her words still made no sense. 'Don't kill him.' That made no sense either. I wasn't going to kill anyone. I tried to clear my mind further and focus on what was happening.

'Why?'

I suppressed my groan and shifted my body in the direction of Adam's voice. His eyes blazed with fury and his mouth twisted into a snarl that brought to mind the image of a jungle cat, poised ready to attack. I couldn't help but shrink from him.

I stiffly turned to follow his murderous stare and found the cause of all my pain crumpled in the corner. Tears rolled down his broad cheeks and his face convulsed. He desperately tried to scream, but his lips refused to part for him, allowing only quiet grunts to escape. His leg was twisted in an impossible angle and his shoulder sat several inches lower than normal.

'Why can I not kill him?' Adam said.

'Because it wouldn't be enough of a punishment.' Maria's severe words were in contrast to the gentle touch of her fingers on my arm. She awkwardly stood and strode over to where Ron lay broken in the corner. 'You shouldn't have gone after my friend, Ron.'

At her approach, he cowered as far back as his injuries would allow. His awareness that his strength was useless warmed me. A voice far back in my mind warned me that I shouldn't feel pleasure at his suffering, but I pushed it out before it could gain ground.

Maria paused before my weeping attacker. She rolled her shoulders and shook her body, as if to rid all tension, before bending forward to grip his face between her hands. He tried to pull away, but she held him steady and looked deep into his eyes.

'Ron, hear me now.' Her voice sounded so soft and gentle, that I momentarily wondered if I was really awake. Ron whimpered once more. 'Open your mind, Ron, and listen to my words.' Ron's face became slack and his eyes vacant. He no longer struggled to push away from her and relaxed against the wall, all the tension leaving him.

'When you leave here,' Maria continued in a murmur, with her hands still cupping his mottled cheeks, 'every person you look upon, you will see the face of someone you have hurt. You will *know* that they are coming for vengeance. You have no power over these people anymore, Ron. You are weak and they are strong. Sometimes they will lie, and tell you that they are there to help, but you will not believe them, because if you let your guard down for just one second, Ron, they will get you. Do you understand?'

Ron whimpered with childlike distress before his face and eyes returned to their almost dead appearance. As I watched, my mind stretched like an elastic band, ready to snap. I heard Maria asking Adam to dump Ron somewhere away from us, yet I continued to stare at the vacant look in Ron's eyes.

All my pleasure at his pain had gone, for all I could see was my face in his, lost in my own craziness, unable to deal with all the madness around me. I had to get away before I truly did snap and become like him. I pulled myself up and staggered from the kitchen, the pain that racked through me only fuelling my ability to run.

I slumped into an empty corner in the bedroom, with my arms wrapped around my knees, and calm descended upon me. My breathing still hurt, though it was dull as if I experienced it through a layer of sponge. My thoughts slowed and I focused my attention on the edge of the duvet, observing the folds in the material and how they changed the pattern of the squares. They made sense, and I relaxed with the gentle harmony they offered me.

Even when Maria entered the room, I kept my attention on the squares. She sat silently down before me with her legs crossed as a small child would, and held out the bottle of water off the bedside table.

'I'm sorry,' she said after a few minutes.

It took several attempts to form a coherent word. 'What do you have to be sorry for?'

'I saw the car,' she said, 'on my way to return your purse. It never occurred to me that he would follow you.'

'I think it's my face,' I told her. 'People seem to find it offensive.'

I chuckled, though it brought to mind how Neave had sounded when she'd had croup as a toddler. A dry, wheezing sound that was not pleasing at all.

'He was going to kill you for just being there.'

'Welcome to my life.' I pulled on the bed to stand but my whole body shook and quivered, and I fell back down.

It was as if a cheese grater had been taken to my throat and I sighed with relief when Gabriel returned. He was here now, so it would be all right.

After running up the stairs, he paused momentarily in the doorway to hiss something unintelligible before swiftly joining me. He held me in his arms, with his hand pressed tenderly to my throat. Maria discreetly left us alone as he healed me.

'How are you doing?' he said once finished.

'I'm okay,' I croaked.

Gabriel left to obtain me a glass of water from the bathroom, to replace the room temperature bottle I held in my hands. I gratefully drank it, relishing the cold water as it soothed the dryness.

'Why is it that I can't go one month without an injury?' I said after a few minutes.

Gabriel scowled and I barked a coarse laugh, a sound void of any real humour but a start at least.

'Don't bother answering that,' I said awkwardly standing. 'Let's go downstairs.' I grimaced. 'I suppose I owe Adam one for this.'

Maria waited for us at the bottom of the stairs, wringing her hands together.

'I'm really all right,' I reassured her. She sceptically looked me up before shrugging. She smiled and turned to Gabriel, who supported my elbow as if afraid I'd collapse at any moment.

'You must be Gabe. Sorry for the trouble, it probably would have been good to meet at a better time, but still, it's nice to meet you.'

He glowered at her. 'How are *you* at fault here?'

I gripped his hand and threw him a warning look.

'Ana here bravely came to my rescue from certain death this afternoon.'

'Hardly.' I felt Gabriel's stare laying heavy on me. Maria could have kept that that part to herself.

'Tell me what happened.' His voice was tight and his expression only became harder as I filled him in on the details. Adam stood expressionless throughout. Maybe Maria had already explained what had happened. More likely he just didn't care.

Once I finished Gabriel glared at me. 'What were you thinking?'

Maria looked from Gabriel to Adam with wide eyes and her mouth open. 'You two aren't human then?'

I groaned loudly, remembering her ability to see their Shi. Gabriel and Adam both glared at me, though Adam with a lot more intensity. Nothing unusual there.

'She didn't tell me,' Maria hastily reassured them. Gabriel stood rigidly by my side as she told them about reading auras and being a witch.

'What do you plan to do with your knowledge?' Gabriel asked her.

'Nothing.' She laughed with childlike wonder. 'I always knew there were things out there, but to actually meet...what are you?'

'Siis,' Adam told her to my surprise. Gabriel glared at him, while Adam just stood idly as if the conversation bored him, though when I studied him, I realised that he watched Maria intently.

Maria glanced around and frowned. 'Do you want me to leave?'

'I suggest you do,' Gabriel said through clenched teeth.

'Gabriel!' How dare he be so rude.

'It's okay,' Maria said with a grin. She embraced me and whispered into my ear. 'Will you be okay here?'

I nodded and hugged her back before leading her through the kitchen. After saying goodbye, I closed the door and leant back against it. I took a couple of deep breaths before heading back to the men.

They stood facing each other, Gabriel tense, with his shoulders back, while Adam's motionless frame held an air of nonchalance.

'Why did you tell her that?' Gabriel demanded.

Adam shrugged. 'I only divulged our name, something Ana would have let slip anyway.'

I gave him an indignant look before forcing myself to relax. There were already too many heightened emotions in the room.

'We could have suppressed her memory of us.' Gabriel took an aggressive step towards Adam. I shifted, ready to come between them, but paused. It wasn't as if I could do anything.

'Hardly,' Adam scoffed. 'Did you not get a sense of her? Her mind would be harder to manipulate than Ana's.'

Both men turned to stare at me and my feet suddenly became a lot more interesting.

Gabriel turned back to Adam, his posture a tad more relaxed. 'We could have tried.'

'You did not see how easily she hypnotised Ana's attacker. The man was screaming with insanity when I left him at the side of the road. It was a surprisingly inhumane action on her part. I—'

'I want to learn how to fight.'

Both men stared at me again, the object of their annoyance with each other forgotten for the moment.

'I am fed up of being the victim, never being able to defend myself.'

Gabriel gripped my shoulders. 'I do not want you fighting. I promise I will protect you better from now on, so there will be no need.'

'You can't always protect me, Gabriel. You weren't even here today.'

'Next time, I will be.'

'What about when you're at work?'

'I'll quit.'

The desire to be with him all day every day was strong. So strong in fact, that it scared the hell out of me. It wasn't an obsession that was wise to fuel, especially as the more time I spent with him, the more I needed to.

'Don't be stupid.' My words were sharper than needed, and I quickly snaked my arms around his stiff body. 'You can't spend every moment with me for the rest of my life. You love your work and I love mine. That is why I need to learn to defend myself.'

'It makes sense.'

Gabriel spun to confront Adam for his words. Before trouble could spark again, I pulled his face towards me.

'Please, Gabriel. I need this, if only for peace of mind.' His jaw relaxed a fraction and I quickly continued. 'Anyway I'm sure I've had my life's quota of bad stuff already, and I will never need to use it but... it would help me sleep at night.'

He stared at me, with his mouth open as if ready to speak, but with no words available to draw on. I had won. He wouldn't be able to resist my request, if only to help prevent my nightmares.

'I will teach you basic self-defence. I won't teach you to go on the offensive. Will that be acceptable?'

I nodded. At least I would be able to break free from an attack, if only to run away. Adam sighed audibly with disagreement, but we both ignored him.

'Great, we can start tomorrow. Now I need to eat, nearly getting killed has made me ravenous.'

Gabriel hissed something barely audible as I left the room.

18

'Are you ready?'

I shifted, moving my foot onto a flatter spot of grass and nodded for Gabriel to continue. He charged towards me with the rubber knife and I side stepped him. Grabbing his extended arm, I propelled him around and pulled his shoulder back as I used my free hand to hit his lower back. He fell back onto the ground.

I threw my fist up into the air. 'Yes!'

'Well done sweetheart. You are doing so well.'

Having mastered the move of deflecting a knife attack, I was finally starting to feel that I might just be able to protect myself.

'Let's do it again,' I said as Adam entered through the back gate. Thankfully, he had found his own place the week before, although much to my irritation, he still turned up every day to see Gabriel and watch me suspiciously. As I was used to him, I ignored his presence and stood ready for Gabriel to attack.

After I successfully caused him to drop the knife again, Gabriel turned to Adam laughing. 'She is doing really well, is she not?'

Adam raised his eyebrows and to my surprise, smiled with amusement. Wonders never ceased.

'Against you she is doing fine, however, I have to wonder how she will perform when confronted by a real attacker.'

Staring him straight in the eyes, I grinned. 'Bring it on.'

He took the rubber knife from Gabriel's reluctant hands and smirked. He stood silently watching. I opened my mouth to tell him to get a move on. His hand snaked forward with a speed Gabriel had never used and I landed heavily on my back. Damn, all the training off Gabriel was useless. He had merely been giving me false confidence in my skills.

Gabriel roared and threw Adam against the wall by his throat.

'Do not ever touch her again,' he seethed through clenched teeth. His muscles vibrated and sharp, stabbing shocks, pulsed off him in waves. Adam held his hands up in surrender.

I struggled up and pulled at Gabriel's hand. 'Don't be stupid,' I gasped, 'he was making a point, that's all.'

'I don't care.' Gabriel kept his eyes on Adam. 'He had no right to hurt you.'

'I'm not hurt,' I said, though the painful ache in my chest begged to differ. 'Gabriel let him go now.'

Gabriel glared at Adam for several seconds before releasing him, his body still tense but the shaking controlled.

'You could have warned me,' I said to Adam.

'Do you think your attacker will warn you?'

He was right. Although I'd started off filled with anger, practicing had soon become fun and I'd forgotten the real reason for doing it. 'So what do I do?'

'You learn to defend yourself correctly. Maybe then you will have a small chance of surviving.'

Gabriel snarled.

'Will you teach me?' I asked Adam.

Gabriel forced himself between us. 'No!'

'Will you teach her then?' Adam said mildly.

'No I will not! There is no reason for her to learn as I will never allow her to fight.'

Adam raised his eyebrows. 'Does she not get a say?'

Beginning to wonder that myself, I tried to push Gabriel out of the way. He remained unmovable, like a boulder and grabbed my wrist, pinning it behind him. Although my first instinct was to hit him over the head, I opted for a more subtle approach, and bent his hand over until he released his grip.

I forced myself between them. 'I am not your property! How dare you presume to treat me as such.' I glared at him, daring him to argue the point.

After a minute of staring each other down, Gabriel threw Adam a cutting look and silently stormed off. I followed him into the house with a sigh, to find him stood in the kitchen, glaring out of the window. I stood behind him and wrapped my arms around his waist. He remained rigid.

'I'm sorry I spoke to you like that in front of Adam,' I said calmly, 'but you really can't tell me what to do.'

He turned to hold me in his arms. 'It's not like that.'

'I get it. I understand what happened to Deonti and I get why you don't want me to fight.' Gabriel stiffened at his wife's name and I quickly continued. 'I'm not planning on being a warrior or fight in any wars. I just need to know how to take care of myself. I promise not to go looking for trouble.' I smiled at him. 'And if it comes looking for me, I'll run as fast as I can in the other direction, I promise.'

'You mean as you did the day you met Maria?'

I winced. 'What about if I promise not to do that again?'

'Is that a promise you can keep?'

Remembering what happened with Ron, I wanted to say yes.

'It's not, is it?' he said in response to my silence. 'I know you and you would not be able to walk away.'

'Fine, I probably wouldn't. But whether I know how to fight or not won't change that, it will only increase my chances of not getting hurt.'

His body stiffened and he tried to pull away.

'Please, Gabriel, I am going to do this either way, but I would really like you to be the one who teaches me.'

'Never,' he said flatly, prising my arms from around him. 'If you insist on doing this, you will have to enlist Adam's help. I will not be a part of it.'

He stared frostily at me before storming out of the house, leaving me to sigh with regret.

I stood in front of Adam making a conscious effort not to wring my hands together. Gabriel had always been gentle, ensuring that I was never hurt. Adam probably wouldn't be the same.

'Relax, Ana. I will not do anything you cannot handle... yet.'

'I'll be the judge of that. Do you think you could start a little slower though? It doesn't matter how much I learn, I won't be able to keep up with the Siis speed. You move like Bruce Lee on an energetic day.'

He nodded and briefly smirked.

'You don't have to look so happy about hitting me.' I said, moving into position.

'Do not tense. Do not try to predict the move your attacker will make, only react to it when they do.'

I frowned at him. How the hell was I meant to do that?

He lifted his right arm a fraction and I moved to block him, focusing on his tense muscles. The sharp ends of his fingers hit between my ribs. I grunted and doubled over. Damn, I hadn't seen his left hand move.

He grinned. 'Had enough?'

I stuck out my chin and narrowed my eyes. 'How about we stop when my discomfort outweighs your pleasure?'

His chuckle rose slowly from his chest, sounding like an engine coming into ear shot. 'As you wish, he said, dipping his head a tad. 'The skill is allowing your opponent to open themselves up for attack. You need to learn to recognise the weak areas and use them to your advantage.'

The training commenced.

He patiently showed me how to execute the moves, never once getting angry when I couldn't grasp it, somehow finding a different method of teaching me. He pushed me a lot harder than Gabriel had and on many occasions I fell down. It never hurt that bad though and the added pressure motivated rather than hindered me.

When I got into bed at the end of the day, I groaned with the aches and pains in my stiff muscles. Gabriel slipped in beside me and hugged my body to his, brushing my breast with his fingers.

'You've got no hope unless you heal me,' I said as I awkwardly turned towards him.

He pulled away and sat up, his eyes dark and lips pressed together. 'I will not heal you when you insist on indulging in this ridiculous notion of learning to fight.'

I groaned loudly. 'Fine. It doesn't look like you will be getting any for a while then.'

I rolled out of bed, unable to get the muscles to work properly. My legs quivered as I shuffled to the bathroom. Hopefully a hot bath would ease the stiffness. As soon as I immersed myself fully, I sighed with relief and rolled my head to help ease the tension.

What did Gabriel hope to achieve by refusing to heal me? If he really thought being stroppy would make me stop, he was sadly mistaken. I studied the bruises that decorated my arms, legs and hips, and sighed. He had taken it upon himself to be my protector and it must be difficult for him to see me covered in the purple marks.

'Well he should make them better then,' I muttered.

Laying my head back against the enamel, I closed my eyes and thought about Adam. Over the day I had been given a new insight into him. He still irritated me quite a bit and on a few occasions during the day, I'd caught him eyeing me with suspicion. Yet I reckoned that over time, I could come to like the moody man, if only a little bit. Maybe like was too strong a word, I could probably come to respect him a little though.

Gabriel opened the door and silently entered. I kept my eyes closed. He muttered something in his own language as he took in the bruises. It wouldn't do him any harm.

He knelt on the floor beside the bath. 'You are so stubborn.'

I raised my eyebrows. He was one to talk. He reached his hands into the water and touched them to my skin.

'Thank you,' I told him once he finished healing me.

'You won't stop, will you?'

'No.'

'It is my job to protect you.'

'How about when you're there, I act like the defenceless woman who needs her man?' I grinned and he gave me a strained smile in return.

'How about you stay out of trouble full stop?'

'I'm willing to agree to that deal.'

Disaster averted, I got out the bath and joined him in bed. I still ached terribly, but I no longer hurt and was now in the mood to be persuaded when he pulled my body close to his.

When time wasn't filled with work or Uni reading (although exams were over, there was still plenty of reading to do if I wanted an added edge in year two), it was taken up with learning to fight. When the weather was good we practiced in the garden, if not we moved the sofas around to create a small area in the lounge.

After a time Gabriel began to watch us work. He continually muttered throughout and stood with stiff folded arms, but at least he stopped glaring at Adam when he hit me. Now and then I even detected a small smile of satisfaction for my growing ability, though he never admitted it. He even involved himself on a few occasions, though these were few and far between.

Maria joined us for some lessons, though her heart wasn't in it, saying she would rather depend on her magic to prevent a situation occurring. When I wryly pointed out that it hadn't helped with Ron, she merely shrugged, choosing to watch instead.

It had been raining for three days straight leaving the garden looking like a marsh, and showed no sign of letting up. We pushed the lounge furniture aside in order to practice. Maria laughed at me as Adam continually knocked me on my backside.

'Use your anger, Ana.' Adam's tone was low as he stood across from me. 'And do not forget to do the unexpected.'

How was that possible when he had taught me everything I knew?

'I am,' I panted, getting ready for the next attack. I raised the long wooden stick and grimaced. It hurt a lot more than the rubber knife when it hit.

'No you are not. You are weak and you will never survive unless you manage to harness the anger I know you have.'

I scowled at him. 'So just think of you then.'

The corner of his mouth twitched, causing a shadow of a smile. 'If that works for you, use it.'

He swung the stick towards me. I managed to block him a couple of times but before long, I landed on my back once again. I leapt straight back up, determined not to let him beat me.

'You need more anger. Remember how the gun felt against you. Remember the Fae who killed your friend. Find that anger, harness it, use it.'

Tears pricked at my eyes and I blinked them back. Instead of dwelling on my loss, I brought Sheah's face to mind, focusing on how she had smiled while her companion killed Lexi. I stood motionless, picturing the Fae stood before me.

Adam swung the stick towards my shoulder. So many times I had tried to block such a move, and so many times I had failed.

I ducked and planted my stick on the floor as I swung up my leg to kick him in the stomach. The stick slipped and I stumbled forwards, under his raised arm.

'What's all this?' Eris said from the doorway.

I waved my arms around, trying to find my balance. It made the situation worse and I fell back into the high book shelf, filled to the rim with Uni and fictional books.

'She is demonstrating how she will get herself killed in the future,' Adam said as the bookcase groaned against my weight. As he dipped his head to greet Eris, the wooden structure swayed before toppling forwards. I quickly rolled, barely missing the side as it collapsed to the ground, but Adam didn't see it coming and it landed on top of him.

Eris burst into laughter as I struggled to my feet. The bookcase rose up before I had a chance to reach Adam.

'You could have stopped that,' he said to Eris as the unit settled against the wall, guided by an invisible force. The scattered books on the floor also rose and returned to their place on the shelves. The sight of the books travelling through the air as one caused the breath to catch in my throat. Would I ever get used to their abilities?

Eris laughed. 'Where would the fun have been in that?'

Maria started chuckling. 'I reckon Ana wins that round,' she said. 'It's about time, I thought you were never going to hit him.'

Even though it had been quite by accident, I was willing to take anything as a victory. I laughed, and much to Adam's disapproval, performed a little victory dance.

'And who are you?' Eris said to Maria.

Maria stared with her mouth open.

'This is Maria,' I said. 'Maria this is Eris.'

'Wow!' was all Maria could say.

'So you're from the Weich family?' Eris asked her.

'That was my great-grandmother's surname,' Maria answered with wide eyes. 'How did you know?'

'I knew her, a very powerful witch. You have the same natural power, though I can see that you haven't fully delved into it yet.'

'Really? You knew her? What was she like?'

'She never liked me much. She didn't get my humour.' Eris shook her head in feigned sadness, before smiling at Maria. 'But I never claimed to be to everyone's taste.'

'Will you stay for dinner?' I asked.

'I can. Where is Gabriel though?'

'He'll be back soon.' I grinned, while beckoning her into the house. 'I'll make us some tea.'

Maria followed me into the kitchen.

'She is something,' she said. 'If only you could see her aura, it's nothing like the men have.'

I poured the boiling water into the mugs, hissing slightly when the steam burnt my fingers. 'I can see that she sparkles.'

Maria shook her head. 'It's so much more than that. The colours are amazing. I mean everyone has colours in their aura, but I've never seen anything like it.'

I laughed, while feeling somewhat disgruntled. 'That's because she's some sort of priestess. I don't really know what that means, except that she can do more stuff than Gabriel.'

She shook her head again in awe. I reached out with my mind and embraced her feeling of respect for the Siis, relishing the childlike joy that came with it.

We returned to the lounge in time to catch the tail end of what Eris was telling Adam. '...leave it alone, I'll keep an eye on it.'

'Eye on what?' I asked.

Eris smiled dazzlingly at me. 'Nothing, I was just telling Adam how I managed to hunt down a colony of the Fae.'

A lump of panic formed in my throat. 'Please tell me you didn't do it alone? You could have been harmed.'

'Ana, were you not paying attention on the night they were here?'

I blanched at the memory and nodded.

'Did you not wonder why they were so afraid of me? That's one of the things I do, I hunt down the Fae.'

'But why?'

'It's fun,' she said causing a shiver to travel up my spine. 'Now, what do you have planned for dinner?' She smiled brightly and I couldn't help but reciprocate in kind. 'I hope it's not going to be anything like those awful sandwiches you made the first time we met.'

'I'm sure I can find something that will be to your usual standard,' I said with a grimace. Not having any idea if that was the case, I excused myself to hunt through the cupboards.

Gabriel slipped his arms around me and I snuggled against him, relishing the feel of his firm body against mine, and his warm breath as it sent shivers down my spine.

'I see Eris finally responded to my message,' he said once he'd cause the strength to flee my legs. He pulled away, muttering something else under his breath. I missed the words but not the tone.

'Play nice please,' I warned him. 'She is a guest in my house and I happen to like her.'

He stared at me intently. 'Why is that?'

'Who knows?' I laughed as I brushed past him to set the table. 'Now leave me in peace and go say hello.'

He groaned and brushed his lips across my forehead, before leaving me to figure out how to fit five place settings around my small table.

Gabriel wasn't openly rude to Eris as we ate, but each time she tried to engage him in conversation he replied with stilted, one worded answers. I repeatedly gave him sharp looks, which he pointedly refused to acknowledge. In the end, I gave up, conceding that it was an improvement on recent behaviour, even if it did cause an atmosphere at times.

For once, Adam was the chattier of the two men, though his speech remained guarded. I even caught him giving Maria the narrow eyed stare I knew so well, not that she paid any attention. Maybe he just didn't like women in general.

Maria continually asked Eris about what becoming a priestess involved, and much to my annoyance, about the Fae, not a topic I wanted to discuss during dinner. I smiled, watching how the two women hit it off and how Maria's face lit up as Eris recounted past events involving her great-grandmother.

We left the men to clean and entertain themselves, and retired to the lounge with a few bottles of wine to keep us company. Gabriel occasionally poked his head around the door at the sound of our hysterics, each time with a scowl on his face, which only deepened as Eris ribbed him about his attitude.

I was feeling fuzzy from the effects of the alcohol when Maria declared, 'Why don't I show you what I can do?'

Eris clapped her hands with joy at the prospect and I marvelled at how after thousands of years of life, she still found pleasure in every experience.

Maria moved her glass into the middle of the table. She closed her eyes and inhaled deeply, before focusing on the wine in front of her. A strange buzz vibrated from her and my jaw dropped as the wine rose from the glass as a mini tornado. It leapt out and spun across the table, leaving flicks of wine in its wake. I watched with wide eyes as it trailed around, heading back to the wine glass where is continued to spin on the spot before promptly losing form. The wine flooded out across the table but I continued to stare with my mouth open. I finally realised that wine was going to run onto the carpet and dragged my gaze away from to table to retrieve a towel.

'Wait,' Eris laughed. The wine flowed back across the table and formed a backwards waterfall into the glass. Even the splashes were gone.

'I always lose it,' Maria said. 'Water isn't as easy to control as fire.'

'I can probably help you with that,' Eris told her.

I sat back in my seat and listened to the two of them discuss how to maintain better control. Life was strange. Who would have thought that I would be sat in the company of a non-human powerful priestess and a witch with more than your average abilities, while being madly in love with someone more special than the two of them put together.

'Did your mother not teach you any of this?' Eris asked Maria.

'Nah,' Maria said. 'My mum died when I was a baby. I grew up in the system, not something I would recommend.'

'That's something you and Ana have in common,' Eris said, causing me to choke on my wine. 'She was adopted as a baby.'

My eyes widened in surprise. 'How do you know that?' Being adopted wasn't something I ever spoke of, purely because it made no odds to me. My parents had been told that they wouldn't be able to have their own children so had taken me into their home. Even when the medical profession had been proven wrong and Beth had been born a couple of years later, I had been treated no differently. They hadn't kept the adoption from me. When I had been old enough to understand the truth of my birth they had both gone out of their way to ensure it made no difference to my life.

I still remembered my mother's words now. *Family has nothing to do with blood ties. That is nothing more than genetics. Family is about the people we love and the bonds formed from that are stronger than blood could ever be.*

'I make it my business to know,' Eris said with a smile. 'Have you ever thought of looking for your biological parents?' She leant forward, intently waiting for my answer. Her face supported a relaxed smile and as always, I couldn't help but respond in kind. But when I studied her eyes, I detected something, a calculated coldness that almost made me shiver.

'My parents offered to help me find them,' I said, 'but I refused. I have no interest in finding someone who left me on the doorstep of the Social Services without so much as an explanation.'

'I don't blame you,' Maria said raising her glass.

Eris' smile widened a tad before she turned to Maria, leaving me with the notion that she had a secret, one that she wasn't willing to share.

19

'Urgh!' I tried to turn away from the sunlight that caused sharp, throbbing pains to shoot across the whole of my head.

'Good morning.'

I groaned and tentatively opened one eye to find Gabriel smiling down at me.

'How is your head?'

'Bad.'

'I'm not surprised. You all drank an impressive amount of alcohol. Adam had to walk Maria home and he was not happy when he returned.'

I gratefully took the water he held out to me. 'Why?'

'Because she sang at the top of her voice the whole way there. Somebody even shouted out of the window for her to shut up.'

'I'm surprised he didn't turn her voice box off or something.' I dragged myself out of bed and staggered to the bathroom.

Gabriel's voice reached me through the door. 'He seriously thought about it.' He laughed. 'And of doing other things not so savoury, however, he figured it wouldn't go down well with relations between us all.'

'What does he care about relations?' I said through the toothpaste filling my mouth.

'Come on now,' he beseeched as I opened the door. 'He is not as bad as you think.'

I climbed back into bed in the hope of another few hours' sleep. 'If only I could believe that.'

He lay on top of the covers and cuddled up behind me. 'I really wish you two could get along.'

'I'm sorry. He really isn't that bad anymore, I'm just still sore from the weeks of him eye balling me.'

He laughed and shook his head. 'He doesn't eye ball you.'

I shrugged and laid my hands over my eyes to block the sunlight out. 'What time did I come to bed last night?'

Gabriel started shaking with laughter. 'You were funny.'

'Oh no,' I groaned. 'What did I do?'

'I woke up to you standing *on* the bottom of the bed, pulsing with light, demanding that I take you there and then.'

The memories came flooding back and I groaned again. 'Oh God, I attempted a strip tease didn't I?'

'Is that what that was?' He bellowed with laughter. 'You sounded like you were trying to hum the funeral march before you promptly fell off the bed with your head stuck in your top.'

'God.' I buried my head beneath the pillow. 'The shame.'

He laughed and pulled the pillow from my head. 'It was adorable. It was nice to see you so relaxed.'

'What happened to Eris? Did she get drunk?'

'Hardly, she left early this morning.' He leant towards me and brushed my lips with his. 'Do you still want me to take you here and now?'

The idea was tempting but my stomach rolled telling me that it probably wouldn't be wise. Plus my breath was still offensive to even me.

I kissed his throat and nuzzled into his neck. 'Maybe you can wake me in an hour when I feel more human.'

He pulled away laughing. 'You have to get up then anyway, there is someone coming to visit.' The distinct air of excitement surrounding him finally broke through my alcohol induced haze.

'Who?' Hopefully it wasn't another one of his friends, Adam was already enough to deal with.

'Suraya.'

'*What?* Your daughter Suraya?' My stomach filled with butterflies, the churning feeling pushed aside.

'What other Suraya do you know?' he said beaming.

I threw back the covers and grabbed the towels for a bath, all thoughts of more sleep gone. 'I wish you had warned me.'

He carefully circled my wrist to halt me. 'Why are you so anxious? Do you not want to meet her?'

'Of course I do.' I stroked his face to try and smooth out the worried creases. 'I just would have liked more time to prepare. It is your daughter, Gabriel. What if she doesn't like me?'

'She will.' He smiled and pressed his hand to my cheek. 'Be yourself, and you will be fine.'

I bit back the words about how that hadn't worked with Adam and stumbled off to the bathroom.

'Stop fidgeting, Ana.'

After a bath, three cups of tea and a fried breakfast I was feeling a lot better, though butterflies still filled my stomach. I had cleaned the house from top to bottom, only stopping to briefly speak to Maria, who had rung to say she didn't remember the end of the night so it must have been good. When I told her about Suraya, she offered to come for moral support. Although tempted, I declined. I needed to do this alone.

I wiped the kitchen side over again, even though it was already as clean as it was going to get. 'What time is it?'

'About thirty seconds later than the last time you asked.' He pulled me into his arms and gripped my chin so as to look deep into my eyes. 'Relax, it will be fine.'

I was about to ask how he knew that for sure, when he grinned.

'She's here!' He gave me a quick kiss and bounded to the door, filled with so much excitement that it rubbed off on me, pushing some of my anxiety aside.

He staggered back a few steps as a petite girl threw herself at him. 'Father!'

'Suraya, I can't believe it has been so long. I have missed you so much.'

After a long embrace, they stepped back from each other. Her sapphire eyes sparkled, framed by long blonde hair. She was just as stunning as Eris.

I fidgeted while silently waiting for them to become reacquainted, not sure whether to wait until they had finished, or take myself into the lounge to give them time alone. They both talked fast, without a pause for breath between words, making it impossible for me to keep up. Eventually Gabriel hugged her again before pulling away.

'This is Ana,' he said gesturing to me.

I smiled, trying to hide the tension within. 'Hi, it's great to finally meet you.'

'Ana!' she exclaimed as if we had known each other for years. 'I can't wait to get to know you. Finally there is someone other than Eris to have all the girly chats with.'

My sigh of relief was a tad louder than I would have liked. She bounded over to me and I uncontrollably tensed as she gave me an unexpected hug, squeezing so hard that I started coughing.

'What have you been up to for the last couple of years?' Gabriel asked her once she returned to his side.

How had he gone so long without seeing her? Then again, I suppose that when you lived forever, a couple of years are just a rain drop in the pond.

'This and that,' she said vaguely. 'Nothing of much importance.' She glanced at me from the corner of her eye. 'I have spent some time with Aaliya.'

To my surprise, Gabriel scowled at her.

Was Aaliya some sort of love interest? I disregarded it immediately. From what I knew about the Siis, when they mated, it was for life. I offered Suraya a drink in a way to diffuse the sudden tension in the room and she agreed with enthusiasm.

As they hadn't seen each other in so long, I tried to give them the space to catch up by pottering around the kitchen. Suraya kindly did her best to involve me in the conversation and eventually, I gave up and settled at the table with them.

'So how did you two meet?' She leant forwards, with her face in her hands as we told her the story of meeting on a rainy evening, not an accurate account of our first meeting but the version that everyone knew.

She grinned and leant back in her seat, taking us both in. 'Bet you're glad that you fell in that puddle now.'

I touched Gabriel's finger tips, caressing the smooth skin. 'I couldn't imagine my life any other way.'

'I couldn't agree more,' Gabriel said standing up. 'Now if you will please excuse me for a moment ladies.'

'Aww, that's so sweet,' she purred. Her voice was nearly as pleasing as Eris', though deeper in tone.

We both watched as he left the room.

'I'm so glad that we get along,' I said, turning towards her. All other words stuck in my throat upon seeing the murderous look on her face.

'Make no mistake, Ana, we are not friends.' Gone was the chatty, friendly woman, in her place sat someone full of malice, her lips pulled back over her teeth, and her nose turned up. The kitchen faded as the air seemed to darken around her, and her eyes flashed as she glared at me.

My skin tingled with shock. 'I'm sorry?'

'I will pretend to like you for my father's sake, but I will never understand why he is with you.'

'I'm confused. What have I done?' To my dismay, my voice came out in a pathetic whisper, all strength having left me.

'You are here and that is enough.' She sneered. 'But no worries, it won't be too long before he tires of you.' My stomach clenched up as she hit on one of my greatest fears. 'I just can't believe that he is shacked up with some pathetic human who is leeching off his life force.'

My lips clamped shut and I leant towards her, though it took all my strength to do so. 'I am not leeching anything.'

'For years I have waited for him to recover from my mother,' she continued, 'and what do I find? Him with a *human.*' She spat the word as if it was something foul on her tongue.

Resisting the urge to slap her straight across the face, I leant back in my seat and forced my hands to uncurl. 'So what? You don't like who daddy fell in love with. That's life, get over it.'

She sat across from me, the rage seething from her. In the space of two minutes, I had managed to make an enemy, a record even for me. With difficulty, I reined my anger in and tried a change of tactics.

'Look, I'm sorry things aren't what you had hoped they would be. Can't we at least try to get to know each other, if only for your father's sake?'

Her nostrils flared and I cringed back in my seat. Her eyes became slits that bore into me, causing my fight or flight instincts to set in, urging me to put as much distance between us as possible. I glanced towards the door, trying to suppress the notion that she would surely kill me if Gabriel didn't hurry up and return.

'I will make sure you are gone soon,' she promised, the words dripping from her tongue like acid.

I forced a strained smile onto my face and reached out with my mind. There was a clinical coldness, similar to when I touched Adam's mind, but unlike him, there wasn't a wall, making it possible to detect something. I stiffened, picking up on the watchful tenseness that flickered over her thoughts, layered with a cold pleasure, almost like she was silently scheming.

'It's rude to snoop you know.'

I jumped. Damn, in my concentration I'd almost forgotten she sat there.

'Sorry, it's not something I can control.'

She could likely detect the lie and I smiled in an attempt to disarm her. She glanced down at my hands. They shook so violently they were almost a blur. I needed to get some control, but the shaking wasn't just contained to my hands, my whole body quivered with tension.

'Guess what I've got,' Gabriel called from the lounge. I barely managed to contain a tight sigh of relief.

Suraya continued to study me until her father entered the room.

'What is it?' She jumped up excitedly, throwing me a dazzling smile, which only made my head reel with the abrupt change.

Gabriel held out a gold necklace supporting a crystal disk, the size of a baby's fist. Inside was a lock of jet black hair. 'It was your mother's,' he told her.

She lifted her hair for him to place it around her neck. Once he secured it, she threw her arms around him.

'Thank you! I will treasure it.' She released her father and practically skipped over to me. 'Do you like it, Ana?'

I could only stare before managing to mumble the words needed. 'It's lovely.'

'Isn't it just?' She held it up to the light in order to admire it properly. 'Oh I'm so glad I came and not because of the necklace.' She put her arm around my waist and it took every ounce of strength not to flinch away. 'I know I turned up with very little notice.' What I could only guess was feigned sorrow shadowed her face. 'But as we have hit it off so well, do you think I could stay with you both for a while?'

Gabriel grinned so hard the backs of his teeth became visible and to make matters worse, he began almost hopping with excitement. I tried to draw on his pleasure in order to hide my feelings, but it made as much difference as a teaspoon of salt would to a frozen lake. His brow furrowed into a slight frown as he picked up on my distress at the idea.

Drawing the misery into myself in the hope of shielding it from him, I smiled weakly and lied like I never had before.

'That would be great. We would love you to stay.'

I needed to get away as I would only be able to hide the turmoil going on inside of me for so long. Ignoring Suraya's fingers as they dug painfully into my side, I pulled from her embrace.

'I'm going to go back to bed now, if that's okay? It was a late one last night and I'm sure you two want to catch up properly.'

Gabriel's eyes shadowed somewhat, though the grin crept back as if he had no control over it. 'Of course.'

I forced a tight smile onto my face and turned to his daughter. 'See you later, Suraya. I am glad I can finally put a face to the name.'

I ignored Gabriel's reaching hand and left the kitchen with the hope that he wouldn't follow. He caught up with me before I even made it to the stairs.

'Ana, are you all right?'

'I'm just tired.' I smiled. My face started to ache from all the effort.

'Are you sure?'

'Too much alcohol last night remember.'

Relying on the confusion of the bipolar and his ability to believe what he wanted to, I reached up to kiss him. After a moment of studying me carefully, he did not disappoint. He visibly relaxed and pulled me into his arms.

'That will teach you,' he said with a laugh. 'Do you want to be woken in a few hours for some dinner?'

The thought of sitting across from Suraya nearly made me shudder. 'It's okay. If I get hungry, I'll grab something easy.'

I kissed him and trudged up the stairs with a heavy heart. What the hell was I going to do about his daughter? If Suraya was anything to go by, I may well have been lucky with Adam's reaction to me. He had always kept it to cold stares and open distain. Somehow I didn't think it was going to be the case with

Suraya. I had a gut feeling that just wouldn't go away and my hackles were up.

20

For a couple of days I remained the model hostess towards Suraya, if only because she was Gabriel's daughter. I listened as she talked and smiled at her weak jokes. I even began to question my level of wariness concerning her as she was nothing but pleasant and helpful.

Then my books went missing and turned up in the most bizarre place, the garden. When I questioned Suraya about it she responded with a wicked smirk behind Gabriel's back, and by saying, 'How could you leave them outside, Ana? You are *so* lucky that they are not ruined.' She said it so sweetly and to my annoyance Gabriel only laughed and said, 'You can be so forgetful sometimes, Ana.' I hadn't even been outside, yet my words of denial were brushed off.

Things fell off the kitchen side when I walked past to smash on the floor. Gabriel always laughed with Suraya about how clumsy I could be and Suraya smiled sweetly in his line of sight, only to turn the smile into a sneer when he turned away. My nerves were constantly on edge and it wasn't long before I had had enough.

I went off to work in a really bad mood. Not only was I on a late shift, which meant I wouldn't finish until ten at night, but my tunic had gone missing and I didn't have to think hard to figure out what had happened to it. My mood only worsened when I arrived at Pinehill. One of our less capable residents, Connie, had an accident in her bed, the kind that meant I had to wear two pairs of gloves and have a strong stomach to clean up.

Robert decided to spend the day pushing my buttons. At dinner he took his usual grumpiness one step further and threw his plate across the room, narrowly missing another resident. As usual he didn't apologise, instead shouting that we were trying to poison him and that he was on to us. The day was definitely not getting any better.

When the shift came to an end, I was grateful to be going home, which hadn't been the case in the two weeks since Suraya's arrival.

There hadn't been chance to grab anything to eat during the shift, so by the time I pulled up outside the house, I happily anticipated the beef dinner Gabriel had promised to save for me.

Suraya stood in the kitchen waiting for me. I gritted my teeth and made a conscious effort not to clench my fists. 'Where's your dad? I asked, throwing my bag onto the table.

'At Adam's. He left your dinner in the fridge.'

Ignoring her hostile stare, I opened the fridge, only to find no plate in sight.

She grinned. 'I threw it in the bin. I can always scoop it out for you if you want.'

I banged the door closed hard enough that the jars inside rattled. 'Why would you do that?'

'Because I can,' she replied mildly.

I slammed my hands down on the side with such force that the shock travelled up my arms to my neck. 'How freakin' old are you?'

She laughed, a sound that may well have been pleasing if I didn't know her true nature. 'It is you who is the infant.'

'Yeah, because I'm the one who is having a two year old temper tantrum because daddy wants to share his time with someone else.' My teeth clenched so hard my jaw ached. It took several deep breaths before I began to relax. 'You know, I'm not talking about this with you. I will just tell your father and you can explain it to him.' I nearly groaned with misery. It was as if I were a child once more, planning on telling tales to my parents.

She laughed. 'You can, but who do you think he will believe?'

'He certainly won't believe I threw a full plate of dinner away,' I said stiltedly as I opened the bin. It took several seconds of staring at the bread wrapper I had put in there in the morning, before I realised that there was no sign of my dinner.

'I never said it was that bin,' she said smugly. 'I wonder if he will believe that you were so tired that you forgot you ate it.'

I slammed the flap closed, only to watch as the lid unbalanced and fell to the floor. I stared at it for several seconds before able to relax my body enough to bend down and retrieve it.

Once it sat back in place, I whirled on her. 'What do you hope to achieve by this? If you think that I am going to leave him, you are sadly mistaken. One day he will see what you really are, and mark my words, I will still be here when he does.'

Her lip curled and her eyes narrowed with loathing. She raised her hand and sprang towards me, like a cat leaping towards a mouse.

'Just do it!' I backed against the kitchen side and she stopped with her open hand still raised. 'Then I will have all the proof I need.'

She lowered her hand, though her face remained twisted in a snarl and the pulse in her temple continued to beat furiously. She rolled her tongue in her mouth as if she had just tasted something bad, leant towards me, and *spat* in my face.

I stared at her with my mouth open as her drool ran down my cheek. I fought hard not to smack her.

'Nice.' I used the palm of my hand to wipe the saliva off. 'Real mature.'

'I will see you gone,' she promised. She abruptly turned on her heels and stalked from the house, leaving me to lean against the side as tremors racked through my body. How had I gone to war over a man, especially against his daughter?

I made a bowl of cereal to replace the lost dinner and tried not to think of what else Suraya could have in store for me.

Upon waking, I became instantly aware of the taunting voice that whispered in my mind. I trudged down the stairs, trying to ignore its promise to make my life a living hell. We'd been through this dance so many times, yet each new bout was a fresh challenge to overcome. I could do it. I always won out in the end.

Three days into the bout I stood gripping the edge of the kitchen side as uncontrollable tears rolled down my cheeks. A thick cloud surrounded me, suffocating me under its weight. My internal demon worked full force and soon progressed beyond general insults. *Give up,* it whispered. *Take all the tablets you have.*

I bit my lip so hard I drew blood, trying to banish the voice from my mind. *Maybe use the knife,* it murmured as I stared at the draining board, gripping the kitchen side so hard my fingers ached. *You can end all of your pain,* it promised. My hand reached towards the blade, and stroked along the cool, sharp edge, as if I caressed a lover's face instead of the item that could end it all.

'No,' I sobbed, wishing the voice would scare me. If it had, at least it would provoke anger, helping to force it back into my mind. It didn't though. Instead its words brought on a sense of stillness, which paused, rather than calmed the storm within.

If only Gabriel was around to prevent the ideas forming in my mind, actions I would never carry out as they were merely a desperate bid to escape my anguish, but still, thoughts that shouted to be heard.

Another wave of torment flowed over me and I crumpled under it. I pressed myself into the corner and curled into a ball. I needed to get out of the house. A strangled sob erupted from my chest and I buried my face in my hands. It was all too hard. Nothing was working. Nothing silenced the demon that created chaos in my mind. How had it gained so much control?

I pressed my hands to my face until stars exploded behind my eyes. My stomach twisted and bile rose up causing me to gag. The demon was right, I was weak. My chest heaved. I quickly pulled myself up and hung over the sink as the vicious sobs tore through me. I was going to be sick.

Even though I heaved again, nothing came out, only my groan as my stomach lurched. The tears continued to flood from my eyes. I was pathetic, good for nothing, a failure to myself. I held onto the sense of disgust, fanning it, clinging to the small spark of strength buried below. I needed it to force myself from the house.

Using the feeling of loathing, I abruptly turned from the side, looking for the car keys. I had to leave before the moment passed and I collapsed to the floor once more. I stopped in my tracks.

Suraya stood in the lounge doorway, her fingers held towards me and a malicious look on her face. It disappeared within a blink of an eye and she frowned at me with false concern.

'Are you all right?' she purred, with a smile so innocent it would have put a baby to shame.

Oh God, she was manipulating me, pushing the chemicals of my brain into overdrive, destroying me in the same manner the Fae would.

She stood watching me, with no sign of her obvious hatred, waiting for me to speak, but try as I might, no words passed my lips. My pulse raced, cutting through the overhanging darkness. The woman stood before me was as dangerous as the devil himself, if not more so.

'Tell Gabriel I've gone to Maria's,' I eventually managed in a strangled sob.

Her heavy stare crushed me as I grabbed the car keys off the table and stumbled from the house, unable to acknowledge the item sat next to them. She laughed cruelly behind me.

Half way down the path, what I had seen finally registered. The full bottle of sleeping pills hadn't made their own way out of the cupboard and I certainly hadn't done it.

Don't, my mind cried as I turned back towards the house. *She will hurt you.* I ignored the voice, pressed my lips together and held my head up, clinging to the small amount of strength that withered with every passing second.

Suraya still stood smiling in the doorway, and she continued to do so as I scooped the bottle off the table. Without looking at her, I headed towards the medical cupboard.

'Did you really think it would be that easy?' I said dropping them into the small box containing the other medications. When I got back to the door, I turned to face her. 'I've already survived so much worse than you, Suraya.'

I had time to see her face twist into a snarl, before I hurriedly exited the house. I may want to try and salvage some semblance of dignity, but it would be wise to remember that she was extremely dangerous.

Never had there been a time I felt so relieved to stand in the dingy hallway that smelled of urine. The dark cloud, filled with the taunting demon still lay heavy on me making me feel as if I'd been forced through an emotional wringer. I knocked on the door, praying Maria was home, unable to sense anything through the darkness.

'Hey,' she said with a smile, 'what are you doing here?'

'I'm sorry, I should have rung.'

She ushered me into her flat, manoeuvring me around the books scattered over the floor.

'I'm not like you,' she said, closing the door. 'I love surprise visitors, it makes the day more interesting.'

I pushed a pile of clothes to the side of the sofa and sat heavily down.

'You're particularly dark today,' she said with a frown.

I started crying and buried my face in my hands. 'I can't bear it anymore.' All the strength I had found to confront Suraya had gone and I was struggling to tread water.

Maria plucked a tea towel from the pile of washing and handed it to me. She probably wouldn't have handed me something dirty to wash my face with, but still, I hesitated for a second before conceding that I didn't actually care enough to worry about it. She went into the kitchen as I dabbed my face. My tears had stemmed by the time she handed me a large purple mug.

It contained a metal strainer, filled with loose tea leaves. When I blew on the steaming drink, an awful smell of mouldy oranges and damp leaves hit me.

I pulled my nose back and grimaced. 'What is this? It smells like a rubbish skip.'

'It's herbal tea. It will relax you.'

'Herbal? Have you put Valium in it or something?'

She chuckled and rolled her eyes. 'Don't be silly. It's all natural and will probably do a better job than Valium.'

I took another sniff and scowled. She pushed the bottom of the mug up so I had no choice but to drink. The taste wasn't as bad as the smell, yet it wasn't pleasant either and I spluttered as it ran down my throat.

I swallowed the nasty tasting liquid with a grimace. 'How do you drink this?'

She shrugged. 'You get used to it. So, tell me what's going on.'

I told her about the things Suraya was doing to make my life difficult, and about the way I thought she was making my depression unbearable, though I kept the bit about the tablets out of it.

Maria's lips clamped down into a firm line. 'Are you sure?'

'As sure as I can be. I don't have any physical proof if that's what you're asking.'

'Have you told Gabriel?'

'What can I say? How can I tell him that his sweet innocent daughter is really a class A bitch? He wouldn't believe me anyway, you know Gabriel, he sees and feels what he wants to half the time and she does act nicely towards me when he is around.'

'Ahh. When you put it that way I can see what you mean.'

'At least Adam was up front with his distaste, not hiding behind false smiles and kindness.' I frowned. I actually missed the moody man.

'What does he think of Suraya?'

'I have no idea. He hasn't been around in weeks, not since she turned up.' It was probably the training I missed more than him. At least it would have given me an outlet for my frustrations. 'Oh Maria, I'm worried she will split us up.' Hearing the dejection in my own voice I gulped down the rest of the tea, if it could be called that, in the hope that I would start to feel better.

'Don't be silly,' she said softly, though with a hard edge simmering beneath the surface. 'You and Gabriel will always be together. It doesn't take someone with abilities to see the bond between you and how strong it is. You should tell him.'

'Then what? Even if he believes me, what would happen then? I doubt he would send her away, and I don't believe she will change if he confronts her, it will just get worse.'

'This is why I don't date guys with kids.'

'No, you just date crazy men who want to kill you.'

We grinned at each other. Maybe it was the special tea or maybe it was just being in her company, but the tension drained from my body and I started to feel more relaxed than I had in weeks.

'Shall I cast a spell on her?' Her voice was stiff and she had a certain gleam to her eyes that reminded me of Eris.

'It would probably backfire on you.'

My words weren't without merit. Not only had there been the attack involving Ron when she had caused him to see things that weren't there, she had told me of other, not so serious incidents, such as when she had tried to get a job in real estate. She had succeeded with her aim, but had to leave her home in the midlands and move up north to take it, which wasn't exactly what she'd had in mind.

'It most likely wouldn't work on her anyway,' I said, 'but thank you for the offer.'

'Maybe so, but then again, maybe not. I could try.'

The idea was so tempting that I nearly told her to go ahead. Instead, being sensible I said, 'Best not. It wouldn't be fair on Gabriel.'

Maria mumbled something under her breath before smiling. 'Well, you know the offer is there if you ever need it.'

I stared at her suspiciously, not sure that saying no would mean anything to her. 'Please don't do anything. You have no idea how a spell will work on a Siis, or what they would do if they find you trying.'

'It would be worth it.'

'Maria—'

'Fine, I won't try unless you tell me I can.' She muttered something else under her breath.

'What?' I asked.

She shrugged and looked around the room. 'I was just thinking about how you're going to make me clean up now.' She grabbed my hand and pulled me from the sofa. 'Depressed or not, you have to help.'

My lips twitched into a ghost of a smile. The day that Maria actually helped with the cleaning, was the day I knew the world had come to an end.

After a couple of hours, I leant back in my seat and sighed. 'I don't want to go home. I actually feel like I can breathe for the first time in days.'

'Stay the night then.'

I hadn't spent even one night away from Gabriel in months and the feeling of loss that accompanied the thought of not being in his arms was so strong, it was disconcerting. But after several seconds of silent debate, I gratefully accepted Maria's offer and rang Gabriel to let him know.

A sliver of guilt wormed its way in when he agreed whole heartedly that it was a good idea. He could most likely sense that I felt loads better and put it down to Maria's infectious personality.

Maria was right. I was going to have to speak to him. I frowned at the idea. Weren't there unspoken rules about slating someone's daughter to them?

If only Eris was around, she would be easier to talk to. Hell, even Adam would be preferable in this matter. If only he hadn't dropped off the face of the earth. We weren't exactly friends, but he knew Gabriel so much better than I did and would maybe have some advice.

It occurred to me that he wasn't around because he had his own bad opinions about the false natured girl. I smirked, considering the possibility that Adam and I might actually share a view, before shrugging it off. It just didn't seem possible.

As the night progressed, my mood lightened further, leaving only a wisp of a cloud hanging over me. Even though smaller than me, Maria managed to find me some pyjamas, and we settled down to a night filled with laughter instead of worry.

The pull towards Gabriel remained, causing me to miss him with all my heart, but the thought of being in the same room as Suraya diminished the effect somewhat. Up until now, I had thought that I had no control over needing to be with him. It seemed that I did have some, even if it was only when the need was overshadowed by fear.

21

I entered the house, grateful to be leaving the heat of the noon sun and could hear Beethoven's moonlight sonata playing quietly in the lounge. I dropped my bag in the lounge doorway and silently watched Gabriel as he sat on the sofa with his eyes closed, his pleasure to the soothing notes of the piano evident in the relaxed smile that played across his lips.

My heart swelled at the sight of him, his beauty causing my chest to restrict with the knowledge of how much I truly did love him. I watched as his fingers moved in rhythm with the music, not wanting to break the spell before me, aware that even with the problems in our lives, I was exactly where I was meant to be.

Without opening his eyes he silently beckoned for me to join him. He stood as I approached and only then looked into my eyes. His burning gaze penetrated me and my head swam as I tried to force the forgotten breath from my lungs. Unable to speak, I stood motionless as he stopped only inches from me.

My breathing became uneven and his breath mingled with mine, intoxicating me. I quivered as he stroked his fingertips across my cheek, leaving a burning trail in their wake.

He removed my clothes before fluidly shedding his and took me in his arms. My body quivered with pleasure at the warmth of his skin on mine. He lowered me to the floor and we lay facing each other, only inches apart. Our skin didn't touch, and although our lips were parted, a small distance remained between us, though we were close enough for our breath to be shared. No words were spoken as we let our light bathe out to encompass each other.

My mind flew high with ecstasy beyond any comprehension. I was lost and wanted never to be found.

I lay in his arms and wept as he kissed away my tears. We didn't speak as there was nothing left unsaid by the quietness between us. His love for me shone in his whole being, my own light speaking the same silent words in return.

'What was that?' I murmured as he brushed away the last of my tears. 'Did we even touch?'

He pressed his lips to mine and smiled, his eyes shimmering with love. 'No.'

'But how...'

'I know.' The iridescent wonder in his eyes matched my own.

He snagged the blanket I kept downstairs for cold nights, and dragged it over us, while pulling me closer into his arms. My senses became sharper and I realised that the house was in darkness, us being the only source of light. The music had finished and must have hours before, yet I could have sworn that it had been playing throughout.

I lifted my head and kissed him slowly. 'Thank you.'

His eyes widened in surprise. 'What could you possibly have to thank me for?'

'For being you.'

'I am only what I am because of you, Ana.' He held my face so as to stare into my eyes. 'Before you I was lost, only a future filled with misery was before me. I have never told you that the night I first saw you being attacked, I was contemplating taking my own life.' I stiffened at his words and he pulled me tighter into his embrace. 'Don't worry, I no longer feel that way. At the time, losing Deonti had broken me and I was tired of trying to hold myself together. Suraya was grown up and was living her own life, leaving me no reason to suffer anymore. There was a small part of me that still wanted to live, though it was diminishing as the years passed. It was that voice that caused me to pray for a miracle, something that would help me live again.'

'Where is Suraya by the way?' I asked a little apprehensively. I enjoyed the calm, relaxed feeling that flowed through me and wasn't in a rush for it to end. It occurred to me that this would be the perfect time to talk to him about what Suraya was doing, but that was the thing, it was the *perfect* time and I didn't want to spoil it.

'She is visiting friends for a few days.'

I tried to suppress my sigh of relief, but his eyes narrowed in response.

'That means we have time all to ourselves?' I said quickly.

'That we do.' He smiled, positioning himself above me. 'And how would you like to spend that time?' He nuzzled my neck and the passion started to build between us. As we made love for the first time, I was dimly aware that I glowed brighter than I ever had before.

Hands clamped my shoulder and shook me, violently and without mercy. I groaned and tried to turn away from the probing fingers. They merely reached further into the flesh, to the joint, demanding I open my laden eyes. I had fallen asleep on the lounge floor. I groaned with the stiffness that seized the muscles and a hand clamped over my mouth, the fingers tight as they pinched my lips together.

'Where's the phone?' Gabriel hissed urgently, snatching away the remaining sleep. I pointed to where I had dropped my bag and sat up, pulling the blanket around me. Gabriel sprung up, seizing the phone out of my bag. With the mobile pressed to his ear, he spoke two words that filled my head with fear. 'They're back.'

They're back? Who was back?

Sheah is coming! my mind screamed. *She's coming to kill you this time.* Her eyes rose up from my memory, cruel, calculated, with no hint of compassion. They drilled into my brain, stilling the breath in my throat, freezing all thoughts. *Remember when Lexi screamed,* my mind urged. *Remember how Sheah's eyes had gleamed with pleasure.*

My heart fled to my throat and I choked, trying to force some rationality into my brain. Sheah was dead. Eris had killed her. Reason didn't halt the words and they continued to shatter through my mind, screaming, *She's coming to get you,* over and over again. *Remember how they tortured Lexi. They want you. They will make you suffer.* I hugged myself, trying to silence the surging thoughts. *Remember the male's hands. Remember the ease in which they reached through Lexi's stomach.* I shuddered, my whole midsection twisting into an agonising knot, as if the Fae was stood before me with his fingers reaching through my flesh to seize my spine. Twisting, raking, spilling the life from me, all the while smiling with glee.

Gabriel hauled me to my feet, leaving the blanket strewn across the floor and threw me against the wall. I hugged my body, fully aware of my nakedness as he stood crouched before me.

'The Fae are here?' My voice was tight, all moisture having fled my mouth.

Think! my mind ordered, this time in Adam's voice. *Ride above the panic. Take control of your fear.* The stern words helped with the torrent within, bringing calmness to the raging storm. Fae or not, I couldn't stand naked, so reached out and snagged the blanket.

Gabriel nodded sharply and continued to scan the room. I wrapped the blanket around me, painfully aware that although Adam had been teaching me to fight, I really didn't know very much. Had I learnt enough to earn my life? Could I survive them this time?

We stood ready for several minutes, tense and waiting. My eyes constantly reached to my clothes, but Gabriel was beyond anxious, his body one vibrating slab of muscle. The Fae could be upon us at any second. What if they came while I was dressing? The image of them spilling into the lounge took control of my thoughts. My jeans half way up my legs, making it impossible to dodge their teeth as they came for me, powerless because of my perceived vulnerability that nakedness brought. The clothes could wait.

The mobile phone rang, the sharp tone causing me to jump. Gabriel answered it immediately.

'Come when it's done,' he snapped. Did that mean the danger had passed? I glanced longingly at my discarded clothes once more.

'What's done?' I asked as he hung up.

'Adam is checking the area.'

I sighed with relief that we were not alone, though still scanned the room, ready for confrontation.

Something heavy landed against the doors, a severe thud causing them to rattle in their frame. Nails scraped down the glass, high pitched, penetrating, bringing to mind the image of a knife being dragged across an old chalk board. A shiver ran down my spine. The doors opened and the curtains billowed in the breeze. Small hands reached around, the nails sharp talons, layered with thick metal, tearing the material effortlessly as the curtains were pushed aside. I dropped the blanket. Skilled or not, it wouldn't help gathered in my arms. The childlike figure stepped into the room. His stare pulled on me, drawing me into his malevolence.

The cold breeze washed over my naked body and I sensed, rather than saw Gabriel shift to attack. My heart raced, yet each beat seemed to be seconds apart.

The Fae took another step into the house. How could a child become so hateful? Even with the intake of heavy energy, how was it possible that their minds could hold such bitter thoughts? There was no doubt of how the small boy, no, small demon stood before us felt. I could almost see a thick fog reaching towards us, glinting as if filled with a million tiny blades ready to slice. Yet when the heavy mist reached me, parasites crawled under my skin and into my brain, devouring flesh and bone as they went.

How many people had the small figure killed? How many children had he taken, changing their fate to a life filled with bitterness and psychopathic thrills? Did their pleas ever make him pause or did he take pleasure in their whimpered words as they cried for their mother to save them?

The Fae lifted his foot to take another step and snarled. Strings of saliva joined his sharp teeth. How much blood had passed over them and down his throat? How many times had they been used to tear flesh?

My eyes darted past him. Where there more? In my experience, they didn't travel alone. They tended to enjoy companionship when stealing the life of an innocent, someone to share in the destruction and pain they caused.

I saw a shadowed figure before the Fae was dragged back into the night, his scream so un-human, my skin wanted to crawl right off my body.

Gabriel's hands unclenched, though he still quivered with tension. A few seconds later Adam came through the open doorway with a dagger in his hand, a spray of fresh blood speckling his face.

'It was a scout party,' he told Gabriel. 'The other one was gone before I got here.' He glanced briefly in my direction, impassively taking in my nakedness before turning back to Gabriel. I reached down to snag the blanket.

Gabriel hissed a single word in his own language as I wrapped it around my shivering body. 'How many?' he said in a tight voice.

'Three, two are dead. They are only the beginning. More will follow now they know we are here.'

My throat thickened, all moisture gone, making it difficult to speak. 'How long?'

'No idea,' Adam replied. 'I would not imagine long though. Maybe a week, unlikely more than a month. It all depends on the size of the assault they are planning.'

The strength left my legs and I slumped against the wall.

'Catch her, Gabe, she is going to faint.'

'I'm all right,' I told him weakly. 'I just need a moment.' I had only just managed to banish the memory of their last attack. It wasn't fair that they would come back.

'It will be all right,' Gabriel said soothingly. 'I promise you I...we won't let anything happen to you.'

'How many will come?' I asked.

Adam spoke first. 'Maybe as many as—'

'It doesn't matter,' Gabriel said, glaring at Adam. 'They will be no match for us now that we know they are coming.'

'I want to know, Gabriel.' I turned to Adam and asked again, 'How many?'

'Most likely about twenty as they know there are two Siis here,' he told me, ignoring the sharp look from Gabriel. 'I have never known them have more than forty in a single attack.'

Forty? My mind reeled with the image of forty Fae crowded around the three of us with murder in their eyes. I tried to find the strength to ask how it could be possible for us to live through an attack of that magnitude.

'Try not to worry,' Gabriel said. 'We will have Eris on our side.'

Even knowing the power Eris had over the Fae, my heart became heavier. All it would take is for one of them to creep up behind her for a surprise attack and she would be gone. The potential death toll had just risen. My blood turned to ice and dropped from my face.

'She's going into shock.'

Gabriel's words penetrated my haze. I wanted to tell him I was okay, but couldn't. I became fixated on the image of the Fae stood over Eris' slender body, Gabriel laid broken on the floor and even Adam, his eyes lifeless in death.

'I'm so sorry,' I whimpered.

Gabriel supported me to the sofa and sat me down. 'Don't fret. It's only a bit of shock, you will be fine soon.' He stroked along the worry lines on my face and spoke to Adam. 'Get a duvet from upstairs to warm her.'

I pushed myself up and gripped his hand. 'No, you don't understand. This is all my fault.'

He forced me back down and pulled the blanket back up to cover my revealed breasts. 'Do not be silly sweetheart. How could this possibly be your fault?'

'If I hadn't gone to the park that day, if I hadn't stared at the Fae long enough for them to notice me, none of this would have happened.' My voice increased in volume as I spoke. 'Don't you get it, because of me Lexi died, and now you may die. First there was the junkie, then the car accident and now the Fae. Maybe Nathan was meant to kill me years ago and now fate is coming for its revenge.'

'Shut up!' Adam's roar stunned me from my self-pity. Throwing the duvet down, he crouched before me, his tone lower, yet still stern, 'So what if you were meant to die. What if it is your fault the Fae are here? The fact is you are here now, alive. You have a choice. Do you want to play the martyr and lie here waiting for fate to catch you up, or do you want to fight for your life and all that you hold dear? Because I have news for you, Ana. Fate is a made up story to make people feel better when bad things happen, nothing is absolute. We all have our free will and have to live with the consequences of our choices, be they bad or good. So what will it be?' He stood up. 'Do you want to wallow in self-pity or do you want to get angry and take revenge for what has been done to you?'

Stunned, I could only stare at him. After a minute in which both men watched me, I found my voice.

'Thank you. I needed that.'

Adam shrugged before walking off. Gabriel touched my chin and looked into my eyes. 'Are you all right?'

'Yes.' I smiled weakly and stood up. 'I could do with getting dressed though.'

He handed me my discarded clothes and I pulled on my jeans, hoping Adam would stay out of the room until I finished, not that he hadn't already seen everything.

'He would make a great motivational speaker.' My voice was muffled as I pulled my jumper over my head. 'He packs one hell of a mental slap.'

Gabriel chuckled, and helped me as I got stuck with my head in the jumper and my elbow wedged, pointing upwards. 'He has been known to get many a person moving, it's one of his skills and what made him a great soldier in his day.'

'One other thing.' I gripped his hand to stop him heading towards the kitchen. 'How the hell are you dressed when I was stood there naked?'

He laughed as he pulled me into his arms. 'Because it took so long to wake you up.' He kissed my nose, before taking my hand to lead me out of the lounge.

I grimaced as I sipped the sweet tea Adam had made. The night shadows pressed against the window as if they were a living entity, determined to force their way into the house. I huddled into the chair, trying to suppress the shivers that threatened to shake me to bits.

'What now?' I asked relishing the warmth, if not the taste of the tea as it spread through me.

'Now we need to contact Eris,' Adam told me.

'But it took her ages to pick up her last messages. How do you know she will get it in time?'

'We have other means of contacting her.'

'How?' Why was Adam the only one with a mobile phone? Life would be so much easier if they just joined the technological age.

The two men stared at each other having some sort of silent conversation and I shifted impatiently. Adam's face was stiff, while Gabriel's eyes pleaded with him.

'Do you really think that now is the time for secrets?' I demanded.

'No, it is not.' Gabriel turned his back on Adam's glare. 'There is a way I can contact her immediately.'

'Why don't you always contact her that way then?'

'Because it's dangerous for us,' he said, causing my stomach to clench. 'I will have to revert to natural form and reach out to touch her.'

'I don't understand. Why is that dangerous?'

'Ana, we don't only stay in human form to blend in with you. We also do it to stay hidden.'

'From what?'

'The Fae, others of our kind who will do harm. There are other threats out there worse than the Fae that I have not told you about.'

'What?' How could there be anything worse than the Fae who were the epitome of evil? Did it have anything to do with the war Adam had mentioned, the one Gabriel assured me wasn't anything to worry about?

'It doesn't matter now. They are of no concern to us for the moment, the Fae are.'

Swallowing my worry, I drew us back on topic. 'How is it dangerous?'

'When we send the message, we shine bright, spreading our distress call out. Everyone from our race will hear it and be able to follow it.'

'But it will draw them here.' My stomach flipped over, and I had to swallow back the nausea. Unable to picture anything worse than the Fae, my mind conjured up the image of hundreds of them, all snarling as they came for us.

'I won't do it from here,' Gabriel said.

'What about you? Will they find you?'

'That is a risk, however, I will be quick and hopefully gone before anyone tracks me.'

'What if there is someone close?' He needed a shake to force some worry into him.

'I will check the area to ensure it is clear. It is a very small risk.' He squeezed my hand. 'I will be fine.'

'I will accompany you,' Adam piped up to my relief.

'No,' Gabriel told him. 'I need you to watch Ana.'

'No!' My response was more forceful than intended. Lowering my tone, I explained my reaction. 'I will not let you go by yourself. You could be hurt, or worse.'

'I am not leaving you here alone. We will be gone for the whole day and although it is unlikely, the Fae could return in that time.'

Determined not to let him get his way, I challenged him with my stare. 'I don't plan to be here alone. I will go to Maria's. The Fae won't know to look for me there.'

'It makes sense,' Adam told him.

'Are you willing to risk Ana's life in the hands of a witch?'

Adam nodded.

'Well I'm not!'

'You don't have a choice,' I told him calmly. 'This is the right thing to do and you know it.' My lips brushed the knuckles of his clenched hand. 'This isn't just about us. It's also about the children who will have their lives stolen if we allow the Fae to win.'

The image of the Fae changing my nieces came to mind and I shuddered. My main concern at the moment was Gabriel. He couldn't be allowed to go alone. His pained expression told me I was winning the debate.

'Anyway.' I smiled. 'It's not like Maria is just any old human, as you know she can do things I can't.'

Guilt flared at the thought of dragging her into our mess, but I squashed it flat. Like I had told him, it wasn't just about us anymore. She would probably kill me if I left her out of it anyway.

'It is settled,' Adam said much to Gabriel's annoyance. 'We will leave at first light.'

22

Gabriel joined me in the bedroom as I grabbed some clean clothes for Maria's. We held each other, not speaking for the air hung heavy with worry for each other's safety. Neither of us wanted to voice our greatest fear, that this was goodbye.

'I promise I will come back to you,' he finally said into my hair. The doubt hung heavy in his tone.

'I know you will,' I replied, pushing his worry to the back of my mind.

We stood kissing and stroking each other until Adam called for us. 'It is time,' he said, the tension for the upcoming mission evident in his voice.

As Adam drove us to Maria's, Gabriel and I sat silently in the back, loath to let go of each other for even a moment. The sun was rising, the reaching light creating a misty red hue to the clouds. They brought to mind the image of blood as if it were an omen of things to come.

'I'll be back tomorrow evening at the latest,' he said as I clung to him in the doorway of Maria's flat. His distress at leaving me was obvious, but buried beneath it was a distinct air of excitement.

'Are you looking forward to this?' I asked.

He pressed his lips together before giving me a small smile. 'You have to understand, it has been a very long time since I've had the opportunity to take natural form. It is something that our race has avoided for thousands of years.' He sighed. 'There was a time that the Siis took human form as a choice, now it is a necessity. I have done this only once since developing my abilities as a child.' He smiled broadly once again.

'Have fun then,' I said in a strained voice, wishing his excitement could diminish some of my anxiety.

After one last kiss, he released me and walked away, leaving me to pray that God would bring him back to me safe, the feeling of loss already laying heavy on my heart.

'I'll make us some tea,' Maria said, her voice pulling me out of my desolation. She placed her arms around my shoulders and led me into the flat.

'Not one of your herbal ones,' I told her, following her into her shoebox of a kitchen. However awful I felt, I wanted to keep a clear head.

She sighed and skipped to the cupboard. 'Fine, regular tea for you then.'

'I'm sorry I dragged you into this Maria.' The guilt became a stone in my throat, causing heat to rise in my face.

'Don't be silly, that's what friends are for,' she said over her shoulder. 'To be honest I wouldn't mind a crack at the Fae myself.'

I inhaled sharply at the thought of my petite, kind friend coming up against the fury of the Fae. Seeing my look of horror, she laughed.

'Come on, Ana, we will be fine, you'll see.'

I took the mug off her. The heat from the tea warmed my hands and they tingled sharply with the sudden change in temperature. 'It's not us I'm worried about.'

She studied me for the first time. 'Do you need to cry? It's okay if you do, better to let it out.'

I smiled weakly. If only it was that easy. Every cell in me was wound up tightly, the tears ducts firmly sealed closed, denying me the release that tears would bring. Would Gabriel survive? Would it work? Would Eris come? Could we really win against the Fae if there were so many? All the questions bounded around my head, without any answers to pacify them.

The hours dragged slowly and my nails bit further into the palm of my hand. Maria gave up trying to talk me out of my unhappiness and instead, turned the CD player on. The squeal of an electric guitar and dull thud of a drum filled the room. It invaded my brain and my temples stung in response, yet it brought to mind the sweet melody of the piano from the night before. The time we had spent in each other's arms was the closest I had ever come to experiencing real bliss. I thought I might cry, but the tears wouldn't fall, as if to cry would be to admit defeat, to acknowledge that he wouldn't be coming back to me. That wasn't an option.

Maria had just given up trying to force lunch into me when the sensation spread through the room. I ran to the window and searched for some visual sign of the message Gabriel had sent out. There was nothing but it hummed inside of me, as if I were a radio picking up a transmission. It was like a sunrise over the ocean on a clear summer's morning and my spirit soared high. Gabriel's voice came through clearly, yet there were no words. It was his essence I heard. Everything he was and had been flowed through me.

So this was how they communicated in their natural form. The music painted a thousand words. Love, friendship, hope, anger, fear and so much more, the emotions ordered to tell the story of what had happened. The message came through clear and the pull towards him became stronger. My feet moved forward with a will of their own before it suddenly stopped and the strong feeling of Gabriel disappeared.

'Did you hear it Maria?'

She shimmered in my vision. I was finally crying, not from sorrow or fear, but from simple pure joy.

'It was so beautiful.'

I blinked away the tears only to see Maria gagging. 'I don't know what you heard, but that was one of the most unpleasant experiences I have ever had.' She started rubbing herself down as if brushing off an army of tiny ants, with her lips pulled back revealing her gums.

'What do you mean? Did you not hear the music?'

'No I didn't.' She swilled her mouth out with her drink before spitting it back into the glass. 'All I felt was my skin crawling and when I tried to focus on where the feeling was coming from, the most God damn awful taste filled my mouth, as if I had just eaten rotten flesh. Yuck.' She spat into the glass again. 'I'm going to brush my teeth. That was disgusting.'

Dumfounded, my eyes followed her as she left the room. Gabriel was now in more danger that he had previously been, yet the light, happy feeling persisted. How could the human language bring him satisfaction when their own way of communication caused the mind to spring open, as if filled with a cleansing breeze?

When Maria returned I tried to put into words the sensation that had reached me, but there were none that could convey the true extent of my experience. Eventually I gave up in frustration. 'I wonder why you didn't feel what I did.'

She shrugged. 'Don't know. Maybe it's got something to do with the energy in you. You are lit up like a star right now.'

'Oops!' The feeling of joy had caused my concentration to slip. I focused and drew my Shi back in, smiling at her once it was done.

'There is a lot more now isn't there?' She spoke gently, though her eyes narrowed with concern. I shrugged and dropped onto the sofa. 'Have you thought about what it could be doing to you?' she persisted.

'I'm fine.' My smile was a bit too wide. Although aware I'd become brighter, I hadn't realised the full extent of how much there was. I was obviously absorbing more of Gabriel's Shi as time went on.

'Really? Are you sure about that?'

'What do you want me to say? That I'm concerned? Of course I am. I would be stupid not to be, but there is nothing I can do about it now. I couldn't leave him if I tried.' I stared at her, daring her to suggest it.

'I know that, I never said you should, but what if it gets worse? Do you even know what you are becoming?'

Her words echoed my own buried thoughts, making them impossible to deny any longer. 'Eris assures me that I am not changing but...'

'But what?'

'I don't know. Sometimes I feel like she isn't telling me the whole story. It's not what she says, more what she doesn't.' Blood rushed to my face as I accused my new friend of lying. 'I'm sure I'm just being paranoid but...I don't know, maybe I'm just spending too much time around non-humans, they can keep things close to their chest at times and it's making me suspicious.'

She bit her lip thoughtfully. 'Why do you think she would hide something about what's happening from you?'

'I don't. Just ignore me, you know what I'm like, I can sometimes see shadows where there are none.' The joy I had experienced started to fade and the anxiety crept back in. 'I hope they're all right.'

'Of course they will be,' she said. 'I bet Adam can take care of more than a few Fae.'

I decided against telling her that there were worse things out there than the Fae. Life was already terrifying enough.

As the evening progressed into night, I became more and more anxious. By calculating how long it had taken them to get there, they should have already returned, and as each hour passed I became more convinced that something had gone wrong. Maria was in the process of threatening to drug me if I didn't stop pacing, when I sensed him.

I ran to the door, only to be halted by Maria's grip on my arm. 'Wait,' she said. 'It could be someone else.'

'It's not.' I shook her off and hurriedly fiddled with the locks on the door, unwilling to spend the time explaining. It would be impossible for someone to mask themselves as him for I knew his presence too well.

'Oh yeah, your spidey senses.'

I threw the door open to find Gabriel stood before me. Without pause, I launched into his arms, knocking him back a few steps with the force.

'Thank God, you're safe. I was so sure that something had happened.' I kissed him between words, making it impossible for him to reply. I didn't care. It was such a relief to have him stood before me.

Much to my disappointment, he eventually pulled away, chuckling wearily. 'I'm fine. You worry too much.'

'Where's Adam?' The hallway was empty but for us.

'Doing a sweep to check nothing followed.' Seeing my frown, he reassured me, 'Don't worry, it is just precautionary.' He peered through the open doorway. 'Hey Maria.' He gave her a smile in greeting, though his eyes were drawn, and his face pinched, making him look ill. How much energy was required to send a message in their natural form?

'Thank God you got back when you did,' she told him. 'My carpet has had just about enough of Ana's pacing. I thought she was going to wear a hole in it.'

Gabriel chuckled. 'Lucky for you we had a free run then.'

'There was no sign of anything?' I watched him for indications of a lie.

'No, we were lucky. We were long gone before anything got there.' Only tiredness shadowed his eyes, showing no signs of deception.

Adam appeared at the door, also supporting dark smudges under his eyes. After nodding to Maria, he spoke directly to Gabriel. 'We should go. Hopefully Eris will be on her way.'

I hugged Maria goodbye and thanked her for putting up with my stress levels, before following the men out. Once in the car, I cuddled into Gabriel's arms and let the quiet hum of the engine soothe the last of the tension out of my muscles.

'Ana, we're home.' My eyes flickered several times. I must have fallen asleep. I stumbled out of the car and allowed Gabriel to support me as exhaustion dragged at me, making it nearly impossible to open my eyes. Climbing the stairs was an awkward process as my legs had turned to lead, and I barely had time to shed my clothes onto the floor before falling into bed.

'Please stay,' I mumbled as Gabriel went to leave.

He lay down beside me and pulled me close, brushing his lips across my ear. 'Sleep now sweetheart, it has been a long day.'

'Mmm.' His breath sent delicious shivers down my spine. 'So beautiful.'

'What is?'

Sleep demanded my attention and it took every ounce of strength to fight it. 'Your song...' Weariness finally won the battle. As I sank into oblivion I thought he said something more, but I could have been mistaken.

23

Sharp pain shot across my head, cause me to groan as I rolled over in bed. I must have drunk fifty million cups of tea at Maria's and I reached for the bottle of water on the bedside table.

Only a little light came through the windows, indicating it was nearly lunch time, but Gabriel's side of the bed was smooth as if he hadn't slept there. It took me a moment of studying the digits on the clock before determining that I'd been asleep for nearly six hours. Why hadn't he joined me?

I trudged down the stairs and became aware of the two figures in the lounge 'Eris!' I exclaimed, running the rest of the way.

'Hello, Ana.' She smiled broadly. 'I have to say you look awful.'

I ignored her remark and sat down next to her. 'You got here so quickly.'

'I flew here as soon as I got the message.'

'What? As a bird?'

Eris and Gabriel chuckled at the wondrous look on my face.

'No,' she laughed. 'Although that would be possible, it would have taken me days to get here if I had.'

'Where did you come from?' I said, trying to ignore the redness that reached all the way to my hair line.

'Africa. I was lucky to get a flight leaving straight away.' Leaning towards me, she shook her head and spoke in a stern tone, 'Have you noticed that there is always trouble around you?'

Gabriel threw her a withering look and I laughed, my earlier guilt buried. 'You know me, I'm just a magnet for it.' Gabriel glanced at me with relief, before leaving for the kitchen, hopefully to make me coffee as my body cried for the kick start. 'What's the plan then?' I asked Eris.

'When the time comes, we fight.'

I stared at her incredulously. 'What? No plan of action to outwit them? That doesn't sound very organised.'

'What would you like us to plan? We don't know when they are coming or how many there will be. All we can do is ensure that we are not caught off guard.'

'What can I do to help?'

Gabriel handed me my coffee. 'You won't be here. I have had word that Suraya will be back tomorrow, and I am sending you both off until this is resolved.'

'Suraya? As in your daughter Suraya?' How could he want to send me off alone with that conniving woman?

'Yes. Don't start now. We need to stay to deal with the Fae when they come. Do you really want to be here when that happens?'

I frowned and shook my head. 'Can't we all just leave until it's over?'

'They won't give up,' Eris told me. 'Especially if they are aware we killed some of their own, they can be quite vengeful at times.' To my amazement, she grinned.

They were right, but it still felt as if I was being thrown out of the frying pan into the fire. 'What if they find us?' I whined.

Gabriel knelt down in front of me. 'Do you really think I would send off the two women who mean everything to me, if I thought the Fae would come looking anywhere other than here?'

'No,' I mumbled begrudgingly. I could always count on his protection. Unfortunately I could also rely on him being blind to his daughter's potential for harm.

'Good.' He bent forward to kiss my nose before standing up. 'I'm going to check with Adam. He is circling the perimeter so that we can get as much warning as possible if they come. Eris will be with you, so there is no need to worry.'

'Be careful,' I said even though he was already out of ear shot. I hugged the mug to my chest, feeling glum and nostalgic for the times before the Fae had come into our lives.

'So you don't like Suraya?' Eris' words interrupted my melancholy.

'What makes you say that?' As much as I had thought about talking to Eris about Suraya, I suddenly felt as if I would be going behind Gabriel's back.

She laughed. 'It may be impossible to read your emotions, but your body language is obvious.'

My eyes flickered to the door and I sighed. 'I can't help it. I have tried for Gabriel's sake, but she's impossible.'

'She's being difficult?'

'That's an understatement.' I bent towards her and lowered my voice. 'She has declared all-out war on me.'

Eris studied me with interest as I explained about broken dishes, doors that were locked even when I turned the key and how she had spat at me.

'...and she is deliberately making me depressed,' I finished.

Eris abruptly stiffened and gave me a sharp look. 'She wouldn't manipulate your emotions,' she said after a heavy pause.

'She is,' I told her curtly.

Eris held up her hands in mock defence. 'Look, I know Suraya can be closed off at times, but I'm confident that she would never do anything to you. She has been spoilt a bit, and that's my fault as much as it is Gabriel's. She didn't have a mother and Gabriel and I both carried our own guilt for that, so I suppose in a way, we tried to compensate for it by giving her more freedom than most.'

If only she understood. Suraya wasn't just spoilt, she was mean.

I wanted to pursue the matter with her, but sensed Gabriel approaching. Maria was right, he would be the best person to speak to anyway.

'Will you help me pack my things?' I asked him when he came in.

'Of course.' He pulled on my extended hand to help me up.

Eris frowned at me and I ignored it. The chances were that Gabriel would be of the same opinion that she was, but I needed to try. I followed him up the stairs, trying to ignore Eris' stare boring into my back.

'You shouldn't need much,' Gabriel said as he pulled the suitcase from under the bed. 'Hopefully it will be over in a few days and then life can return to normal.'

I stood, twisting my hands together as he pulled my clothes from the wardrobe.

'We will be fine.' he said as he folded up a blue jumper and put it in the case.

'It's not that,' I said nervously.

He finally got the depth of my distress and quickly took me in his arms.

'What is it?' He took my chin in his fingers and lifted my face so as to look into my eyes. My courage dwindled under his tender smile. 'Ana, talk to me.'

'It's Suraya,' I said.

His eyes narrowed and lips tightened as he pulled away.

He started throwing the clothes into my suitcase. 'I am not having this discussion now. I know you have not exactly taken to Suraya, however, this is not the time to discuss those issues.'

'I don't want to go with her Gabriel. She keeps doing things to me, and she is manipulating me, making me depressed.'

He twisted the jeans in his hands and turned to me. Never had such a cold look filled his eyes while looking at me.

'That is enough.' He spoke stiltedly and without warmth. 'I will not have you speak such slander about her.'

'It's not slander if it's true,' I said weakly.

He threw the jeans down onto the bed and stalked towards me, causing me to stumble back into the wall. Only then did he stop before me. He didn't raise his hand, or threaten me verbally, yet for the first time ever, I was truly afraid of him.

My eyes so wide they threatened to pop right out of my head, I stared at him with my chin trembling.

His hands remained clenched at his side as he glared at me. 'Are you saying that my daughter is no better than the Fae?'

My mouth stayed locked closed.

'Well?'

A deep, shuddering breath rattled through my chest. 'I'm just saying what she has been doing to get me away from you.' It came out as a pathetic, hurt whisper, not the determined confidence I'd been aiming for.

His hand shifted and I threw my arms across my face. Nothing happened, yet my heart still beat wildly against my chest and in my ears as I cringed against the wall. His hands circled my wrists and I shuddered, before realising that the touch was soft, not the aggressive pull I had expected.

'Ana,' he said lowering my hands. 'I will never hit you.'

I stayed silent, unable to stop the trembling of my chin, so violent my teeth knocked together. I started crying. Gabriel led me to the bed and sat down next to me. My eyes focused on my lap as he took my hand in his.

'I apologise for causing you to fear me,' he said, 'that was never my intention. However, you have to understand what you have accused Suraya of. Using our ability to harm someone in such a way is something that we would not do. Such actions are against one of our highest laws, one I *know* she would not break.'

Even though my fear gradually evaporated, I stayed silent.

'I know you have been extremely low recently, however, do you not think it is more likely due to everything that has happened? That your paranoia is causing you to blame Suraya?'

'You think I'm imagining it?'

'I believe that your illness is convincing you of things that are not real.'

I sharply pulled my hands from his. 'Did it make me imagine her spitting in my face?'

'She *spat* at you?'

'Yes.'

His lips pressed together as he closed his eyes and rubbed his hand across his face. 'That is unacceptable,' he said eventually, 'and I will speak to her about it. However, she is not the one making your depression worse. You need to believe that. I know my daughter and I can promise you, she would never harm you in any way.'

How well knew his daughter was up for debate, but even if there was physical evidence to prove it, my protests would fall on deaf ears.

'Can't I go to Maria's instead?'

Gabriel sighed loudly. His hands didn't clench but they twitched as if he had only just stopped himself in time.

'I don't want to argue with you today. Suraya can protect you if the need should arise. Which I'm sure it will not, however, just in case, I want you with her.'

I looked down and bit my lip.

'Do you trust me?' he said.

I nodded, though when it came to Suraya I wasn't so sure.

'Then trust me with this,' he said moving to kneel in front of me. 'Please.'

He was giving me no choice. If I trusted him, I had to trust her.

'Okay,' I said against my better judgement. 'I'll go with her.'

'Do you promise you will be careful?'

Eris rolled her eyes at my worried question. I had finished packing up the few things that I would need if we were away for a while, Gabriel was off talking tactics with Adam, and Eris had been left to baby sit me as my anxiety levels rose.

'Ana, this is what I do remember.' She paused to beam at me before continuing. 'To be honest I have to thank you. I'm really looking forward to it, the more the better.' A hard glint came into her eyes and she gave me a deadly smile.

'I know. I can't help but worry about you all.' I sighed and dropped to the sofa. 'Maybe I should stay in case I can do anything to help.'

'You would just be a liability.' She joined me, settling at the edge, so that her body turned to face mine. 'Anyway do you really want to be here?'

There had been many occasions since the night of the Fae that I'd fantasised about being able to confront them. The problem was that the reality would most likely turn out very different to my imagined scenario.

'Of course not,' I told her. 'I just feel guilty about leaving you all with my mess.'

'Self-pity isn't going to change the situation,' she said sternly. 'This may well have happened anyway, even without you capturing their attention. The Fae have been a problem for us for many years now, one that I hope to eradicate in time.'

As we sat in silence, I thought about the upcoming battle that they would all have to face. 'Can I ask you something?'

She laughed. 'You can, but I don't promise to answer.'

'Why do you do it? What makes you chase down the Fae?'

'Like I said, they are a problem and I take pleasure in wiping them from existence.' The coldness of her voice left no doubt of the dark satisfaction she took from killing them.

'I get that, what I don't understand is why. You don't just kill what you come across. It's almost as if you are looking for something in particular, like something is fuelling your passion to find them.'

She sighed loudly as she relaxed back into her seat. 'You are quite perceptive on occasion. I wonder if Gabriel really understands how much you really see.'

Unlikely, though it was difficult to tell at times.

'So I'm right then?'

'Yes.'

I waited for her expand, but she sat silently.

'Well?' I prompted.

Eris sighed. 'There are things happening that are so much bigger than the Fae, and Gabriel will be annoyed if I tell you.'

'Maybe Gabriel should stop deciding things for me. Maybe if he had told me about the Fae to start with, I could have been better prepared when I saw them.'

'That's not fair on him,' she chided. 'He only wants to protect you and prevent you living in fear.'

'I know.' My eyes dropped to my hands. 'It's too late now though, I am already as afraid as I'm going to be. At least if I know everything I can be better equipped to deal with it as it comes up.'

'That's true,' she sighed to my surprise. I'd expected more of a fight. 'But how about we focus on one problem at a time?'

'Will you tell me after this is over?'

'If and when it's needed,' she said. Even though she hadn't exactly promised, there was no point pursuing right now. She was right, there were other things that needed our attention at the moment.

'Where will I be going with Suraya?' The thought of spending time alone with the devil woman played heavily on me.

'Gabriel will organise it with her. Don't worry, it will be somewhere safe.'

'From the Fae.'

'Let it go, Ana. Why don't you get your bag down and put it in the car. Suraya will be here soon.'

Maybe they were all right and I was just over reacting. Somehow it didn't seem likely.

213

My teeth clamped together as Suraya sauntered through the door. If only Eris had accompanied me to the kitchen as I wasn't eager to start my time alone with Suraya just yet.

'Can we talk please?' Her voice startled me as it wasn't full of the spitefulness normally directed towards me.

'What?' My eyes narrowed with caution. What torrent of grief was she going to send my way now?

'I just want to say I'm sorry for everything I have put you through lately. I know I have been hard.'

My eyes narrowed further. There were signs of remorse on her face but she had a knack of convincing people of her innocence.

'There is no one here to hear it,' I told her icily. 'You should save that line for when Eris comes downstairs, maybe she will buy it.'

'Please, Ana.' She reached her hand towards me and I flinched. 'I really do want to make amends with you.'

'Why?'

'Because I love my father.' She sounded genuine, but her love for Gabriel had never been up for debate, only the morality of her actions towards me. 'Because it hurts him that we don't get along,' she continued.

Damn, Gabriel must have spoken to her.

'Sorry, Suraya. I don't buy it. Why don't you just tell me what you are up to and we can carry on with the charade in front of your father?'

'I know you have no reason to believe me,' she said with wide doleful eyes. 'I would expect nothing else after the way I have treated you. But I do really mean it when I say I want us to rectify our differences.'

A single tear started its way down her cheek and my resolve began to weaken. Was it possible that Gabriel was right? That my own paranoia was at fault, fuelled by her actions towards me? It didn't seem likely, but Gabriel and Eris were so sure that she would never do such a thing. For the first time in years, I began to question my own instincts.

My back pressed painfully into the wall as the tear reached her jaw line and dripped on the floor. When another one welled up to take its place, I sighed loudly, if not a little hesitantly, praying to God that she wasn't just playing me.

'A fresh start?' I said, holding out my hand.

She smiled as she shook it. 'Definitely.'

The atmosphere in the kitchen was heavy with tension and excitement, the intensity of it making me feel jittery.

'Your instructions to the safe house,' Gabriel said as he handed me a scrap of paper.

Unable to speak in case I should cry, I nodded. I was never any good at goodbyes and this one was harder than ever before. Determined not to let him sense my feelings, I swallowed them down while smiling weakly at him. I stepped back to allow Suraya the chance to hug her father farewell.

All the excitement came from Eris, she practically buzzed with it.

'You have Adam's number in case you can't reach Gabriel on the house phone?' she said. When I nodded, she continued. 'Hopefully they will attack sooner rather than later.'

'You don't have to sound so pleased with it.'

She grinned and stuck out her tongue. 'Don't spoil my fun,' she said with a laugh. I couldn't help but smile, if not a little weakly.

'To think, I had begun to wonder how I was ever afraid of you. You are scarily relaxed Eris, it's disconcerting.'

'*Me?*' she exclaimed. 'I just know how to have a good time.'

I laughed faintly. Adam stood stiffly without expression. 'Good luck,' I told him. He responded with a curt nod and stalked off. Some things just never changed.

Gabriel gave me one last lingering kiss goodbye. It took every ounce of strength to let him go. I hesitated several times as I trudged down the path, sure that my body would refuse to let me leave. I only continued as Gabriel would never allow me to stay.

Suraya asked me if she could drive. My first instinct was to refuse, but Gabriel gazed at us from the doorway, so I bit back my words and nodded in agreement before reluctantly getting into the passenger side.

Although I still felt her anxiety, all outward signs of her distress disappeared as she started telling me the things we would do while away. I tuned out her excessive chattering, which were probably was due to nerves, and prayed to God, promising him anything, if only he would allow the three people left behind to survive.

After a couple of hours on the road Suraya finally stopped talking. Taking in my surroundings, I checked the instructions Gabriel had given me before saying anything.

'Umm, Suraya, I think we may have gone the wrong way. Shouldn't we be on the motorway by now?'

'I know a quicker route,' she said with a smile.

Unsure to how country roads could be quicker than the motorway, I settled back uneasily in my seat. There were no houses in sight. If something went wrong we were probably miles from help. I checked the phone and groaned upon seeing no signal.

'I would feel more comfortable if we followed the route your father gave us.' I smiled nervously in response to the change in atmosphere building in the car. Ignoring me, she stared at the road as she drove. Her face was set like rock, yet her eyes held the same look I had seen so many times before. 'Suraya, what's going on?'

'I am protecting my father.' Her cold tone sent a sliver of ice along my spine.

'How?'

'By handing you over to the Fae.'

Bile rose in my throat as my stomach clenched. Individual rays of light pierced through the leaves of the thick, moss covered trees, filling the car with dazzling light, highlighting the maliciousness in her eyes. The road was now little more than a track, the half-buried rocks causing the car to shudder as we travelled along it, indicating it wasn't well used.

Her apologetic words had fooled me, her false tears touching on my love for her father and the desire to make him happy. Even so, my blind faith had been stupid. The mobile phone still had no signal. I was all alone, with no way to get help. I was screwed.

Suraya slowed the car as it groaned against the unevenness of the track. If I was going to do something, it had to be now. I quickly released the clasp of the seat belt and grabbed for the door handle, desperate to be out of the moving vehicle, frantic to be anywhere that she wasn't. A cry of frustration escaped me when it wouldn't move.

'You're not going anywhere,' she said stonily. 'I fully intend to fulfil my end of the deal.'

The hatred that vibrated through me overshadowed any fear I had. Grabbing the steering wheel, I yanked it towards me. The suddenness of my actions caused her grip to slip. She pulled my hand off, but it was too late and the car headed straight for the thick trunk of a tree with no curb to stop us. The tyres squealed as she hit the brakes and the car went into a skid. With no time to control it, we braced for impact.

Smoke rose from the tyres, invading the car. The scent of burning rubber stung my nose and caused my eyes to water. My seatbelt was off and I tried to move my legs up onto the dashboard. They moved too slowly.

The car impacted and the engine buckled, throwing me forwards. My head hit the windscreen and the glass shattered. Greyness crept over my vision. I needed to fight it, but it couldn't be beaten and I cried out with anger as it pulled me away.

24

Garbled shouts broke through my haze. Something was wrong. A hazy red film covered everything making it impossible to see properly. I shifted to rub my eyes and sharp pain exploded in my head. My hands came away red, covered in blood. Everything flooded back to me, but too late. Suraya grabbed me from behind. The roots of my hair screamed in protest as she dragged me from the car.

'You stupid whore! Now I'll have to fix the car.'

She threw me face down onto the dirt road. I coughed from the dry, dusty mud I accidently inhaled and sat up. My head span and I tried to focus while taking deep even breaths.

As soon as the world stopped turning, I sprung unsteadily to my feet and ran into the trees. I only managed to travel a few metres before Suraya grabbed me from behind. Wishing I had cut my hair short, I spun, ignoring the pain as the roots ripped from my head.

Her eyes widened in surprise as she stood with my hair hanging limply in her hand. My foot hit her full force in the stomach. Silently thanking Adam for his ruthless teachings I ran, the air wheezing from my lungs. I made it further this time before the weight of her body hit me, forcing us both to the ground.

A blow from her fist caused my ears to ring, drowning out the words she screamed at me. When she lifted her weight off me, I sprang up ready to fight, hoping that my training would give me the added advantage needed against her, thanking the adrenalin that coursed through me.

I managed a couple of blows to her face, but she was so much faster than me and moments later she knocked me to the ground again. My fighting skills may well be good enough to help me against a human, or maybe even a single Fae or two, but Suraya had the speed of the Siis to her advantage. She lifted me and threw me against the nearest tree.

'This would have been easier if you hadn't stolen my father's Shi,' she seethed, wiping the blood from her split eyebrow and lip.

'How could you do this to him?' I forced the words between shuddering breaths as I glared at her. My lips curled in hate as I fought uselessly in her grip.

'I am doing this for him!' she screeched, the high pitch vibrating around my injured head. 'You bewitched him and brought the Fae down on him, and you are stealing his life force from him.' Her chest heaved as she stood looking at me with a hate similar to the Fae.

God, I wanted to wipe that look off her face. 'You crazy bitch!'

Dry, dead leaves covered the ground. Could I unbalance her? But then what?

'What the hell do you hope to achieve by this?' I continued in the hope of keeping her occupied long enough to formulate a plan.

'I have made a deal to save my father, you for him.'

She released me with one hand and reached behind her. If she was going for a knife I would be royally screwed, if I wasn't already.

She smiled. 'The Fae will be here to collect you soon.'

Before she could do anything else, fear broke my paralysis. Using the tree for support, I thrust my legs out, snaked one foot around her ankle and kicked with everything I had at her knee. As she dropped screaming, I pushed away from the tree and kicked her full force in her side, while silently thanking God that although the Siis could deflect weapons easily, they still experienced the pain of any blow or wound from someone who has Siis energy within.

There was no time to pause. She rolled over from the force of the kick and I gripped her arms, yanking them behind her. Her whimpers only fuelled my rage, giving me the strength to pull her up. I shuffled back and pressed against the tree, grimacing as her feet repeatedly found my legs.

She started laughing, a high pitched hollow sound that reminded me of the haunted house rides from my childhood. 'You can't beat me, Ana.'

She gripped my wrist hard, digging her nails into my flesh. I cried out, unable to keep my hold on her. Once free, she turned to me once more.

It wasn't a blade she had been reaching for, but handcuffs, about two inches thick and dark grey, with a thick bar joining them. My brain worked furiously as she forced one of the cuffs onto my left wrist. The hollow click as they closed sounded so final that I very nearly gave up. I didn't though. Instead the cartoon my nieces continually watched popped into my head. It was a strange thing to think of when in so much danger, though it gave me an idea.

I looked up over her shoulder and forced a surprised, grateful look onto my face. 'Gabriel?' I said.

Suraya's eyes widened and she looked back. For a second I remained motionless, stunned by her stupidity. I quickly recovered and yanked the other cuff from her hand. If it was made from a normal metal she would be free in seconds, but I had a suspicion that it was Daku, the one that the Siis had no control over unless they were a priestess. Thank God she wasn't that.

As soon as it closed around her wrist, she screamed with rage and hit me once more over the head. I grunted as pains shot down my spine and my vision swam out of focus. Her rage showed I was right about the Daku, but where was the diminished strength Gabriel had spoken of?

'You stupid bitch!' she screamed, spraying spittle all over my face. She went to hit me again, and this time I managed to block her approaching fist. My free hand was restricted by hers, making it impossible to hit her back. I grunted in annoyance for my lack of movement, before consoling myself with the fact that she also had the same problem.

She pulled on my bound wrist and held up a small square of metal, maybe some sort of key. I twisted her hand, hissing with pain as I turned my own wrist in a painful angle to execute the move.

She dropped the metal square and I scooped it up before she had a chance to move. A heavy blow landed on the back of my neck, causing a painful springy sensation to travel up to my head, threatening to buckle my legs beneath me. I gripped the small piece of metal, able to feel the groves on the surface.

'There is nowhere to run,' Suraya sneered. She looked off into the distance and a smile found her lips. 'They are not far from here.'

My insides froze. There was no sense of the Fae as of yet, but her relaxed, spiteful smile left me with no doubt that she spoke the truth.

'Can you fix the car?' I asked.

'If you release me.'

My heart sank. She would flee as soon as she was free, leaving me to be killed by the Fae. I could run, but where to? We were in the middle of nowhere and I would soon be caught.

'Run,' I said anyway. I pulled on her, but she resisted with the relaxed grin still plastered on her face, obviously confident that the Fae would give her free passage.

Her calm attitude told me all I needed to know. She definitely wasn't going to help me and by being cuffed together she was only a hindrance. A knot formed in my throat. There was very little time until the sun was completely gone, leaving me in darkness. I was taking too long.

Turning my back to her, I studied the small metal square in my hand. Raised markings decorated one side. Both bands of Daku contained a slight indent for the key to slip onto. It would be possible to unlock myself while leaving Suraya stuck with the cuff on.

Suraya struggled as I pressed the card against the cuff, causing it to nearly slip from my fingers. I sighed with relief as it clicked open and quickly slipped it off.

I kicked her forcefully before taking off with the key still gripped in my hand. She couldn't be allowed to escape and regain her Siis powers. There was already enough to deal with.

I ran while thanking God that I was less clumsy since I had started training, else I would have ended up on my face. There wasn't any point in trying to be quiet as she could sense me. The dim light revealed a potential weapon. I barely slowed as I reached for it on the way to the open road.

Everything Adam had told me about the Fae ran through my mind. They could change molecules only by touching them, though not anything containing Siis energy like me. They couldn't heal themselves, so if they went down, they generally stayed there. Also, they were fast and strong, more so than a regular human.

'You cannot hide from me.'

She was right. She could sense me more precisely than I could her. I leant against a thick trunk with the sharp branch clutched to my chest, trying to still my erratic breathing. The shadows were deep and small movements kept catching my eye, increasing the fear until I thought I might choke on it. I had to calm down and think. But the image of the Fae consumed my thoughts, their sharp teeth catching the moonlight as they snarled.

'Did you ever really think you had a chance against me?' Suraya called.

She was closer, making it possible to sense her presence, but still far enough away that her exact location remained undetectable.

'The Fae know that you are the reason some of their own died. When I told them I could bring you to them, they agreed to leave my father alone.'

I wanted to scream, *Are you really that stupid?* but kept my mouth closed. Not because she could follow my voice, she already knew my location, but because I needed to save to breath to run again. A cold breeze blew through the trees and I nearly screamed when something snagged on my arm before realising that it was only a branch.

My only chance was to go back the way we had travelled in the hope of out running the Fae, but first Suraya needed to be dealt with. The square key was still gripped in my hand. Without it, Suraya would need the help of a priest to get free, something that would need an explanation on her part. I quickly crouched down and pushed the key into the mud, thankful that the dirt was loose, allowing me to bury it deep. Hopefully I'd get to see her explain the cuff to Eris.

Something scurried over my foot forcing a tight yelp from my throat. It was only an animal, just going about its normal business. Every shadow became a potential attacker, every movement somebody coming to strike me. Even though it went against every instinct, I closed my eyes. The woods were filled with shadows, drawing my attention and fuelling my imagination. It was a distraction, one that could get me killed.

For a moment the area only became more daunting, and it took several slow breaths before I calmed enough to focus. Then I got it. Suraya was closer than I had hoped, only a couple of metres behind the tree. She was stronger than me, but her skills in unarmed combat seemed no better than mine. Thank God Gabriel was protective over all the women in his life.

The question was, how far was I willing to go to stop her? Could I really kill someone? With an equal measure of dismay and relief, I realised that the answer to that was yes. But could I really kill the daughter of the man I loved?

Suraya was now directly behind the tree. I kept my eyes closed, focusing on her presence. She moved around to my left and I turned, ready with the branch held high.

It was a strange sensation. There was no sense of the surrounding area, but I could see Suraya in my mind's eye. Not her solid form, but the Shi that she was made up of. There was no sense of the tree that separated us, but her location in place to mine was clear, as if I really looked at her.

She moved silently, yet she couldn't hide. I opened my eyes, and swung the branch around, heading straight for her head. I didn't want to kill Gabriel's daughter, but I had no intention of dying by her hand either.

She didn't expect me to attack with such force, so wasn't prepared to defend herself. Unfortunately, the branch only glanced off her shoulder as she moved. The light had nearly gone, leaving the woods filled with darkness. Enough light remained to show what she gripped in her hand. It was a dagger.

I leapt back and held the branch out before me. It had been a mistake not to check her for weapons. So many times I had practised this, but she wasn't holding a rubber knife, she gripped the sharpest weapon I knew of. If she managed to land a blow, it would most likely be a killing one. It just wasn't fair.

'I am really sick of your crap!' I screamed.

Suraya took a step towards me and laughed, a sound that echoed out through the woods, stilling the woodland creatures that had begun their nightly hunt for food.

'You think you can beat me with that?' She laughed again as she took another step.

I forced myself to stay still. During training I had found it hard to remain motionless, but this was almost impossible. Every inch of me screamed to run, but if I did, it would only be a matter of time before she caught me.

'You are just a human,' she continued with a sneer.

'So you keep saying,' I retorted. 'Yet, since you have met me, you have treated me as a threat. You hate that I can have so much power over your father, especially when you have no idea why.'

'He would soon have tired of you,' she snarled, taking another step towards me. The distance between us was barely more than the length of the branched gripped in my hands.

'No, he wouldn't have and you know that else you wouldn't be doing this. You are no longer the only important person in his life and that leaves a bitter taste in the back of your throat, doesn't it?' She snarled once again, the sound more animal than human and tensed ready to pounce. 'Just think, Suraya,' I continued, 'a lowly human managed to steal Daddy's affection. What does that say about you?'

Intense rage flashed from her, exactly what I'd been waiting for. She sprang towards me with the dagger held up, not looking at the weapon I held, but at my face, boring her glare into my head, consumed with the need to kill me where I stood.

Even though my eyes settled on her twisted face, I took in everything. Her left hand reached for me, heading straight for my throat. Her right hand held the blade down and out, ready to thrust up into my side. Her left leg bent, taking the weight of her body.

Look for the joints, Adam had said. *They are the weak point.* Without hesitation, I ducked down, avoiding the outreached hand, and swung the branch around to hit the back of her knee. My position was awkward and the blow not hard, but when it made contact Suraya collapsed onto her side. She quickly rolled onto her stomach, trying to scramble onto her feet and I brought the branch up. Using both hands, I stabbed her right shoulder.

The end didn't pierce deep, but her scream was loud enough to warm my heart. Her grip on the blade loosened in response and I quickly pulled it from her grasp.

She reached for the dagger. 'I will kill you!'

I stumbled back, throwing the branch into the woods. I positioned the dagger in my hands so that the blade was pressed against my arm, ignoring the sharp sting as it cut straight through my clothes into the skin.

'So you keep saying,' I panted, 'but so far, your words have been nothing more than empty threats.'

The situation was dire, but I couldn't help but smile in victory. Some of my pleasure dissipated when she smiled back. Why didn't she have a look of defeat on her face? Suraya sat up, supporting her arm against her chest as blood flowed from her shoulder wound. She closed her eyes and tilted her head to the right.

The smile drained from my face. 'What are you doing?' I did not like the look one bit.

She opened her eyes and smiled. 'Morton will be here soon.'

My heart sank. Gabriel had once told me that when two Siis were fully bonded, they shared thoughts and memories. She wasn't working alone. As if she wasn't enough to deal with, now there was another Siis added into the equation. Even though I had the weapon and she was defenceless, she still wasn't worried. If only she wasn't Gabriel's daughter. If only she wasn't so confident that I wouldn't kill her because of this.

The hairs on the back of my neck rose and my heart sank even further. Something more terrifying than her approached. It was the Fae. I couldn't tell how close they were, or which direction they came from, but the sense of them crawled at my skin and over my brain.

I stumbled back against the tree. 'Damn it.'

Suraya grinned broadly. 'You may have defended yourself against me.' She laughed, a cruel sound filled with malice and pleasure. 'But there are many Fae coming. Let's see how well you manage against them.'

She had a point, and it wasn't something I wanted to put to the test. I turned to run, and then thought better of it. Suraya was still a problem. I swung my foot out. She didn't see it coming and it caught her straight across the face. Her nose crunched and blood splayed out as she fell back. A springy sensation travelled up to my knee and I flexed it, making sure it wouldn't seize up. She would be out for a while.

I ran, hopefully in the right direction.

I finally emerged from the woods several metres up from where we had entered. I paused, looking for signs of the Fae. Their presence crept over my skin, but I still couldn't detect their exact location.

I turned around with the blade gripped securely against my arm, wondering which way would be best to go. There was always the car. That was a stupid idea. The car would be nothing more than a trap.

The Fae came into range and I nearly cried out in despair. They were all around me. Moments later they came into sight. Their shadowed forms approached, their eyes shining as if they were lanterns to ward off the darkness. There were so many. It was too late to escape.

They advanced, chuckling harshly with the knowledge of their victory. I stood firm. The panic that had been bubbling away calmed. There was just no way I would survive. I drew on my hate for the Fae and silently vowed to take down as many as possible before they overpowered me.

They came towards me slowly, creeping low as animals stalking their prey, crowing gleefully. I stood silently, awaiting their approach with the blade of the dagger pressed up against my forearm, hidden from their sight.

'If it isn't the girl from the park.' The song like, raspy voice was familiar.

It was the male from my first meeting with the Fae. He approached ahead of the rest. A face of an innocent child, but with a smile of a beast, filled with sharpened teeth that glistened in the moonlight. His eyes narrowed. So much malice, so much need for death, not a glimmer of the child he had once been. The engraved dagger glinted in the moonlight, giving the silent promise of pain and torture. His voice cut through the air, harsh with venom, filled with centuries of bitterness. 'You killed Sheah!'

I stood firm and silent.

'She was my mate,' he hissed. 'We will not tolerate one of our own being slaughtered.' His voice spread out, clear and strong, and shouts erupted from the surrounding Fae as they brandished daggers before them. 'We will avenge her death and in her honour, we will create more Fae.'

The air hummed with anticipation. By speaking aloud to them he was rallying them, fuelling their anger ready to attack. Not like they needed it. In spite of the hidden dagger, I was defenceless against them.

The games began to tire me. Even with the increased adrenalin in my system, the weariness was present as a barely noticeable cloud in the horizon, yet one that would catch up with me eventually.

'She deserved nothing less.' My teeth were clenched, the words barely audible, yet he had no trouble hearing them. His face contorted as his lips pulled back into a snarl, and he screamed a high pitched squeal that made every hair on my body stand up in protest. He crouched, preparing to spring. I didn't move. I was ready.

There was no way to kill them all. Even a Siis such as Gabriel would have trouble doing that. But if I took down the Fae stood before me, it would at least be something.

Something had changed. I was different, transformed by the horrors brought on by Gabriel's world. Dying no longer scared me.

They came for me as one.

I didn't pray. The time for that had gone. The Fae from the park reached me first. I didn't think, or even plan, I briefly drew on a memory of Gabriel's face before thrusting the weapon up towards him. His eyes widened in surprise as the blade sank into his chest with an ease I could never have anticipated. He had expected little resistance from me, believing that I was still the frightened girl he had once met. As the blade slid easily from his body, I took pleasure in his shock.

There was no time to relish the feeling of victory before the rest of the Fae reached me. They were quick. Each time I managed to knock one down, another took its place. They came with daggers and it wasn't long before they started piercing my skin, the sharp pains barely noticeable in my lucidity.

Something hit my leg and I collapsed to the ground with a scream, only able to stare at the bone protruded from my calf. Someone pulled the dagger from my grasp. I was powerless, only able to hold up my hands in defence as a smaller Fae came towards me. The blows smashed through my arms and they continued to stab, beat and tear my flesh with their teeth.

My vision began fading and I welcomed it, willing to leave it all behind. I was no use in the fight anymore. At least I'd been able to kill some of them. Hopefully now Adam would realise that I wasn't completely useless, not that it mattered.

A scream echoed out into the night, high in pitch, yet deeper than the Fae's. It was Suraya. My eyes were almost too heavy to force open. The Fae surrounded her as she lay on the ground. She had obviously come forward, still confident that they wouldn't harm her. I took solace in the fact that she had been wrong as I drifted into unconsciousness.

25

'Shall we drain her first?'

Panic forced its way into my mind at the sound of the coarse words.

'No, we will perform the ritual on the Siis first, she is more dangerous.'

The words fully broke through my unconsciousness, but with it came the agony from my injuries.

Unable to stop from screaming, I tried to move, but it only made everything worse and my thoughts started to cloud over again. I gritted my teeth and desperately tried to focus. An icy spear stabbed at my heart. How many children would the Shi within me change? How many innocent souls would be lost?

I carefully peered around to see we were in some sort of wooden shack. A couple of old kerosene lamps hung on hooks, offering enough light for me to view my surroundings. The stars were visible through the missing ceiling, only the walls still intact, though the wood looked rotten and unlikely to hold up to a strong storm. The floor consisted of dry dirt with weeds growing through, large enough to show that the place had been abandoned for a long time.

A cool breeze blew through the closed door, making me shiver. I cried out as fresh pain racked through my body. Blood splayed from my mouth and I choked on it before mercifully, darkness claimed me again.

Screaming brought me around. The air was thick, as if I tried to breathe in water. My eyes opened with difficulty. Four Fae had hold of Suraya, though she continued to put up a fight. Even though her arms and legs were shackled she managed to break free, only to get a few steps before they overpowered her again. A slight glow pulsed from her as she tried to transform, yet it never reached full brightness. It was as if she was a dead battery on a car, with enough power to rev, but not enough to actually start.

They threw her onto the ground next to me and locked the chain to a metal ring, bolted to one of the studier sections of the wall.

One of the male Fae laughed as he crouched in front of her.

'This was not the deal,' Suraya shouted, with a wilting edge to it as her strength failed. 'He told me I just had to hand her over.'

The Fae laughed again. 'Deals change.'

Suraya's head hung down in defeat, her once beautiful hair now matted with dirt and blood. Seeing her injured and broken I could almost forget that it was she who had betrayed me. Our fight in the woods was a distant memory as if it had happened weeks instead of hours before. I felt so alone with every inch of my body filled with sharp pain. We were both going to die. I tried to tap into Gabriel's emotions, but my agony overrode all sense of him.

Suraya's narrow eyes locked with mine and she snarled. If she managed to break her bonds, she would make sure to kill me before escaping. I didn't want to die with her looking at me in such a way.

I rolled halfway onto my back and paused as darkness rushed in. The pain rolled over me like waves, each time threatening to force me into a dark nothingness. Part of me wanted that, but first I wanted to turn away from her penetrating glare.

Fresh blood streamed across my vision. My nose was clogged with the scent in the air, the iron of the blood spilt, the fear and defeat that hung heavily, bitter like ammonia and old sweat, and the murderous lust of the Fae, filling the barn with a sickly aroma that clung like syrup. There was no need to see anything, it was evident I was in hell.

'I hurt so much,' Suraya choked.

To my dismay, my lips curled with bitterness. I didn't want hate to consume my last thoughts. I wanted to die with the memory of my love for Gabriel, the times we had shared, not thoughts of the future that was now lost because of his hateful daughter.

The door opened and more Fae entered. The will to care had gone. I silently begged God for death before they could take my Shi, and for him to protect the children that would be lost. Three Fae grabbed Suraya and her screams filled the barn, deafening me as she grabbed at my extended hand which lay uselessly in the dirt. My screams joined hers as she pulled me forwards with her. A heavy blow hit my back as they yanked her away.

I thanked God as I lay helplessly on my back, all feeling in my lower body gone, not even a twinge, aware of the blood sliding down my throat, yet not caring. I couldn't see Suraya and that was at least one small blessing. I drifted, accompanied by the sound of her screams. This time I wouldn't come back. I was ready. I tried to bring Gabriel's face into my mind, but I couldn't, there was only blackness and then nothing.

26

'Breathe, Ana, breathe.' The man's voice tried to pull me away from the measure of relief I had found in the darkness. I didn't want to go back to hell and fought against the pull of the tide.

'Adam, get her out,' another voice said. Once I recognised it, a measure of my peace was robbed from me. I could have sworn it was Eris. I clung to the receding darkness as it must have been a dream, something my mind had conjured up to make me fight some more. I'd had enough fighting and now wanted to sleep.

Pain shot through my chest, forcing my eyes to open. Blood flew out of my mouth and my body instinctively drew in a painful breath.

'Just keep breathing,' Adam said. 'You will be healed soon.'

A cool breeze flittered over my face, the air fresh and clear. I was somehow outside with Adam bent over me. Terrible screams came from close by, echoing through the woods as the eerie cry of a dying animal.

He hissed a word I had heard before, but could never quite grasp, an obvious curse. Something was different, he felt different.

'Am I dreaming?' I garbled.

'No,' he said soothingly.

'But I must be,' I persisted.

'Why do you think that?'

'Because you're worried for me.' All strength left me and I battled to keep my eyes open. 'And I know that could never happen.' The pain receded and I closed my eyes. Maybe it would all make sense when I woke up. 'It's very strange,' I said, drifting off once more.

Voices roused me again.

'Eris?' My voice was barely a whisper, yet she came to my side.

'You're safe now, we are here.' Her words were reassuring, but a frantic edge lined her voice. Was it worry or excitement? Did I really care?

'Gabriel?' I said.

'He came too, don't worry.' I tried to ask where he was, but she turned to Adam cutting me off. 'Take her home when you've finished, I'll make sure he is all right.'

Adam nodded without taking his hands off me and she sprinted off into the woods.

The feeling came back into my legs with a sudden rush. I only had a moment to marvel that my back was no longer broken, before I cried out as the pain of my injuries set in. The broken bone no longer protruded from my leg but the many stab wounds remained, hidden amongst the blood covering me.

'I apologise,' Adam said. 'I should have healed them first.'

I gritted my teeth and held still so he could heal the wounds. When he finished, he helped me to sit up, leaning me against the fallen trunk of a large tree. The bark was dry and flaking and it must have fallen a long time ago. It was strange to notice this.

Although he had healed my injuries another pain spread through me, this one different to that caused by the Fae. A vacuum took up residence in my chest, drawing my internal organs into it. An agonising groan escaped my lips as I pulled my bloodied arms around my chest, trying to hold myself together as my heart shattered into a thousand pieces.

'Oh my God,' I cried, unable to do anything as I was drowning in the sea of emotions. 'What is happening?' There was no way to survive this. My very essence was being sucked away, leaving a sharp, twisted agony in its place.

'You are feeling Gabriel's anguish.' He gripped my shoulders and brought his face to mine. 'Construct a wall in your mind, Ana. Block him from you.'

I gasped as another wave coursed through my body. My lips parted to ask how it was possible to block a pain that wasn't just in my mind, but the clarity to form the words escaped me.

'Block him,' he urged again.

I seized him, twisting his top around my clawed hands, pulling him towards me as if he could somehow block the hole that my insides were falling into. I tried to form barriers against it, but any defence I had was crushed under it the ferociousness of the attack and whisked away into the thick, dark cloud that was now my body.

So many times I had blocked people's emotions, but Gabriel was now part of me, making it impossible. I needed a wall like Adam had, but when I tried to ask how he managed it, the words were snatched away, leaving me able to do little more than groan with despair. I reached out with my mind and found him, but it was weak, barely a shimmer in the darkness that consumed me. I had to touch that wall. I had to draw off his strength.

I hauled myself up and grabbed at his shoulders. My head hurt, my body was no longer mine, rather a tool with only one purpose, to destroy me. The metal door in Adam's mind became stronger and I reached out in body as well as conscious thought. My head touched his and I clung to him, forcing my mind against his, drawing the strength I needed in order to survive.

Adam hesitantly reached up to touch my arms. He became my life raft in the sea that tried to drown me and I gripped him as if my life depended on it. The pain racked through me and so did the sobs, the tears falling freely to soak us both.

Eventually my mind managed to bury it. Having suffered so much already, it protected itself from the pain of Gabriel's sorrow. I settled into Adam's arms, allowing his warmth to soothe me.

'Suraya?' I asked.

'She is alive,' he said to my surprise. 'However, she may not survive.'

Fresh tears rolled down my cheeks. I hated her for what she had done, but she was Gabriel's daughter and he would never heal from the loss if she died.

'What happened, Ana?'

My words were stilted at first, though soon gained momentum. By the end, my speech was a garbled mess that he most likely struggled to understand. Once finished, I huddled into his hard chest. I had never been this close to him before. He smelt like a summer's day, as if the air and sun had been trapped in his skin.

'I should have known something like this would happen.' His voice was tense, but I couldn't find the words to reassure him. None of us could have predicted the extent that Suraya would go to, to get rid of me.

'How did you know?' My mind still struggled with the turn of events. I had been so certain I would die.

'Gabriel sensed your fear,' he told me. 'We flew here as fast as we could.'

'Not by plane this time.'

Adam let out a surprise laugh. It was small and without much humour, yet echoed around the open space we sat in. 'You will be all right,' he told me. That was up for debate. 'We came as falcons,' he continued, 'it was faster than driving.'

The image of them travelling across the skies, their great wings spread out in flight, should have filled me with wonder. But apart from the pain transmitted from Gabriel, I felt nothing, as if I had actually died in the barn and now was merely a ghost, destined to wander the world with only Gabriel's pain to keep me company.

'Is he with her?' It was selfish, but I wanted him with me, not her. I needed to be in his arms, yet at the same time, how he would react terrified me.

Adam nodded.

'The Fae?' I asked.

'Eris is finishing them up now.'

The image of the Fae surrounding me flashed before my eyes and I shuddered violently. I wasn't feeling so strong and calm anymore.

I tried to wipe the tears from my face, before realising that I was only transferring more blood to my cheeks. My hands dropped to my lap. Who cared what I looked like.

'You're not as tough as you like people to think,' I said.

'Why would you say that?' He sat up on the fallen tree, staring off into the woods.

'Well, you don't hate me as much as you like to pretend.'

'I beg your pardon,' he said, turning to me.

A high pitched scream came from close by and I shuddered once more. 'Well?' I prompted.

'Well what?'

'You don't hate me anymore?'

'Does it matter?' he answered stiffly.

'No, but I would still like to know.'

I tried to get a sense of what he was feeling, but he was a vault once more, leaving me with only guess work. Upon focusing, I detected something simmering at the edge, a glimmer of anger that wasn't betrayed by his features.

'I felt your worry,' I reminded him.

'I was concerned for us all.'

I chuckled darkly. 'Somehow I don't believe that.' He wouldn't have left Eris to deal with the Fae on her own if he thought for one minute that she wouldn't be fine. Also, my ability to read people had improved somewhat. His worry had been aimed in my direction.

'Your beliefs are irrelevant,' he said stonily as he turned to scrutinise the woods once more.

'Ouch,' I replied.

'What do you want me to say, Ana?' He turned to stare at me with an intensity that in the past, would have pinned me to the spot.

'I don't know,' I sighed. 'I'm just making conversation.'

The silence between us was deep, though broken by the remaining screams of the Fae as Eris hunted them. The sound should have disturbed me, but it didn't. Another scream echoed out into the night, cut off at its highest pitch. Was it the Fae who had broken my back? Maybe it was the one who had sliced his blade along my thigh. Each scream brought me a sense of satisfaction that chilled me. They may have set out to kill me, but how could I feel such pleasure at their demise?

'I do not hate you.'

'That's good.'

'It does not mean I trust you.'

'I would expect nothing else.'

I looked down at my torn and bloodied clothes. I was in dire need of a shower. A momentary flare of intense anger speared through me upon seeing the torn holes in my favourite pair of jeans. I smiled wryly. It was stupid and irrational to be annoyed about clothes when so much had happened.

Gabriel was still inside the shack, less than twenty metres away. I desperately wanted to go to him, but it took several minutes of battling with myself before I found the strength to stand. I stumbled forwards a couple of steps and nearly fell. Adam gripped hold of my arm.

'I'm fine,' I told him once steady.

My feet became heavier as I walked towards the shack. The pull to be with Gabriel was strong, but a cold, dark anger brewed in him, threatening to halt me. When I reached the rotten door, I hesitated. Maybe it would be best to wait for him to come to me. After all, as much as I hated his daughter, he needed to be with her right now.

Before I could make a decision, I sensed him approaching. I stepped back in order to avoid the door, but didn't manage it in time. The wooden panel flung open so hard that it ripped from its hinges and the corner of the door caught my shoulder as it was thrown forwards. I stumbled back and would have fallen, but Gabriel grabbed the front of my top, hauling me up towards him.

'You!' he bellowed. Light flowed around his body, moving like the rushing waves of a stormy sea. His face stopped inches from mine, and I nearly gagged on the intensity of his rage. 'Because of you, my daughter may die.'

My attempt to speak failed miserably as the words stuck in my throat. Gabriel lifted me by my arms and shook me so hard that my brain spun within my skull.

'Get off!' I screamed.

His fingers dug painfully into my muscles and I cried out. Someone had once told me that love and hate were two sides of the same coin. I had never understood how that was possible, until now. It was as if all Gabriel's love for me had been twisted into a snarly rage. Only hours before he had held me in his arms, telling me how he loved me more than life itself, now he wanted to kill me. He released my arm and raised his hand up, ready to strike. I had survived Suraya, and had even managed to live through the Fae, but now I was going to die at the hands of the man I loved.

Everything had gone so wrong, and I could only stare into Gabriel's eyes, the eyes of a stranger. They were no longer the electric blue I had come to love. They had darkened to the colour of the midnight sky and blazed with a fire from within. I couldn't see that. I couldn't watch yet another person I loved attack me. My head reeled with the change in him, and I closed my eyes in anticipation of the pain that was sure to come.

'Stop this,' Adam said. I opened my eyes to see that he had hold of Gabriel's raised arm. 'Gabe, go back to Suraya.'

Gabriel glared at me with his lip curled and his body shaking, before dropping me to the ground. There was no love or regret as he watched me scramble away and he remained tense as if still preparing attack. He glanced towards Adam, who stood watching and ready, before stalking back into the barn.

Adam reached his hand out to help me, but I ignored it and did my best to contain my groan as I stood.

'I want to go home now,' I told him.

He studied me before nodding and leading me along the road towards the car. My brain had reached its capacity for the day and I needed to be in the safe confines of my house.

We passed the bodies of the Fae killed by my own hand, eight in total, more than I would have predicted possible to take down. I paused by the Fae I'd first met in the park. His mouth was open in a final snarl, revealing the sharpened teeth that could tear easily through flesh. There was something else, something different that I couldn't quite put my finger on.

'They become visible to humans in death,' Adam said, startling me. I couldn't move away. Another Fae, a female, tore at my gaze, dragging my attention to her small slender body. She lay on her side, with her knees tucked into her stomach and her fist pushed gently under her chin. Her red hair trailed over her face, framing long, thick eye lashes that rested against her skin. Her lips were only slightly parted, hiding the teeth that I feared so much. The essence of the Fae had gone, revealing the child beneath, a child once stolen from her bed, once loved by a family.

A desperate sob forced its way from my chest. I barely had time to make it to the twisted bush that lined the road before the contents of my stomach forced their way from my body. I choked, only briefly, but enough to cause a moment of panic when air couldn't make its way to my lungs.

'I can't do this,' I stammered, straightening up. 'I really can't do this. I can't be this person. This isn't right, it just isn't right.' I pressed my shaking hands to my lips. 'How can you live like this? How can you do this? They are just children, just poor little children.' My throat thickened and tears flooded my cheeks.

Adam gripped my wrists to pull my hands from my face. 'They are not children. They may look like that now, but many of them are thousands of years old and have committed many atrocities. You would be wise to remember that.'

The breath wheezed from my lungs in fast, forceful gasps. My head vibrated with all the information waiting to be processed. Maybe I would go crazy after all.

I snatched my arms from his grip. 'I can't do this.' My head began to swim and I took several deep breaths in order to try and calm the rising storm, for if I didn't, it would consume me. 'It's all too much. Everything that's happened, you, the Fae, Lexi, Siis that talk to other Siis in their minds, I can't cope with it.'

Adam gripped the top of my arms, digging his fingers into my flesh until it hurt. 'What do you mean Siis talking in their minds?'

'Get off me!' I yanked free from his grip. 'You have no right to touch me. None of you do. And I'm sick to death with you all thinking that you can control my actions.'

His eyes flashed before he forced himself to relax and took a step back from me. 'This could be important,' he said calmly.

'Suraya.' I breathed deeply to try and curb my anger. 'She tilted her head and then said someone called Morton was coming.'

The sight of the lifeless Fae caught my eyes again, their petite bodies more lifelike in death than they had been in life.

'They're just little kids,' I moaned into my hands. 'I killed little kids.'

'I understand how difficult this must be,' Adam said.

'You have no idea what I'm feeling.' I turned away from him and hurried towards the car. 'I'm not doing this anymore,' I shouted over my shoulder. 'I have had enough of your crazy world. I have had enough of being in danger. I have had enough of all of you. I have just had enough and I want you to stay away from me.'

Adam followed, causing a spark of rage in me, so intense, that I thought I might explode.

'You believe that you can simply walk away?' The light amusement threaded through his tone only flamed my rage further.

'Just you watch me.' I increased my pace, only to groan loudly upon seeing the raised bonnet of the car. 'Just fix the car,' I demanded, ignoring his amused smile.

Even the sight of the bonnet becoming liquid metal and smoothing down as if it had never happened, couldn't reduce the anger that brewed within. Up until now, I had taken everything in my stride, dealing with every problem as it arose. But now it was as if I'd dived outside of my own body and for the first time was able to have a really good look at everything as a whole. I didn't like it one bit.

Once he finished, I started the car. The engine roared into life as I pressed down heavily on the accelerator and I grabbed the handle to slam the door. To my annoyance, Adam gripped the side, stopping me.

'It does not work that way,' he said, bending down to peer at me. 'You cannot merely decide to abandon this life.'

'Watch me,' I retorted, tugging on the door. When I couldn't budge it, I leant back in the seat and crossed my arms. He finally released the door with a loud sigh.

'You need to take this,' he said holding out a sheathed blade.

'I don't want it,' I barked. He tossed the dagger onto the passenger seat and hunkered down so that he was at eye level. The amusement had gone, and his dark stare demanded my attention, robbing me of all protests.

'Whether you like it or not, your life has changed. The sooner you accept this, the more likely you are to survive.' He stood without waiting for a response and closed the door before striding back towards the barn.

'To hell with that.'

I turned the car around to head home, scraping the bonnet across a tree. Maybe he was right, maybe this was my life now. I shuddered at the thought, before forcing it into the back of my mind. I couldn't accept that.

The car bounced along the track, groaning with the pressure I put it under. I pushed against the image of the Fae, forcing it into the back of my mind. After a time, I managed it and focused my attention to the task of driving. When the voice in my mind piped up, warning me that there would be consequences for the day, I ignored it. Right now, I couldn't deal with that. Right now, I needed to get home, have a long shower and sleep. It wasn't the time to worry about tomorrow. The day would come as it always did and I would deal with the problems then.

27

Adam placed the sheathed dagger on the kitchen side.

'I only get two?' I asked.

He shook his head and rolled his eyes. 'If you need more than that, then you will most likely be dead.

'Fine.' I took one of the daggers and turned it around in my hands. It felt unnaturally heavy, more so than it ever had before. I briefly closed my eyes against the image of the Fae, not how they were in life, but how they had looked in death.

'They are not children, Ana.'

'Since when can you read minds?'

He laughed. 'Your face paints a clear picture of horror. I merely made an educated guess.'

Adam watched with interest as I carried the dagger over to the sink. The screwdriver sat on the kitchen side from when I'd used it minutes before, along with the dirty dishes. I was really going to have to get a grip and get my life sorted. The wash basket was full to bursting as well. I tried to slip the dagger under the kitchen side, onto the newly fitted tray.

'Damn it.' The tray was too small, only by a few millimetres but enough to be useless.

'A clever idea,' Adam said peering over my shoulder.

'Don't look so surprised. Anyway, it wasn't that clever, it doesn't fit.'

He shook his head and smiled. 'Try again.'

'I said it doesn't fit.'

He sighed. 'Try again, Ana.'

'For God's sake,' I pushed the dagger into the slot again. 'See, it doesn't...' I stopped short as the dagger slipped easily into place. 'Huh.'

Adam smiled at me.

'Thank you,' I said. 'I suppose you want a cup of tea.'

'That will not be necessary.' He held out some Daku cuffs. 'I brought these for you. If for any reason Suraya returns, they will help.'

'Do you think she will?'

'I doubt it,' he said with a sigh. 'However, I cannot be sure.'

I bit my lip, chewing on it until it tingled. 'Will Gabriel come back?'

He studied me for a moment before sighing again. 'I do not know that answer to that either.'

'Thank you,' I said, 'for everything.'

He dipped his head and gave me a small smile. 'Take care, Ana.' Without another word, he left, closing the door quietly behind him.

I watched him through the window as he strolled down the path. This would probably be the last time I saw him. I fiddled with the cuffs, trying to ignore the light sense of loss I felt. It didn't really compare to the pain of losing Gabriel, but still, it was there.

A light *pling* came from the sink as water dripped from the tap, a continual beat that got louder as the seconds passed. The house was always silent now, more like a physical presence than a loss of sound. How was I going to survive it? How would I live each day with the pain of Gabriel's anger?

The phone began ringing, disturbing the quiet. I sighed and answered it.

'It's me,' Carl said. 'I need you in right away. I've had to send the agency worker home for slapping Robert's hand.'

I smiled, only a small movement, but my first attempt in days.

'Well?' he demanded. 'Are you coming in?'

I sighed and rolled my eyes. The day Carl was polite and respectful was the day hell froze over. 'I'll be there straight away.'

After hanging up the phone, I collected my stuff and headed out, making sure to lock the door behind me. Half way down the path, I paused and looked up at the sun. I smiled again, only lightly but with more feeling. No matter what happened, there would always be someone demanding my time, be it Carl, Beth or even Maria. The world continued to turn, regardless of my problems and life carried on, unheeding of my urge to hide from it. Of course I would survive. I had no choice.

I continued down the path, wishing I had been there to see Robert get a slap. I always missed all the good stuff.

THE HIDDEN LIGHT

(VOLUME TWO OF THE ANA MARTIN SERIES)

Ana believes that Gabriel's absence will keep her out of harm's way. Little does she know, it is too late for that. She already contains some of Gabriel's Shi which allows her to sense the bad intent of others. This ensures that wherever she goes, trouble will find her.

After a run in with a local psychopath and more dealings with the Fae, she finally resides herself to the fact that life has changed.

Then children start going missing from the local area, leaving the police mystified as it appears a different person is taking each one. Against her better judgement and with the help of Maria, a natural witch with a stubborn personality, she decides to investigate.

Suddenly, she is drawn further into the world of the Siis and Ana finally realises that her troubles have only just begun.

Dear reader.

Night of the Fae, is the first volume of the Ana Martin series. The next two installments, HIDDEN LIGHT, and, FROZEN FLAME, are available now.

As always, I love to hear about your reading experience. My preferred place to leave a comment is on Amazon, however, you can leave a comment on Goodreads, or the Ana Martin series Facebook page.

I look forward to taking you on the rest of Ana's journey in the future.

Kind regards

Lyneal.